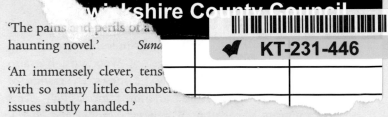
'The pains and perils of a... haunting novel.'    *Sunday*...

'An immensely clever, tense... with so many little chambers... issues subtly handled.'

Jim Crace, Man Booker Prize-shortlisted author of *Harvest*

'Among his many gifts is Woodward's extraordinary skill in taking all the big themes – sex, truth, faith, obsession, existential crisis, the works! – and wrapping them up with such deft lightness of touch that the pages all but turn themselves. This is contemporary family drama at its most compelling, and with a brutally exquisite ending.'

Nathan Filer, author of *The Shock of the Fall*

'An unsettling tale of passion, faith and identity . . . The set-up to Gerard Woodward's unsettling new novel has all the creeping sense of unease one might find in a chilling horror movie . . . Woodward has always been a keen observer of the family dynamic and here he deals confidently with love, marriage, betrayal and suburban stasis . . . the way in which Woodward navigates these choppy waters is engrossing . . . Polly and Arnold feel like such authentic characters.'    *Observer*

'Woodward's prose has a rare and wondrous texture that comes from his ongoing play between the comedic and tragic moments of his characters' lives. *The Paper Lovers* is a beautifully wrought narrative with a devastating ending – an intimate exploration of requited and unrequited desire in all its forms. I couldn't put it down till I was done, and then I wanted to laugh and cry all at once, at the sheer absurdity of being human. An epic novel that should draw comparisons with Greene's *The End of the Affair*.'

Nikita Lalwani, author of *The Village*

'By the end of the book, after a couple of almost surreal twists and turns, the deep meaning of ordinary life, which Woodward is good... ...ives, has crystall... ...kes this book so impressive and enjoyable is the writing, whether it is Woodward's occasional tongue-in-cheek similes or his convincing insights into all manner of things . . . Woodward has also published several books of poetry, and it shows. The reading of straightforward poetry, neat and undiluted, increasingly seems to be a minority activity, but Woodward's candid and lateral-thinking prose is alive with similarly pleasurable jolts, sneaked between the reassuring covers of a novel.' *Sunday Times*

'A mordantly ironic novel . . . Paper, we're reminded at one point, has an edge, and there are plenty of those to Woodward's discomforting tale.' *Daily Mail*

'A man finds religion after embarking on an adulterous affair in this closely observed allegory of obsession and redemption . . . Woodward's way with metaphor reminds you that he, like Arnold, is a poet academic . . . Woodward has crafted a subtle allegory of obsession and redemption in which the mysteries of paper-making closely resemble the Christian sacrament itself.' *Guardian*

'The wry truths that Woodward teases from [the characters'] ensuing identity crises are universal in their poignancy.' *Mail on Sunday*

'One of Gerard Woodward's gifts is the ability to focus on a very small section of time and describe the minutiae of feelings or happenings second by second, giving his prose at times a television-camera quality. He asks interesting questions . . . a strange, inconclusive book, which lingers with you long after you've read the last page.' *Church Times*

'It's a fantastic book and an interesting example of a dual-narrative novel . . . Gerard Woodward deftly explores the big issues (love, religion, family, home life) at once sensitively and destructively. And it is in the destruction, when everything is torn apart and in pieces, that we really know what we are dealing with and what makes these characters so frighteningly human.' *surreyedit.com*

# The Paper Lovers

Gerard Woodward is a prize-winning writer of poetry, short stories and a number of novels, including an acclaimed trilogy comprising *August* (shortlisted for the 2001 Whitbread First Novel Award), *I'll Go to Bed at Noon* (shortlisted for the 2004 Man Booker Prize) and *A Curious Earth*. He was born in London in 1961. He is Professor of Creative Writing at Bath Spa University.

Also by Gerard Woodward

August
I'll Go to Bed at Noon
A Curious Earth
Caravan Thieves
Nourishment
Vanishing
Legoland

*Poetry*
Householder
After the Deafening
Island to Island
We Were Pedestrians
The Seacunny

GERARD WOODWARD

# The Paper Lovers

PICADOR

First published 2018 by Picador

This paperback edition first published 2019 by Picador
an imprint of Pan Macmillan
20 New Wharf Road, London N1 9RR
Associated companies throughout the world
www.panmacmillan.com

ISBN 978-1-5098-4801-0

1 3 5 7 9 8 6 4 2

A CIP catalogue record for this book is available from the British Library.

Printed and bound by CPI Group (UK) Ltd, Croydon, CR0 4YY

Visit **www.picador.com** to read more about all our books
and to buy them. You will also find features, author interviews and
news of any author events, and you can sign up for e-newsletters
so that you're always first to hear about our new releases.

# Part One

# 1

They had bought a sewing machine for Evelyn's seventh birthday realizing, only after she had unwrapped it, that it was too old for her. Although she herself had asked for one, when she was confronted with the reality, she fell into an embarrassed silence, almost as though a stern, elderly relative had entered the room. The sewing machine had been her main present of the day, and was the last to be opened, but the girl would not warm to it, and withdrew to the comfort of her other, lesser presents.

Her parents realized their mistake. It had been a child's version of the machine Evelyn had wanted, not the full-size model they had given her. It must have felt like receiving a fully-grown, serious-looking dog when she'd been expecting an adorable puppy. What made matters worse was that neither parent knew how to operate the machine, and so couldn't demonstrate its delights for her. They had unpacked it and had read the instruction manual, but without comprehension. They quickly came to regard the machine as an over-complicated, slightly dangerous piece of equipment, and they put it back in its box, and took it down to the cellar, where it stayed, untouched, for two years.

Then one evening when Arnold came home from work he noticed, even before he entered the front door, that the house had changed. He didn't know precisely in what way it had changed, and to every outward appearance the house was identical to the one he had left in the morning – a solid Victorian terrace with red-brick walls and a stained-glass front-door window. The fig tree in its tub, the wheelie bin half-hidden round the far side of the bay, the expensive circle of Zen pebbles – they were all as he remembered. Yet they were different. Inside, the sense of change seemed stronger, as if someone had redecorated but in the same colours, so that everything was fresher, brighter. There was a smell of flowers, and he looked around the hall carpet to see if there was any evidence – fallen petals or leaves, but there was none.

In the lounge-diner, which he entered still carrying his work briefcase, he came upon a scene that he found puzzling at first. The room seemed full of women, though in fact there were only two – his wife and her friend Vera, whom he knew a little, and his daughter Evelyn, and Vera's three children – he couldn't remember their names, though one of the girls was the same age as Evelyn, and had recently become her best friend. And there was the household's newly acquired kitten, as yet unnamed, also female, but black and spidery.

They were all gathered at the far end of the living

room, near the bay window, and sitting on the floor, around the coffee table. Vera was kneeling. Polly, his wife, was sitting on her haunches. Their daughter had draped herself across her mother's shoulders, while Vera's children were engrossed with something colourful and knotty. They were, all of them, absorbed and preoccupied to such an extent that no one noticed him enter the room.

The smell here was overpowering, the waft of perfume that came from this huddle of females, though he realized almost immediately that it came from only one of them, Vera, that it was a scent she was wearing. He was drawn in by this scent, at the same time as he felt excluded from the group at the far end of the lounge-diner, indeed the room itself had become a space in which he didn't properly belong.

The object of their attention, around which they were all sitting, was the sewing machine. Arnold took a moment to remember it, and to understand what it was. He felt a pang of relief that this gathering was now so easily explained, and a certain sense of pleasure that the machine they had consigned to the cellar two years ago had been resurrected, and that it might have a use, and be appreciated, after all.

Vera was leading the project to get the sewing machine working, the others were merely her attendants. Polly had the instruction manual and was reading from it when directed to do so by Vera. On the floor was a slew of packaging and haberdashery that the kitten was playing with. The women conferred over details of the instruction manual, and discussed how they could be applied to the machine itself. They were clicking and slotting things together, unjamming and unwinding things, and trying to thread cotton through hooks and eyes that they strained to see. It appeared that Vera, unlike Polly, knew about sewing machines, but even she was having trouble remembering exactly how they worked. For a moment it looked, to Arnold, that the task they were engaged in was something of far greater import than it actually was. They were like surgeons fighting for the life of a baby, or technicians defusing a bomb. There was something devotional and serious in what they were doing. But there was also tension. They seemed captured by the machine, as though they had woken an apparently gentle beast to find that it had many tentacles and was gripping them tightly. They were becoming impatient, and wanted to move on to other things.

He felt he had been standing there for hours before anyone noticed him. Then Polly swung her head briefly in his direction and gave him a distracted smile. This prompted Vera to do the same thing, dutifully giving him a glance and the same smile (as though she had borrowed it from Polly), a slightly apologetic smile, he felt, as if to say, sorry for taking over your living room, Arnold.

Although he didn't know Vera well, and had only met her a small number of times, he understood that she had caused a stir among the circle of friends his wife had made since having a child. There had been a time when Polly and her group were always talking about her, just after she moved to the area. She had had problems at her children's old school. One of the daughters had been bullied, he vaguely recalled. Polly and her friends were always thinking of ways they could help her, anxious that she should settle in and be made to feel at home (she was perhaps foreign? Arnold couldn't remember). At times it seemed their anxiety was that they might lose her to one of the other tribes of mothers who centred on the school, and they were adamant that Vera belonged to them. So when their daughters formed a friendship, it felt as though Polly had won a coup, claiming Vera for herself and her friends.

Now Arnold was beginning to feel he understood the fascination. As she knelt before the sewing machine, directing the operations, he noticed her as though through the refracting lens of her scent. The gorgeousness of her smell seemed to give her a halo, to make her shine, radiate. Indeed the scene before him was like a religious image, a depiction of an epiphany, *The Adoration of the Sewing Maidens*, as painted by El Greco.

He took a step closer, not quite sure of what to say or how to react. He was surprised by their indifference to him. He guessed that half an hour ago they had been full of playful excitement at what they were doing, that had since been overtaken by a sense of duty. The machine had convinced them that it was not a mere toy but that it was a serious, practical device. It had won their respect, and they were treating it accordingly. But he was surprised by the fact that they had assumed that he, as a man, would not be interested in their project. The sewing machine had not only won their respect, it had revived their long-rejected notions of gender-based labour divisions.

'I'll give you your family back in a moment, Arnold,' said Vera, without looking up.

'We can't let it win,' said Polly, also without looking up, 'not at this stage.'

Realizing he wasn't going to be asked to help, Arnold offered to make tea instead, and went into the kitchen.

Once there he rested his hands on the worktop and leant on them, taking deep breaths. He looked up and saw himself reflected in the glass doors of the kitchen cabinets. He looked sweaty and dishevelled. Drunk. He wiped his face with a tea towel, then called through to the living room for tea preferences. Polly always drank Earl Grey, very weak, with a half-spoon of sugar. No milk. Vera, he wasn't surprised to learn, was equally particular. She asked first for peppermint, then seemed surprised when told they had none. What about camomile? No, none of that either. Arnold fingered through the small library of infusions that filled one of the shelves, boxes of teabags that he riffled through like card indexes – blackcurrant, sage and sunflower, honey and chrysanthemum. There was everything but peppermint and camomile.

'What about lemon and ginger?' he called.

'You know what, I'll just have a glass of water.'

Bitch! Arnold said to himself as he poured boiling water onto a frail bag of Earl Grey. Then immediately he wondered where that sudden little spurt of anger had come from. He gnashed his teeth together. He clenched his fist and brought it down on the counter, and disguised the noise by slamming the cutlery drawer. Through the door he could just see Polly turn her head in a puzzled way. The anger had passed, although it wasn't anger, but a little thrust of adrenaline or testosterone that had surged through his body, and which he'd dissipated with a sudden release of energy, for saying that she would rather drink plain water than any of the teas they had. Surely that was a kind of insult. Who did she think she was, taking over his family, reviving that pointless machine, frustrating his wife and children, making a mess, causing disruption, spoiling his evening routine, filling the house with that gorgeous smell?

'How's your eyesight, Arnold?' Vera called to him.

It took him a moment to understand that he had been addressed. She had turned her attention, her thoughts, towards him. He poked at the teabags as they lay slumped in the hot water, puffed up with air like the anoraks of drowned trainspotters. 'Oh, you know, gradually deteriorating.'

Both Polly and Vera wore glasses, and it was partly their poor eyesight that was causing them problems with the sewing machine. That was why it was on the coffee table, so that it could be near the light from the bay window. They had brought over a small table lamp and had angled it to shine on the machine. As it had grown darker outside this had increased the sense that the women were involved in some sort of devotional activity – they seemed to be working on something that was glowing.

Arnold tried to remember what else he knew about Vera. She had been, like him, a lecturer at the university, though before his time, and in a different department. He had seen her at children's birthday parties, whenever it was his turn to collect or deliver Evelyn. She had been at a library storytelling event, where they had had a short and friendly but entirely forgettable chat. On the few occasions he dropped off or picked up Evelyn from school, he had seen her there. He once noticed her for the amount of time she spent waving to her daughter as the little one departed into her classroom. She waved far more than the other parents waved. And there was real feeling in her wave. It expressed both love and amusement at this particular expression of love. He watched her leaving the playground, walking half backwards, waving all the way, and smiling. The image stayed with Arnold, because it was such a charming expression of motherly affection. To be on the receiving end of that wave, as a child – what would that be like?

There was one other thing he knew about Vera – that she was religious. As Arnold made the tea he tried to remember how he knew this fact. Polly must have mentioned it in passing. She had said something like – Vera told me that someone in her church had had her car stolen, but the conversation had probably followed the car-theft route rather than the church route, and Vera's religiousness had not been discussed any further. At the back of his mind the news had disappointed him. He could not, he believed, have any sort of meaningful friendship with a practising Christian. He had had religious friends before and everything was fine up to a certain point, and then the cloud of their faith would descend and a common ground of communication be lost.

As he delivered the drinks, he realized Vera's religiousness had touched everything he'd seen and felt that evening, from the moment he smelt the overpowering scent of her perfume, to the epiphany-like scene of adoration around the sewing machine. It wasn't the feminization of the living room that had so disconcerted him, but its desecularization. She had raised a little chapel in the heart of his own home.

The arrival of the drinks caused a small amount of panic, because there was nowhere to put the steaming mugs that didn't risk upsetting all the work that had been done so far. He placed them on the nearby dresser out of harm's way, aware that they would be forgotten about and turn cold unsipped.

'This is so ridiculous,' said Polly, 'my eyes can't be that bad. I haven't threaded a needle since I was fourteen, but it has no right to be this difficult.'

He was closer to the women now than he had been since he first came in the room. He was standing right next to them. As they crouched on the floor he towered above them. All he could see of them was the crowns of their heads, both golden and spiralled. Polly and Vera, both blonde, slim, slight and bespectacled, looked, at times, like bookish twins.

'I'll bet Arnold's eyesight is better than both of ours

put together,' said Vera, suddenly looking up at towering Arnold, and being visibly shocked at his nearness and toweringness. Her eyes moved quickly the length of his body, up and down, in that comical, who do you think you are? way. It delighted him. His presence had amused her.

The children by now had lost all interest in the sewing machine and were playing a game which involved stuffing the kitten into Evelyn's Georgian dolls' house. Arnold, at last called upon to assist, and more aware of the perfume than ever, his eyes almost watering with it, entered the sacred space, and knelt down. Vera was wearing a dark blue T-shirt and an unbuttoned cardigan over her shoulders. Her neck was immediately noticeable, the strong length of her throat, the way it seemed to shine in its own theatre, created by the curtain of golden hair that enclosed it on three sides. In their stooping and kneeling and re-arranging they were thrown into sudden and unusual physical intimacy. His face was brought within an inch of the back of her head when she turned to rise and give him space, and he was startled by the clean, pine smell of it. She smiled at him and offered him the thread, the end dampened to a straightness with her spit. He was the surgeon who would make the one life-saving stitch that was beyond the dexterity of his fellows. He bent down and to his astonishment, threaded the eye of the needle, which he could hardly see, in one go.

'That's bloody ridiculous,' said Polly.

'See how it takes a man to do a woman's job,' said Vera.

'You are the most impractical man I have ever met, and yet you thread the needle in one go.'

'Poets must have a good eye,' said Vera, 'a good eye and a steady hand.'

It thrilled him that she remembered he was a poet.

'Well, poets do like games of precision. They like golf, and darts, and they make good carpenters,' said Arnold.

'OK, you can go now. You've impressed us enough.'

'My grandmother had a sideboard made by T. S. Eliot.'

The women ignored him, having turned their attention back to the machine. After some more clicking together of plastic parts, Polly pressed a pedal and it purred with life, the busy sound of mechanical stitching, and a sudden burst of energy from what Vera had called the 'business end' of the machine. The little girls looked up from the dolls' house as the kitten escaped from a bedroom window, as if from a house on fire. It was the first time in their lives they had heard the sound of a sewing machine and they found it unexpectedly beautiful. They had not anticipated such a vigorous, mechanical and scientific noise to come from the device. It put the machine in the same realm as motorbikes and chainsaws, of things that possessed tremendous power, that could be controlled by the lightest of touches. And it made them a little afraid of it as well, as though it might start suddenly dashing around the room. But it seemed to call them, as if it was singing. They were drawn to it, as Arnold had been to the scene in its entirety. And Arnold himself felt pushed away again, and retreated to the distance, observing the females at their work, not knowing quite what he should do. All attention was on the machine again, and its possibilities.

He imagined that, having got the machine to work, there would be an end of it. It was nearly dinner time. It was not that Arnold expected his meal on the table at a certain hour, or that he had any outmoded views on the wifely role, but the rhythms of the household had fallen by chance into a pattern that reflected exactly those views, so that an outsider might think that it was a household run on Victorian values. But in any case, this archaic routine had been disrupted by one of even greater archaism, patriarchy had been trumped by matriarchy, and the sewing maidens had taken control of the house. Vera began directing operations again, ordering Polly to go and get material that they could work on, and Polly obediently went in search of fabric, returning with a bundle of throws, sheets, tablecloths and curtains that had long been folded away somewhere. The operations became tense and urgent, because both women knew their games had overrun, and that Vera needed to get back home as well to (Arnold supposed) get her family's dinner ready. It was as though it had taken the sewing machine to make them realize how little they had developed, after all, in this liberated age. And Arnold pondered the irony with an inward chuckle, as he stood there helpless, with a well-stocked kitchen behind him.

Scissors were produced, thick fabric was snipped through, stitching was unpicked, hems were torn open.

Then the machine was put to work. Now that it was set up, Vera was able to demonstrate her skills. It was no longer a puzzle, she had command of it. The others sat around her enthralled at the wonderful busy sound of the machine as it jiggered through the material, making a munching sound as it went. Arnold crept closer again, to observe. He marvelled at how the machine seemed to travel through the fabric, yet stayed still. Cut squares of random textiles were stitched together. In just a few minutes Vera had made something new out of the old materials, a patchwork quilt, a little landscape emerging from the busy needle, the children gasped with delight. 'Look, Daddy,' Evelyn was saying, acknowledging him for the first time, 'look what Irina's mum's made.'

And with that, Vera suddenly realized how late things were. She was meant to be home an hour ago.

'I am sorry for turning your house upside down, Arnold,' she said just before she left, looking back at the overturned room. 'What a mess I have made.'

'Don't worry about it,' said Polly, 'it's a lovely mess. I'll get Arnold to clear it up while I make the dinner.'

Both women laughed.

But no one cleared up the mess. Arnold found, in the quiet of the living room post-Vera, with Evelyn now upstairs with the kitten, and Polly in the kitchen, the space had changed from a place of fraught chaos into one of peacefulness. He had thought for a moment that he might tidy things away, but he felt the same form of compunction he experienced when, for whatever reason, he had to break a spider's web. It had taken so much work to create the disorder of the room that it would have felt destructive to tidy it. And if he did clear it up, the chances were that the sewing maidens would never reappear. He didn't articulate the thought to himself, but he left the room untidy as a sort of charm to ensure Vera's return.

It worked, because not only did Vera return, but others came with her, and a regular series of sewing evenings were formed as others in Polly's circle of friends became interested, and soon the living room was crowded, once a week, with enthusiastic needleworkers. They assembled after dinner, and mixed sewing and haberdashery with wine-drinking and cheese-nibbling. The sewing machine was again at the centre of everything, but some women brought their own machines, saying they hadn't used them for years, and expressing gratitude for being given this opportunity to use them again. Polly was praised for reviving their interest in what everyone agreed was a dying art. They would reminisce about their mothers' sewing skills, and how they had loved to watch them, as children, making things. They would bring along books and magazines on sewing, discuss projects, and take turns trying out the machines, comparing the quality of stitches and seams.

Arnold was again transfixed by how the house became a different place on these occasions, even more so with the growing membership. And as the membership grew, so did Arnold's sense of exclusion. In fact the living room became a place of such clustered, concentrated femininity he couldn't have felt more out place if he had stumbled into the dressing room of a troupe of Tiller girls. Polly suggested he simply not bother coming home on the sewing evenings – he could go for a drink with his friends, or work late. He could go and have dinner in town.

He joked, at first, that they would need him to thread the needle, and he strongly desired to be there, as part of the group, because he wanted to observe Vera again, to see if her beauty was a permanent, enduring thing about her, or whether it had existed only in his perception of her on that one occasion. And he had no friends, at least none that he could rely upon to be available for a drink in the evening.

Once, tired of making himself scarce and longing to look at Vera again, he tried his best to become involved. Unlike the first time, his entry into the room drew much attention and was a cause of amusement, because he was so obviously out of place in a room of nine women and five or six little girls. Their excitement at what they had done and their anticipation of the possibilities of the new group had made them playful and foolish. So when Arnold entered a cry went up that was both a cheerful salutation and a warning.

'No men! No men! Sorry sweetie, this has become a women-only house . . .'

It felt almost as if he was in front of a class, and he felt gripped in the same way as he felt when confronted with a new seminar group, by the responsibility to say and do something. Yet he didn't know what to say. All he could do was smile and survey, as quickly as he could, the room. On all the available chairs and on the floor the women sat, some of whom he knew well, others only vaguely, some not at all. There was Geerda, a doctor on extended maternity leave, who always looked as though she was about to lose her temper, and in the far corner the hippyish woman whose name he didn't know, dressed in her high-priestess robes and beads; Tamsin, the sweary but golden-hearted teenage mum who worked in Polly's shop, whom Polly and her friends had taken rather under their collective wing. And more women, laughing, turning their heads, reaching for an olive, flushed and smiling, and in the centre of every-thing there were the sewing machines, most of which looked like the one they had bought for Evelyn, although there was one that was much older, a black and silver model that looked like something from the Victorian era. And everywhere there was fabric; two women were at that moment examining together a long length of magenta curtain, holding it out between them as if stretching a safety net for someone about to fall from the ceiling.

After Polly's exclamation all faces turned towards him in expectation of a riposte, as if some sort of battle of the sexes was to be played out before them, for their entertain-ment. But still he felt the dumbness that had overwhelmed him since he had entered the room. What existed there now was an entire garden, in the full force of its blos-soming, whereas before it had been a single plant with its evocative, enticing perfume. He held up a defensive hand. 'You know I've never approved of sweatshop labour,' he said at last. It was the best he could do, and although some of the women laughed, most of them looked at each other with fixed smiles, wondering if there was something darker behind what he had said.

'Why don't you go off and buy a box of cigars and smoke them while reading a car magazine?'

The woman who said this was one of the overdone, tinted and glossy types who didn't really belong among Polly's friends, and whose husband probably did exactly the things she'd just recommended, regularly. It didn't play well with the other women, who saw genuine antagonism in the remark, and Arnold began backing away, and the group very quickly began to lose interest in him.

He stayed for as long as he could to observe Vera, who so far as he could tell had taken no notice of him at all during the whole comedy of his entrance. All the time she had seemed preoccupied with the Victorian sewing machine. She may have given him a half-glance, but otherwise she was busy with threads and bobbins, using her mouth to break a length of cotton, her golden hair spilling forward as she bent to the task. But she filled his attention as she had done before. It was an agony to take his eyes away from her, to pretend uninterest. And the scent was as powerful as the last time. The room was a mixture of smells now, a stew of perfumes, but the original one dominated, the hyacinth tang that had amazed him before and amazed him again.

He withdrew, first to the kitchen, then he slipped upstairs, and from there he listened.

At first he listened from the spare bedroom that he used as a study, but was soon drawn out of that room and onto the landing, where he could hear more clearly. He was alone in the upper part of the house. His daughter was downstairs with the rest of the females. From his perch at the top of the stairs he could eavesdrop without fear of discovery, but he had trouble making out individual words. Why did they talk so much at the same time? He worked his way slowly down the stairs. Someone had shut the living-room door, which made it very hard to hear clearly, though he could make out enough to tell they were talking about sewing and sewing machines, about fabrics and stitches and threads. They were sharing recently uncovered memories of childhood sewing, of watching their mothers sew, of holding wool for their grandmothers. From what he could make out, they never deviated beyond this general subject area. And then he heard it – Vera's voice. That was all he was waiting for, he realized. He didn't care about the sense, he just wanted to hear the voice, the music of it. From the general hubbub of the women, Vera's voice broke through and silenced everything around it. He was entranced by its music. All the other voices held back, allowing it to do its work, which was probably the telling of another sewing anecdote of no import, and although her voice had no great strength, it had the power to quieten the other voices, the only voice among the women that was able to do that.

They listened to her story until it reached its conclusion, and then they laughed and responded, as though released from a spell.

Then he noticed something that fixed him with a sudden whelming of energy. The vestibule at the end of the hall where they kept their shoes and coats had thickened and swelled. The women had brought coats and hats with them, and Polly must have hung them up there, because leaning over the banister he could see several strange garments he hadn't seen before, and he wondered if Vera's coat would be part of that little crowd of empty clothes.

Barely had he had a moment to think through what he was doing before he was down in the hall and in among the coats. He had to pass right by the door to the living room, and pass close to the voices that were now much clearer. He put to the back of his mind the problem of what to do if that door should open now, as he was feeling his way through the visitors' coats trying to identify Vera's, what he would say if Polly saw him. He was too busy following the smell, which was rich and deep here, and helped him pull out from its hook the black duffel coat that he remembered he had seen on Vera, and to take it in his arms and engulf it. No one opened the door. He held the coat close to him, pushing his face into its lining, enveloping himself in the hood. He was surprised by its texture, expecting a duffel-coat roughness, a bristliness, but instead there was a softness to the fabric; the big black muscly coat was tender and yielding, so much so that it

felt as though the coat was touching him back. He felt
suddenly joyous, for the stupidity of what he was doing,
making love to an empty coat, playing with its silly,
childlike toggles. Rather than feeling ashamed at having
executed such an underhand, proxy assault, he felt the
triumph of a little boy who has obtained some forbidden
treat from the adult world. He thought for a second about
taking the coat upstairs, kidnapping it entirely, taking
possession of it, imagining the quandary when it came to
home time – where was it? Where had Vera's coat gone?
Are you sure you brought a coat with you? I don't remember you having one? Yes, the black one, the duffel coat,
it's my favourite coat, the nicest coat I've ever had, the
warmest, the loveliest . . .

# 2

Since he regarded himself as someone to whom women were not inordinately attracted, Arnold did not see much risk in indulging his fascination for Vera. He also felt that, because she was a practising Christian, he was doubly safe from any danger of straying. Even if he had wanted to, he could not have tempted her into infidelities, her beliefs and her commitment to her family were too strong. There were three barriers, then, to any chance of dalliance – family, Church and his own lack of sexual appeal. This all-surrounding triple-layered fender of prohibition made it seem perfectly safe for him to encounter Vera and play with the possibilities of what could happen between them, if those three barriers hadn't existed. It also enabled him to deny to himself he had any physical longing for Vera, and to feel instead that he was merely enjoying the richness of a particular type of human presence.

Outside of the sewing-machine circle, the only other opportunity Arnold had to meet Vera was at the school when dropping off or collecting Evelyn. Polly did this, even though it would have made more sense, given their working hours, for Arnold to have done so, but Polly felt it kept her in touch with the other parents, and with their daughter's teachers. In the evenings it was normal for Evelyn to go to a friend's house to be picked up from there at around half-past four or five o'clock, which was usually the earliest Polly could get back from her shop. Now that she had a new best friend in Irina, Vera's daughter, she most often went to her house after school to be collected.

In usual circumstances Arnold only did the school run if Polly had some other commitment, and it was a task he generally hated. It meant standing in the playground waiting for the bell to go (a reminder of his own dismal school days) with the other mothers and the occasional father, with whom he felt he had very little in common. He would endure the scanty conversations he had with these parents, which were mostly confined to enquiries about Polly and why she hadn't shown up, or else things about the children's education that he tried hard to appear interested in, when really he was just waiting for the bell to go so that he could make his escape.

Now Arnold grabbed every opportunity for taking Evelyn to school. If Polly showed the least sign that it was too much for her, if she was running the littlest bit late or worrying about the pile of things she had to do at the shop, he would step in and helpfully volunteer for the school run. It was ridiculous, he said, that on mornings when he didn't have to be at work till ten, he didn't take Evelyn. It was actually on his way to work, whereas Polly's shop was in the opposite direction. He even had a research day each week, when he didn't have to go to work at all. Why not let him take some of the burden? And Polly agreed, after a moment of doubt, that it did make sense when he had the more flexible work pattern, to take on some of the ferrying duties. It would be a relief, she said. And so once or twice a week, and sometimes more, and to the child's delight and puzzlement ('Why are you taking me to school, Daddy?') Arnold took his daughter to St Clare's primary.

Vera was always there. She was usually part of a small group of two or three other mothers. Now that their daughters were best friends, he had permission to join this group, indeed he had little choice and could even make a display of being the reluctant follower as Evelyn led him across the grey playground, to where Irina and her mother stood. And as soon as they were together the children would go off to play or talk, leaving the adults to themselves.

Arnold then found he couldn't do much more than observe Vera, as she would be in conversation with the others, and in some ways he felt satisfied with that. In fact he felt a terror of being alone with her, for fear that he would suddenly blurt some inappropriate remark, or even take hold of her, hug her, as he had done already her coat. But he was happy to be part of the small crowd, to laugh at the right moments, to offer his bland, innocuous comments when required, to add to all the other bland, innocuous comments that made up the typical playground conversation.

Sometimes a father would be part of their group, dressed for work in the real world of business, wearing a suit and tie, and Arnold would feel overshadowed by the way this man handled the group, dominating it in such a way that the women didn't seem to mind being interrupted and spoken over, since it was done with such good humour. Then Arnold would wonder if he was doing something wrong, that he should follow the example of this man, and do what he did, which was somehow to entertain the women, as though they were in his charge and he had responsibility for them. And when the man was in the full flow of his entertaining, charming the mothers with work anecdotes – he was a sales and marketing manager for a firm that made something Arnold had never heard of – Arnold felt a responsibility to assert his own presence, and to match the father's stories with stories of his own. He didn't because he felt that doing so would put the two males in competition and somehow imply a sexual motivation for his presence in the group. So he held back, remaining silent and unobserved.

Once or twice a week his day started in this way, to be followed by the familiar routines of teaching and research. In his classes there were many beautiful students, yet none of them held the remotest interest for him, and not simply because they were more than twenty years his junior. The beautiful faces seemed like exquisite masks with no character or expression, fragile artefacts compared to Vera's older, living face. And then once a week the sewing evening, when he would eavesdrop if he could, or linger in the kitchen to get a glimpse of her, and feel sorrowful and even heartbroken if for some reason she wasn't there.

As far as he could tell, she had taken very little notice of him in return. Beyond polite pleasantries, nods and smiles, she seemed mostly unaware of his interest. He was not surprised and it confirmed his feeling of safety and protection. It would be hard to design a person less inclined to have an extramarital affair than Vera. She, like him, was still devoted to her family. For his part he was not even bored with his. They still interested and excited him. In this way he found his attraction to Vera quite inexplicable. He had no needs that were not being met. He was satisfied with his life, his love, his work, everything. He also sensed that Vera's beauty was something most people wouldn't see. She was beautiful in her own way, and this set her apart from other women. She was not like certain females he knew – that tinted and overdone woman in the sewing group, for instance – who seemed finely attuned to the subtleties of male attention, whose attractiveness had made them skilled in fending off or courting it, according to their highly specific preferences. Vera had not turned many heads in her life, he imagined, and was mostly overlooked by the male gaze, but not by his.

She had, if anything, a slightly odd face, rather distended and awkwardly put together, and her glasses made her eyes look little and sad. Yet being in her presence had an effect on him that was like the feeling of his heart being lifted out of his body. An intoxicating sense of gladness and relief that she was there. He began to feel about her in the same way that he understood some people felt about the natural world, birdwatchers and the like, that they felt a constant reassurance from observing it, having it in front of them, the solid, empirical evidence of its existence. A twitcher catching sight of a rare warbler on a twig has their trust in the forcefulness of nature restored. That's what he was beginning to feel about Vera, the whole bundle of her physical existence, the four-limbed, bipedal feet-on-the-ground substance of her.

He would have dealt with her in poems if he could, but writing poems about people had never been where his talents had lain. He longed, rather, for painterly skills, and was surprised that he didn't have such a talent, since he considered himself a far better observer of the world than most people he knew, including the handful of artists he'd met in his life, those sloppy splashers of colour and scrapers of pigment, who seemed to think paint itself was the important thing, and not the stuff out there. And Vera was stuff, she was the essence of stuff. When he was close to her he felt as though he was within the remit of something infinitely benevolent, that he was inside a charmed circle, and that the source of this energy was located in the form of her physical presence – her body, her clothes, the breath she emitted, and the invisible, intangible things that her body gave off – pheromones, DNA, molecular chaff.

But these thoughts were going on at the back of his mind, below the surface of his conscious, moral self, which maintained, so far, respect for those around him, and to whom he had responsibilities and obligations.

It was a few weeks before anything that could be called a friendship developed between them. Sometimes he found that they were the first of their group to arrive in the playground and so had a few minutes of conversation, or otherwise after the bell had gone they found themselves taking the same route out of the playground gates towards their cars, this again giving them a few minutes of private chat. At these times the talk would remain on the well-worn topics, the safe ground of children and schooling. Arnold laughed when she told him that she had been in their children's classroom and had heard a teaching assistant telling them how to spell the word Zebra, 'And she said it was spelt Z-E-D-B-R-A, but I couldn't correct her, not in front of the class.' And immediately Arnold realized he shouldn't have laughed, because this wasn't funny. And they agreed that something terrible was happening in the school, teaching assistants were being used increasingly – untrained, sometimes not very well educated – and teachers were allowing them to run whole lessons. 'And Irina thinks it's all right to say "he was sat on the chair", because that's exactly what Mrs Dalrymple, the teaching assistant, taught them was correct. We should do something about it. The government are getting away with murder. Handing over our kids' education to cheap, untrained labour.' Arnold agreed, knowing how the teaching assistants often came from a background of low-grade office jobs. 'And they bring their small-minded, office-dogsbody mentalities into the classroom.' They were both chilled by the thought that their children were being taught by fools.

But Arnold felt uncomfortable talking about their children. They were the common ground between them, but they were also the constant reminder that their lives belonged to other people, within the closed circles of different families. Sometimes, on the way out of the school, if they happened to be the last parents to leave, he felt momentarily free of that sense of belonging elsewhere, and that he and Vera could talk like two carefree and unattached friends. At such times he would try and steer the conversation away from subjects related to parenting and children.

He tried talking to her about the coincidence of them both having connections with the university, and he learnt that she had left academia with some bad feelings. She felt she had been pushed out of her job, was overburdened with teaching, given no chance to do research, then punished with a heavier workload for having such a poor research profile. It was a vicious spiral Arnold knew well, and was himself having to struggle with.

He had published nothing but a single collection of poems, *Macroscopia*, more than a decade ago. He had started working on a second but the flow of poetry had been slow since the success of his book. *Macroscopia* had won a major prize, and had been widely praised. For a year or two he had been famous in the small world of poetry and poetry studies. Following up on the success of the first book had been harder than he'd imagined. Although he had now accumulated enough finished poems for him to think about assembling them into a collection and offering them to his publisher, he balked at the thought of it, deeply worried that the new poems did not live up to the promise of the old. He feared that he had been in the grip of something very muse-like, that had enabled him to find poetry in anything, and he feared that that moment had passed. He struggled now to find poetry in things that had once seemed bedecked with it.

He didn't like to talk about his work as a poet, and she, it seemed, didn't like to talk about her life as an academic. He tried probing what she had wanted to research, but given that she had been an academic in the department of religious studies, he didn't want to steer her into talking about religion for fear that her moral consciousness might be unduly exercised, that she might suddenly awaken to the darker side of the intentions he barely acknowledged to himself that he had.

So they talked about mundanities. Things they'd seen on television, newsy gossip. There were some trashy TV programmes they both secretly liked. He was delighted that he seemed to be able to make her laugh very easily, and he found the way she laughed enchanting – the tilted head, the crescented eyes. Usually slow and deliberate in his conversation, he found himself possessed of a fluency he'd never had before, so that he couldn't quite believe it was himself talking. It was almost as if she was talking through him. It astonished him. Whatever came out of his mouth seemed to charm and amuse her. And he was conscious at the same time that he was talking rubbish, nonsense, inconsequential tittle-tattle. He suddenly wondered if he was actually a fool. His default position, conversationally, was surfaces and appearances. These were the things he liked talking about.

He began noticing that she seemed pleased to see him when he arrived in the playground. It became expected that he should talk to her. It became a routine, a normal thing. One morning, when by chance she was in conversation with another mother when he arrived, he stood apart, and felt conspicuous and out of place. Another morning, when he arrived, Vera was crouching down, attending to some problem with her daughter's shoes, so that she looked up at Arnold as he approached, her face filled with a smile, and her look passed all the way up and down his body, and her gaze settled on his body just for a moment longer than would have been normal for a friend. She seemed to enjoy looking at him.

The effect of knowing Vera, of being in her presence, even for that ten-minute morning drop-off, lasted with Arnold for the rest of the day, all through work and into the evening. He came home bright and elated, full of joy. But it was a general joy in life and its apparatus that he experienced, that through the day had become dissociated from its source, so that he couldn't have explained, exactly, why he felt happy, and mistakenly thought it was simply because he was home with his wife and daughter. It took him quite a lot of thought and reflection to realize that the happiness originated in that morning encounter, and that in a strange way the blissful energy that came from Vera was fuelling his joy in his own domestic life. She was giving him the energy to enjoy what he treasured most, even as she tempted him away from it.

As soon as the night came and the day was finished, when he'd eaten with his family, enjoyed them, helped his daughter with her homework, played with her, watched television with her, watched the late news, showered and gone to bed, he woke the next morning as if scraped and scaled of every last vestige of Vera's influence, and felt the need, the overwhelming urge, to revisit her, to see her again, as if she was a place, a beautiful building or land-scape that held strong and comforting associations for him. Yet he couldn't go every morning, and sometimes he couldn't go for several days. There were long separations. The hosting of the sewing evenings was now shared with friends, and they met at Polly and Arnold's only on alter-nate weeks now. So the chances of seeing Vera were reduced even further. Then a half term and no school runs for a week. How was he to cope? He hoped he would begin to forget about her, but in fact her memory seemed to grow stronger in his mind the longer the absence.

He felt an urge to talk about Vera with his wife, principally to find out more about her, but also because of a rather dangerous need he experienced, to have Vera established as an abstract presence within the family, someone they could both talk about and share opinions on. In a curious way he wanted to share his feelings about Vera, just as he would want to share his thoughts about a good book he'd just read. But he realized the profound risk he was taking in even mentioning Vera. The only way he dared do it was by contriving a conversational exchange in which Polly herself might be prompted to mention her. So he would ask how the sewing evenings were going. Had anyone made anything fantastic? Yes, said Polly, Geerda had started making velvet watermelons, using a special stitching technique. And Beverly had made a cover for her husband's iPad. Gillian was making a clown costume for a fancy dress party . . .

'Is that what you do, then, bring in pieces you've been working on and talk about them?'

'Yes, that's it. We talk about what we've been working on, then we take turns using some of the machines, sharing new techniques any of us have learnt. Then we have a drink and start gossiping.'

And what has Vera been making, he wanted to say, but it seemed she had made nothing of note, at least not enough to be among the examples Polly brought forth.

The only other subject he could think of was religion. If he could engage Polly in a religious discussion, then she would inevitably bring Vera into the conversation, because she was the one example she had, among her friends, of a religious person. She might cite and quote things Vera had said. But it was difficult to get Polly to talk about religion. She was, like him, an atheist, but more vehemently than him. Arnold liked the idea of religion, even if he didn't believe in a god, but Polly didn't even like the idea of it, was adamant that it was the product of fear and stupidity, that it was a force for bad in the world and that only the frightened and the stupid could believe in it. Which was Vera, he wondered, frightened or stupid?

'I've got this religious fanatic in one of my writing classes,' he said to her one evening in as casual a way as he could, which was difficult because he was doing something unusual in talking about his work. They were side by side on the couch, in the blaze of the television, wine glasses in hand, and Evelyn upstairs in bed.

'Have you?'

'Yes. Whenever the discussion moves on to sex, she asks if she can leave the room.'

'Why?'

'I'm not really sure. I suppose it offends her religious sensibility. She's very polite and apologetic about it. She behaves like someone with asthma might behave if someone started smoking. She just has to go outside, and comes back when the air has cleared.'

'So how often do your writing classes involve talking about sex?'

'Unfortunately one of the other students writes about nothing else, and of a quite extreme kind. But then most students think detailed sex scenes are compulsory in a novel. They don't seem to think anyone else knows how to do it. And they think they are the first ones ever to write about it.'

'And I suppose you take extra care in evaluating their descriptive powers in this area.'

'Well, I usually tell them to cut it out. I say if you're writing a story about two people and at some point they make love, there is no need to then go into several pages of detailed description. They wouldn't lavish the same amount of attention on them cutting their toenails, so why focus on the sex?'

'And, well, you're the writer, but I've always felt that including explicit sex scenes in a novel is just – bad manners.'

'Spoken like a true Englishwoman. But anyway, I feel sorry for the religious fanatic.'

'Oh, she sounds idiotic. An attention-seeker. Passive-aggressive. If she was in a class of mine I'd have sex there and then, just to annoy her.'

In fact, the student didn't exist. Arnold had made her up for the purposes of talking about religion.

'I think it's rather sweet that people can still be offended by it, in this day and age. It is strange, the religious mind.'

'Stupid, you mean.'

'Isn't one of your friends religious?'

'Oh, Vera? Yes, she is a bit.'

'And is she stupid?'

'Well, I suppose in some fundamental way she must be stupid, but otherwise I think she's very clever. I like her, actually. She never talks about religion.'

'So how do you know she's religious?'

'She says things like she went to church on Sunday, but she doesn't talk about her beliefs  that's what I meant.'

'Has she ever tried to convert you?'

Polly laughed. 'Of course not.'

'Why "of course not"?'

'Because I don't think she's that sort of religious – an evangelical. And she knows that we would have to stop being friends if she tried anything like that. I couldn't stand it. In fact just thinking about her religion is starting to put me off her. If I don't think about it, then I can like her.'

In a strange way this was a relief. Their friendship only went so deep. They weren't soulmates or kindred spirits. Religion acted as an impediment to deeper friendship. In the mind experiment that Arnold was playing, in which he entered into a full-blown affair with Vera, the damage he would do to Polly was softened a little by this fact. And then he went on to have the thought that Vera's religiousness made having an affair with her a less insidious crime than if she was an atheist. It would demonstrate that the passion between them was so strong, so irresistible, that even the strictures and prohibitions of one of the world's great religions couldn't prevent it from happening. Not even God could have stopped it. If a devout Christian couldn't resist the temptation, then what chance did he, a faithless little poet, have?

'What church does she go to?'

'What church? You mean the actual building, or the branch of Christianity?'

'Both, I suppose.'

'I don't know the answer to either, actually. But I know it's not a regular church, not a traditional church with a steeple, it's some other place.'

There were several churches with steeples in their neighbourhood, mostly Victorian neo-Gothic structures with billboards outside that said things like Jesus Saves, or He is Watching You. Arnold had taken little notice of them before and felt glad that she didn't attend one of those, because they seemed institutions of unbearable sadness, akin to old people's homes. But then the modern churches seemed even sadder, the Kingdom Halls with their feeble attempts at inspirational architecture, an out of town supermarket was a more uplifting building. Then the terrifying thought – supposing she was a Jehovah's Witness, or a Seventh Day Adventist? Someone bound up in rigid dogma and governed by peculiar laws and prohibitions. How could he have a relationship with someone who might think him evil, for obscure, irrational reasons?

He satisfied himself that her religion could not be extreme in any way. She seemed too relaxed, too at ease with the vulgarities of secular society. She would be at the softer end of the scale of religious belief, the tolerant one, the one that doesn't really believe in miracles. She would not be like that woman he once met at an airport who said that aeroplanes flew because they were borne aloft by angels. But then again, she did look religious. What did that mean? He could have picked her out of a crowd, if told there was one believer in a crowd of unbelievers. She looked unadorned, pure, clean. There was nothing decorative about her. She looked fresh and healthy. But she also looked serious and a little bit stern. He began to wonder if that was what he found attractive about her. And in that way she was similar to Polly. He had always felt attracted to studious, serious, quiet women, which he thought must have been a legacy of falling in love, as a child, with so many of his teachers. She also looked peaceful. It was impossible to imagine her committing an act of violence, or shouting. That was why the experience of causing her to smile or laugh, to animate her in any way, felt so fulfilling.

Arnold still did not fully understand the force of Vera's attraction for him. He could see that her looks were plain at the same time as he felt a sense of helpless devotion to them. Perhaps it was purely chemical, or olfactory, or perhaps she resembled closely some childhood goddess who had transfixed him once, and then been forgotten. At times he felt afraid of the force of attraction he was experiencing. He tried reassuring himself that her spiritual beliefs, her religiousness, her moral uprightness and her commitments to her husband and family were all strong enough to ensure that nothing could ever happen between them, and that his own family was safe and secure. But then, when he saw her again, when they had their easy little playground chats, when he saw her full of smiling and laughter, these certainties would melt away and he would feel himself in the current of something irresistible, that he was being pulled willingly towards uncertainty and danger.

And then, one morning, she said something about her body. They were standing side by side in the playground, waiting for the bell to go. Each morning a different child was given the privilege of ringing the large brass handbell that signalled the start of the school day. This morning, for the first time, the privilege had been given to Arnold's own golden-haired daughter Evelyn, who insisted that she would only do it together with her best friend, Vera's daughter Irina. The two girls went over to the far end of the playground where the teacher on duty was standing with the bell, and the two parents watched side by side from afar. A mother and father, of different families, but both looking on in shared pride, as though they were part of the same family. Arnold noticed a little moment of pain pass across Vera's face.

'Are you all right?'

'Just a headache,' she said. 'I get lots of headaches. I think it's to do with my neck.'

'What's wrong with your neck?'

'Nothing, it's just too long.'

He was touched by this reference to that part of her,

and a little shocked. He felt flushed in the face. It was because he found her neck so attractive, so gorgeous, that by acknowledging it, it was almost as though she had made a sexually provocative remark. It was almost as though she had said 'my breasts are too small'.

'It's a nice neck,' he said. Too quick. Too sudden. He hadn't thought about it. He had just said it. He said it in an encouraging tone of voice, as if in reply to a remark of self-deprecation, as though she had said 'I've got an ugly neck'. No, it's a nice neck. You should be proud of your neck. You should make a display of your neck, you should wrap it with jewellery, a choke of pearls, or black velvet. Actually no – such ornaments would look silly on Vera's neck. She would look like something on a hoop-la stall. She would look like one of those tribal women who increase the length of their neck by the means of stacked rings.

'I wasn't fishing for a compliment,' said Vera.

'I know. I shouldn't have said that.'

'It was nice of you to say it.'

Evelyn and Irina marched across the playground, shaking their brass bell, and all the children began to move away from their parents and into the school building.

It was as though she had said – 'Here is my neck, you are free to adore it.' He had wondered – did she really have a long neck? Was it longer than other people's? Necks are all the same length. They consist of the same set of bones, the seven segments, C1–C7 of the cervical spine. Everyone has a neck of seven bones. Well, he supposed these bones could be bigger, thicker, taller in some people than others. All mammals, not just humans, have a neck of seven bones – dogs, gazelles, camels, even giraffes. Seven cervical verte-brae. Thoughts about Vera's neck filled him. He had been given her neck, she had offered him her neck, to think about, and he thought about it, just as he thought about everything she said during that morning encounter, for the rest of the day, so that he could process it and analyse it for any clue as to her feelings towards him. He imagined planting kisses along that pale column, planting kisses all the way along – how many would it have taken. Seven? A kiss for each vertebra?

When he got home he felt relieved and thankful to find that his family was as it always was – busy and messy and preoccupied. He imagined that he had harmed it merely by harbouring the thoughts he'd had about Vera, the thoughts that had been in his head all day since that morning encounter and the conversation about her neck. All day he wondered what he had done. It was a simple remark, but he had complimented her on an aspect of her physical appearance, he had told her that he appreciated a part of her body. And she had received the remark will-ingly. It was a nice thing to say, she had told him. She appreciated the remark, as though people didn't appreci-ate her neck often enough. That she had a neglected neck. You should wear your hair up, he had said, venturing further than he thought he'd ever dare, yet somehow he felt it was all right to say this to Vera. But the cheek. Who was he to start saying how she should wear her hair? You should wear your hair up. Show it off, your neck. He had put playfulness into his tone of voice, which took energy, because the actual tone of voice he wanted to use was one of hushed, devoted seriousness. And she had smiled and responded to his playfulness – 'No, too much work. And I need to protect it from the cold.'

Now, at home, he could hardly believe the conversation had ever taken place. Not here, in his home with his daughter, in the lounge-diner and Polly busy in the kitchen. At times like these his house reminded him of a workshop in which people are hard at the task of creating themselves. His daughter had a pack of cards and was sitting on the floor, bent over them. As soon as he entered the room she claimed him, springing up and going over to the dining table, demanding he sit down opposite her. He felt compelled to obey, because at this time of day it was understood that he was under his daughter's command.

He thought at first that Evelyn had a deck of ordinary playing cards, and he was anticipating a game of pairs or snap, or beat your neighbours out of doors, one of those interminable games with few rules. But when he sat down he saw that they were not ordinary playing cards. They had plain symbols on them, in heavy black outlines – a square, a circle, a star . . . . He recognized them. They were mind-reading cards.

'Where did you get these?' But he vaguely remembered

that they'd come in a box of magic tricks she had been given for Christmas a year or two ago, and never used until now.

'I can read minds, Daddy,' said Evelyn, in a cheerful voice.

Without quite knowing where it came from, at first, Arnold experienced a cold sense of threat. He felt like someone walking the length of a causeway who suddenly finds they are cut off by the tide. Then he realized this sense of dread emanated from his own daughter.

'Is that a good thing?'

She ignored his question and handed him the cards. 'Pick one,' she said, 'but don't show me.'

With dumb obedience he took the little pack, aware all the time that his wife was behind him in the kitchen, busy with important things. He picked a card. A set of wavy lines. They represented water, which made the sense of threat all the stronger.

'You're not thinking,' said Evelyn.

'I am.'

'Think harder.'

He couldn't help being reminded, by the wavy lines, of Vera's hair, and for a moment felt afraid that Evelyn might say, 'Irina's mum. You're thinking of Irina's mum.' But instead she said, 'Water.'

He had been prepared for playing a little joke on his daughter, and switching the cards to make it seem as though she'd given the right answer, and he was taken aback by the fact that he didn't need to. In fact, he was momentarily horrified. He showed her the card, and she took the news of her success in her stride. Mind-reading, to this young girl, seemed nothing exceptional.

'Let's do it again,' she said.

Reluctantly he took another card. A star. Evelyn concentrated, a little frown appeared on her forehead, above her closed eyes.

'You're not thinking hard enough,' she said.

Arnold realized this was true, he had not thought about the star at all. When he did, staring and trying to make it big in his mind, Evelyn suddenly relaxed her face and said, 'Star.' He hardly had to show her the card, she seemed to know she was right.

Polly appeared. 'Are you still playing with those silly cards?'

'She got it right twice in a row,' said Arnold, disconcerted by his daughter's apparent ability.

'I told you I can read minds,' said Evelyn, 'I can read Mummy's too.'

'She got two out of three with me,' said Polly, as if confidentially to her husband, half-smiling. 'It would be a useful ability, if it worked with anything other than those cards.'

Polly was setting the table at which they were seated. Arnold had a clear view of her as she made a space for the plates that were on her arm. He wondered when he had stopped observing her so closely, and realized it was only within the last few weeks. Up until then she had had all his attention, but in the short time since, he had almost forgotten what she looked like. He noticed her neck. It was a beautiful neck, but it was not Vera's.

Evelyn was urging him to pick another card, but Arnold declined as gracefully as he could. He knew it was a game that could only end in disappointment, after however many lucky guesses. And perhaps it was better to preserve the magical moment in which the child genuinely believed she could read his mind.

Polly dropped a handful of cutlery onto the table with a sound like chains being severed.

# 3

It was a harder thing for Arnold to have an excuse to collect Evelyn from Vera's house if his daughter went there after school. Polly always fetched her because she was usually back from the shop before Arnold was home from work. There were only two days of the week when Arnold was home earlier, and these only rarely coincided with the days that Evelyn went to Vera's house. Nevertheless he prepared himself for the occasion when it did happen, that he could leap in and offer to collect Evelyn from Vera's. He didn't feel it was something he could just volunteer to do, he had to have a good reason. And so when the time came he picked his moment carefully and said he had to go out and buy a new ink cartridge. That was the kind of modern emergency that fitted the situation perfectly, one that every poet and academic knows – the empty ink cartridge and the dissertation to print out by tomorrow. They sold his cartridges at a place on the main road that didn't close till 6.30. 'I'll pick Evelyn up on the way back, if you like.'

'OK,' said Polly, mildly surprised, 'if you don't mind.'

'No, I don't mind.'

And he drove straight to Vera's house.

He had only been there once or twice before, and hadn't taken much notice of it then, but now he studied it in every detail. He took in the frontage, rather similar to his own house, Victorian red brick, stained glass in the front-door window, tasteful curls of art nouveau in the side panels. The glass in the windows was dimpled and crisp. There were net curtains, which Arnold thought rather odd. His generation had done away with net curtains, so he had assumed. But here were net curtains, greyly opaque, such as his grandmother used to have in her windows, from which she observed the world as though from inside a muslin bag.

There was a short front garden that had been pounded into submission by the pouring on of pebbles. In a wooden tub an olive tree was trying to grow. A garishly yellow and orange plastic tricycle sat crookedly on the pebbles. Unmistakably a family house, even without the tricycle – there was an aura of the siege, of a household under the constant bombardment of its children's demands.

He pressed the bell, which worked. Vera answered the door and didn't immediately register his presence, saying hello without looking who she was speaking to, assuming him, he supposed, to be his wife. She did a kind of double-take, and her face immediately brightened, her eyes dilated and doubled their fullness. 'Oh – hello, it's you.'

She couldn't hide or deny her pleasure in seeing him.

'Hello again. Can I come in?'

'Of course,' she stepped back from the door, and he passed her closely as she held it for him, almost as if she was expecting a kiss, the kiss of a husband home from work, the polite friendship kisses that had become commonplace now, and which provided Arnold with endless opportunities for awkwardness (to kiss or not to kiss, one cheek or two? Lip or no lip?). But he passed her without making physical contact, though he had to mention her hair – or should he? She had put it up. It was piled on the top of her head now, with some stray strands hanging down. The whole neck was revealed.

Since their initial exchanges he felt he had gained permission to make slightly personal remarks about her appearance. He had made the suggestion about her hair several times, and she had always come back with some riposte, some reason for not wearing her hair that way.

— Why don't you ever wear your hair up?

— Why – do you think it would cure my headaches?

— It might do. But it seems strange, when you have grown your hair long, not to do things with it.

— Oh, so you are saying I'm strange?

— No, not at all. It's just that your neck – you should show it off more.

— Oh no, my neck is too long. People would laugh at me.

They had talked about make-up. Vera never wore any because she had sensitive skin. She had never in her life worn mascara or eyeshadow. Not even when she was a teenager, when all her friends were obsessed by it. Arnold said that she didn't need it.

— I can't imagine you with make-up. It would look wrong.

— Another way of putting what you just said would be – it might make you look quite nice.

— But you already look quite nice.

— Angus is always trying to persuade me to wear make-up. He buys it for my birthday. He once bought this stuff for my eyelids. It was like a bottle of ink, with a paint brush. I said, what am I supposed to do with this? It looks like something to lacquer shoes with. He said I should paint it on my eyelids. And so I tried it, but it was ridiculous. Without my glasses I couldn't see to put it on, so he tried doing it for me, but I couldn't keep my eyelids still for long enough, and he didn't have a steady enough hand, and the stuff kept dripping. When he'd done it I looked like a zombie. And then my eyes became inflamed and I couldn't see for the rest of the day.

These were the sort of things they sometimes talked about. He loved to hear her criticize her husband, which she would only do indirectly. She said he was frustrated in his job, because it was a nine-to-five job with an hour-and-a-half commute each way, which meant he felt he didn't see enough of her or the children, and this sometimes made him sour and grumpy when he was at home.

Half-past six was his time for returning home, though quite often he could be as late as seven. But he was never,

ever, home before half-past six. Arnold had memorized this fact. It was half-past five when he arrived at the house to collect Evelyn. A whole hour before the nine-to-five man was due home from work.

Arnold decided not to say anything about Vera's hair, not immediately. She had not been expecting him to call, so she couldn't have done it for his benefit. Nevertheless he was excited by the possibility that she had responded to his observations about her. He passed through the narrow hall with its tide of shoes and wellingtons and turned right into a rather dowdy lounge-diner. The last time he had seen this room it had been prepared for visitors, swept and dusted, with toys back in their boxes, DVDs back on their shelves. Now he saw it in its raw state, with its litter of childhood. The table still carried the trash from the children's tea – smeared plates, spilt juice, flakes of food on the floor. The room had an air of defeat about it. He sensed the presence of a slightly more argumentative family than his own, of children who answered back, who had bedtime tantrums, who had the upper hand in the household's power struggles. It became immediately apparent when Vera went to call the children, who were in the playroom at the back of the house watching a DVD. There were loud cries of protest. Arnold followed behind and saw a small group of children gathered on the carpet before the glow of a large, cumbersome television.

'Daddy, it's nearly finished, can we watch to the end?'

He had almost forgotten Evelyn was in the room, and was startled for a moment to see her face down there among the other childish faces. He didn't say anything but looked at Vera. There was nothing he wanted more than to stay. He wanted to stay for as long as he could, and hoped she was thinking the same.

'It's got about ten minutes to run,' she said, 'I could give you a tour of the house.'

They left the children. Arnold took one last glance at them, making sure they were settled. There were four of them. Vera had two more children, one older, one younger than Irina. They all got on very well together. Everyone noticed it, commented on it, how well they got on. Evelyn was becoming like a new sibling for them. What struck him at that moment was how uninterested in him they seemed. Apart from Evelyn, none of them had acknowledged his presence at all, even though he was a rare visitor to the house. When he tried to remember his own childhood, the entrance of strangers into the house had always been a cause of excitement and fear, of awe – who were they, these visitors? What were they doing, why had they come? What did they know? What powers did they have? For these children nothing seemed remarkable. He was something slow and colourless by comparison to the more vivid reality of manufactured narrative that absorbed them now.

Back in the lounge-diner, for the moment an adult domain, he and Vera inhabited what seemed a far more solid and logical world. He wanted to say something about the children, about how horrible it was that the television captured them so completely, but he was aware of how thankful he was for it, for the invisibility it conferred on them. And anyway he wanted them both to forget about the children as quickly as they could.

'We've been wanting to decorate this room for ages, but I don't see the point until the kids have grown up a bit. They'll ruin it as soon as it's done.'

From there they went upstairs. The same scuffed quality to the walls of the stairwell, wallpaper torn aside as though someone had tried to turn it, like the page of a book. A dent in the plaster. On the landing there was no decoration at all. Walls had been stripped in preparation for paper that was never hung, but scribbled on with pencils and crayons instead. Bare floorboards. A heap of dirty washing piled by the bathroom door.

Vera led him through into a bedroom. The atmosphere in here was very different. The room had been decorated in dark blue, the bed was plump and neat. There was a sense of crowdedness of things, but of a careful order as well. Arnold noticed a row of ties hanging on the back of a chair. A desk was by the window with a big, out-of-date-looking computer on it. They suddenly seemed to be in a separate world from the children downstairs.

'This is where we sleep,' said Vera, with a slightly embarrassed hesitation in her voice, as if she was suddenly not sure why she had brought Arnold here. Arnold's attention was drawn to another corner of the room, where a sewing machine sat, identical to the one he had first seen her working on, at his own house, the one that still occupied a corner of his lounge-diner. Alongside it was the older black and chrome one she had brought to a sewing evening. The lives of the husband and wife here seemed represented like two fighters in a boxing ring, occupying opposite corners. Was that a reflection of their relationship, Arnold wondered, poles apart, adversaries? But the sewing machines bothered him because they were also a reminder of Vera's friendship with his wife. Their presence halted any thought he had that Vera had brought him in here so that they could make love, even though at that moment he had to use all his reasoning and willpower to hold himself back from reaching out and touching her. Nevertheless the privilege of being admitted to this sanctum, the place where the object of his fascination slept, albeit with the nine-to-five man, was intensely thrilling to him.

Vera looked exquisite to him at that moment. She was wearing the simplest of clothes, jeans and a dark blue T-shirt with a neckline low enough to be revealing when she bent down. Tantalizing glimpses were given when she picked a stray toy off the floor, of smooth, deepening skin, white inner fabric. But then she was gone and he was following her back onto the landing. The house seemed to go up and up. There was another staircase, a short one that led to a mini-landing which opened onto another bathroom. This was ancient, with a copper boiler, and a white enamel bath on clawed feet. The silver taps were encrusted with white crystals. Yet there was an intense brightness about the room, a freshness despite the agedness of everything.

They visited other rooms, went up more stairs, finally they were in the attic, which was one of the children's bedrooms, and here they made love.

He reached out and put his hand against the side of her neck. He felt confident that his touch was desired and would not be rejected. She had brought him up here for no other reason than to be as far away from the children as they could be, to have the longest amount of warning if they were interrupted – all those staircases to clump up. He could see in her face that she was waiting for him to do something, the eye contact was prolonged and meaningful. She looked a little afraid, knowing that they had reached a boundary and were preparing to cross. She almost seemed to wish there were more stairs to climb, that her house went up and up for ever. But they had reached the top. They were crushed in beneath the low attic roof. And he reached out and touched her neck, placing his hand on the side of it, in a gesture that was reassuring, gently affirmative, encouraging, as if she had been a frightened child, or he was seeing her off on a train. And she held his gaze as his hand rested there. He could feel her pulse in the palm of his hand. And she lifted her hand and placed it on top of his, cementing the grip.

He had always imagined that, if this moment were ever to occur, something would hold him back, some moral force – guilt, a sense of wrongness, fear for what he was putting at stake, and if not that, then Vera's religious sense of right and wrong would prevail and prevent anything happening. But in reality, those forces proved to be as weak as a baby's hand, and Arnold suddenly became aware that what he had been doing in all these weeks of chatting with Vera and complimenting her on her looks and talking about her neck, was laying the ground for precisely this to happen.

They kissed, and he remembered how complicated the procedure seemed when performed with a near-stranger. He didn't know her mouth and their teeth clashed. She put out her tongue at the wrong moment, so that it was left hanging in the air, before he went back and took it in his own mouth. There was no taste in her mouth other than the taste of her. She put a hand to his crotch. The sensation of being touched there by her knocked the air out of him. He was becoming so solid he had to wriggle slightly against the sudden ache, and had to free himself of his own arousal, in order to let it gain strength. Her hand against his jeans pinched lightly at the stiffened length as though gauging its thickness. His hand went to her abdomen and stirred the fabric at her waist, untucked her and went inside. The warmth of her skin was slightly cloying, she felt softer than he'd expected in one so slim, it seemed she had no skeleton, no edges. He pulled back from her and lifted the T-shirt higher, exposing her white bra. He suddenly became aware that he would do anything to have her breasts revealed to him. Their disclosure seemed, in that moment, like the greatest goal of his life; he would have done anything to guard and maintain the privilege that had, out of nowhere, come to him, of witnessing the moment. If a child had run into the room he couldn't have stopped himself. He would have killed someone. He was that closed off from things. At the same time, he wanted to hold back that moment of disclosure for as long as he could, knowing it could never happen in quite the same way again. It was the moment, as much as the thing, that contained the beauty.

His breath went away again when they were uncupped. He couldn't help but utter, barely audibly, the single word, 'Jesus', because they seemed to him miraculously perfect. He was aware that she was making a mewling sound as he put his lips to her tightened nipple and sucked. Her mouth was at his ear, her tongue travelling along its grooves, voice filling it. His mouth tugged at her, extended her, she snapped back, there was a taste of something on his tongue. In his mind he pictured her neck, her long neck, her swan's neck, her Alice in Wonderland neck coiling like a serpent, like a serpent, coiling down on him. She had found a way through his clothing and her fingers had lightly touched his cock, then slowly began to take a firmer hold. He wanted to cry like a baby. He felt helpless, as though his body had come undone and she was fastening it. He felt as though he was bleeding somewhere. Then he felt powerful, gigantic. He could have kicked a door down.

And then they were finished. They had reached a point where they could go no further, not without risking everything. High up in the attic of the tall house they felt as though their children were trapped at the bottom of a well, but even so, they might come tumbling up the stairs at any moment on some spontaneous expedition. A form of sanity returned to the two adults and settled on them and they adjusted themselves, tucked themselves away, buttoned themselves up. Still breathless they hugged and kissed in a reaffirming way, at the top of the stairs. At the landing they kissed again, telling each other, by so doing, that they didn't regret what they had done on the floor above. Only when they came towards the stairs and passed the open door of the master bedroom did they break off contact, became separate and distinct again. Arnold experienced a sense of exertion, as though he had been running, or climbing. He felt as though he had rescued Vera from a crumbling building. He felt as though she, in turn, had rescued him. He felt like they were survivors of some unimaginable disaster, that they had saved each other, and were returning to their old life as if reborn, ready for anything.

The children amazed him by showing no sign that anything had happened; they were just as he'd left them, in the gaze of the television, even though their DVD had finished, and they were watching something else. It seemed impossible that what they had done upstairs had not wrought some change in the world beyond them, but everything was the same, nothing had been affected. Even Vera was back to the woman she'd always been on the ground floor of the house – sensible, polite, serious. But he could still see the flush on her skin, the fullness of her eyes, as though she'd been crying.

As he took his daughter out of the front door which Vera held open for him she was all practical, polite primness. He looked at her carefully for any sign of regret, and she gave him a smile of intense warmth as he passed, a momentary glimpse of her upstairs face, that lasted barely a second, but which was enough to signal she had no regrets about what had happened.

He held his daughter by the hand as he walked her to the car. The feel of her hand in his was terrible, for what his own hand had so recently been doing. He felt he was passing the essence of his wrongness from his hand to hers, that he had infected her with his own vileness, that she was permanently marked with it, yet he couldn't avoid holding her hand, because he couldn't reject normal contact with her either. And at the same time, the feeling of rebirth stayed with him. It was a feeling of exhilaration that was so strong he was shaking, and had trouble driving. When he spoke he had no idea what was going to come out of his mouth, and his daughter laughed at him, because he was talking nonsense. He was so exhilarated it was all he could do to prevent himself from telling his daughter what he had just done, he was overspilling with the joy of it, he wanted to share it, to relate it. At home, the same with Polly, he wanted to tell her what had just happened, not as a confession, but in order to let her know how he was feeling, to share the joy of the experience. But the sane part of him placed its restraints on his behaviour. He understood quite plainly how badly he had behaved with Vera, and he understood how that behaviour would be seen by others. But from that point on he felt as though there were two of him living parallel lives, the part of him that cared about and loved his family, and the part of him that loved Vera, and he was able to separate one from the other with an ease that surprised and worried him.

The wrongness of what he had done seemed nourishing. And he wanted more of it. He wanted to do it again and again. He wanted to do nothing but that thing he had done with Vera. He could not stop thinking about her. Not even for a moment. It was as though she had written herself onto him.

# 4

It was during a holiday in Wales, when Evelyn was still a baby, that Polly discovered she had a talent for paper-making. On a guided tour of some slate caverns they had come across a little paper-making workshop near the exit and Polly had volunteered to have a go herself after the paper-maker had given a demonstration. She had fallen instantly in love with the process and as soon as she was back home had started making it herself, filling the bath with paper pulp and the house with piles of scrap paper to use as raw material. She had become so quickly adept at the craft that it turned into a hobby, then an obsession. After doing some short courses in business management and accounting she decided to try and make a living from it. She was convinced there was a demand, in an age where paper was being used less and less, for a hand-made high-quality version of the product. Artisan stationery. Two years after Evelyn's birth, and in partnership with a small group of friends, she opened a shop in a good loca-tion off the High Street in the tourist area of the city centre, near the cathedral. She called it, simply, Papyrus.

Arnold objected to this name, saying that papyrus and paper were completely different things, but Polly insisted, because it was etymologically the root of the word paper and therefore, somehow, a purer form of it.

She had never run a business before, but she seemed to discover a talent for that as well. She filled the shop, as much as she could, with her own paper, which she made in a workshop at the back – itself open to visitors. For the rest of the stock she relied mostly on high-quality paper bought from other small-scale, specialist paper-makers, alongside other stationery items – envelopes, pens, note-books. She also sold original artwork and some other crafts made by her friends. Terri, one of her partners in the business and co-manager of the shop, made greetings cards and jewellery.

Polly sometimes liked to claim, half-jokingly, that she had reinvented paper. Arnold had to agree that, as a writer, he had never thought about the surface upon which he wrote more deeply than when confronted with the beautiful leaves of paper that came from Papyrus's pulp tanks. The shop and Polly's hand-made paper seemed to remind a public that had forgotten how to look at it that paper had a texture, a thickness and an edge.

Polly ran a programme of events at Papyrus as a way of raising the profile of the business and bringing potential customers into the shop. At first she organized paper-making courses, and then drawing and painting sessions in which home-made paper was used. It then seemed to her an obvious idea that the next step in promoting her paper would be to use it for the publishing of books, which could then be read to an audience at the shop. Since she would only ever be able to make small books in short print runs, poetry pamphlets seemed a good idea. With a modestly famous poet husband as editor, they might even be able to attract well-known poetry names to publish with them. Arnold was reluctant, at first, to take on the role of editor for the Papyrus Press, even though he could see it was a potentially good idea. Polly said that the paper would be individually made for each book, and would incorporate something that responded to the content of the book. So if a book contained references to a particular material, or colour, those things could be used in the making of the paper. And so the Papyrus Press published a small number of poetry pamphlets each year with Arnold as the general editor, Polly the designer and papermaker. They were, so they believed, the only publishing press in the country that produced books using their own bespoke paper.

Other than this joint venture, Arnold had little to do with Papyrus, and it was recognized as entirely Polly's business, in which Arnold didn't even have a share. She often said how it had kept her sane in the years after Evelyn's birth, being something that could fit in with the raising of a child. Evelyn as a toddler could be kept quiet for hours when given a role in the paper-making process. The profits, after a slow start, were reasonable, and the future of Papyrus was looking good. Polly employed a small number of staff in both the sales area and the workshop.

In the evening she would often be full of news about her day, which she imparted to her family during the evening meal. This evening, over a lamb tagine, she told them about a visitor they'd had.

'Someone came into the shop today and told me I was wrecking the planet.'

Arnold was having trouble with the tagine, it tasted hot to him, like a curry. Polly insisted there were no chillies in it. Yet his lips burned.

'Oh dear,' he said. 'Well, you are.'

'He seemed to think I personally went out and cut down all the trees that go into our paper. And he wouldn't stop going on about it. He kept saying we have to cut down on paper use. He said the computer was at last putting a stop to the need for paper. He said that the total world production of paper is starting to decrease for the first time in human history, and here was I, doing my bit to keep it going.'

'What did you tell him?'

'I told him the truth, that nearly all the paper we sell is recycled, and the rest comes from sustainable forests.'

'And what did he say to that?'

'He said that it didn't matter where it came from, the point is a tree has had to be cut down to make it. So I said what if the tree was planted for that purpose only, but he wasn't listening to rational argument. He just thought paper was evil.'

Arnold sighed. He was bothered, as Polly knew, by the current movement of physical culture into digital form.

The death of the film camera and the long-playing record were losses he was still struggling to come to terms with. The threat to paper and, beyond it, the book itself, posed an unimaginable tragedy. He seriously wondered if he could live in a world where physical books had disappeared. 'When we were young,' he said, 'we were enthralled by the possibilities of technology, but the last thing I would have expected of the future was that it should become a place where paper was thought of as wicked. But there do seem to be people about who regard paper as the embodiment of evil, as something that has to be wiped out.'

'Are you wrecking the planet, Mummy?' said Evelyn, who previously had not given any sign that she was following the conversation.

'No, I'm not, darling.'

'But Daddy said you are.'

'Daddy was being funny, but I'm not wrecking the planet more than anyone else, and probably a lot less than most.'

'Is Daddy wrecking the planet more than you?'

'I should think so.'

How beautiful that Polly should be so concerned with paper, with the history of paper, the future of paper. He felt rather proud that she was someone who could draw the ire of an environmental extremist. When they first met he'd never dreamed that she would be an entrepreneur, even of this softer, gentler type. He would never have thought that she would ever take up occupation of retail space on a busy shopping street, unless it was to protest against unethical trading. And now here she was, being protested against. She was exciting. He felt proud to be associated with her. And yet he still could not get out of his head the miracle that had happened earlier that evening, of having been locked in sudden, hot-breathed intimacy with another woman. More exciting by far, but was that simply because of the newness, and the wrongness of it? Polly could see nothing on him, there was no betraying mark, as she looked at him full in the face, stared at him as she related her story about the paper terrorist, about the plans he said he had for blowing up paper mills. 'He spoke to me like I was an idiot. Tried to tell me about how paper is made. I own a paper shop and he thought I knew nothing about paper. White China clay. Quarries have to be opened up just to feed the paper mills. Chlorine, zinc, sulphur. Water wastage. He said he was organizing protests against all the big consumers of paper. Printers, news papers, book publishers. He said I was a legitimate target, because my work depended on virgin paper. I said rubbish, some of our paper is made from vegetable pulp. I tried rea-soning with him, but he was mad, he wouldn't listen to argument. I told him to fuck off and he laughed at me.'

In some ways it was a typical, and typically charming Polly story. Odd people often came into her shop and did odd things – though he couldn't remember anyone ever protesting about her shop before – and Polly told it so wonderfully, rounding it off with the expletive that made Evelyn blush and giggle.

'I wonder if you should notify the police,' Arnold said, 'if he is talking about blowing things up.'

Polly laughed at this.

'He was the most unlikely terrorist you could imagine. I don't think the shop is in any danger.' And she concluded her remark by silently signalling to him that he shouldn't talk like that within earshot of Evelyn, who seemed not to have picked up on what they were saying.

'You were the one who started talking about bombs,' said Arnold, loudly and indignantly.

For no good reason Polly insisted on taking Evelyn to school the next day. It wasn't her turn, but she could not be talked out of it. For the last few weeks they had alternated, but this morning Polly said she might as well go because she didn't have to be at the shop till ten o'clock – Tamsin was opening up early.

'Then you might as well take the opportunity for pottering around at home for an extra half-hour,' said Arnold.

'No, I'd like to take Evelyn in, I just feel like it.' Arnold dared not push the point, in case he aroused suspicion, and he felt Polly was already on the verge of saying something like, Why are you so desperate to take her to school all of a sudden?

It was almost as though she sensed something subconsciously, and Arnold wondered if there was some subliminal chemistry at work, that the same pheromonal tide that had drawn him to Vera in the first place was perhaps now signalling danger to Polly, that his body was giving off subtle evidence of their liaison, that he was marked after all. He could think of no other way of dissuading her, and so had no choice but to let her take Evelyn to school.

It frustrated him on two counts – the first was that he would not see Vera until the next day at the earliest (and Polly might well take her again then, because it was her regular turn), and secondly, his absence from his regular school run the day after their intimate embrace might send a signal to Vera, that he had regretted what they had done. It might even make her think that he had confessed to Polly, and so she might be driven to make a confession as well. Perhaps she would do so anyway, perhaps her faith, her Church, her religion had got to her. So he had to wait, and began to dread what he might find when he got home. He waited the whole day, through one lecture and two tutorials and a tedious departmental meeting, and in the evening he tried to find out how things had gone in the morning. But there seemed nothing to worry about, Polly was preoccupied with other things.

'It is very puzzling that the phrase "as slippery as a mango" has never become established in this or any other language. They are such slippery things.' For the second time she nearly cut herself as the fruit spun on the chopping board.

'So, how did things go this morning?' said Arnold.

'This morning?'

'Yes, did you manage to drop Evelyn off OK?'

'Yes,' she said, 'why shouldn't I?'

'No reason. Just wondering.'

Arnold felt desolate. He felt as though he had gone for months without seeing Vera, when it had only been a day. And the next morning he was dismayed to find that Polly was going to take Evelyn to school again, because it was her regular day for taking her. He was unable to raise much of a protest, and then it was the weekend. It would be Monday before he could see Vera again. He vainly hoped that there might be an opportunity to pick Evelyn up from Vera's house on Saturday, but nothing had been arranged. So it was an empty weekend for him. And on Sunday they were due to make their monthly visit to Polly's parents, who lived an hour's drive away in the green belt south of London.

Polly's father was a retired builder, and had been married to Polly's mother for nearly fifty years. They liked to joke that they were bound together by cement. Arnold had once asked them if they thought they would ever need some repointing, and they had not laughed, nor even smiled. And they clearly thought that he and Polly were joined together by a less powerful mortar. They had, for more than a decade, politely declined to show any interest in Arnold.

They lived in a house that Polly's father had built himself, that seemed to Arnold to be a construction of unparalleled ugliness, a parody, almost, of the English country house of the Cotswold type. The mellow lime-stone blocks were a synthetic concoction of moulded concrete, which seemed to blow a raspberry at the past, rather than honour it. Everything felt solid and heavy and far too clean.

Apart from Polly, no one he knew thought ill of the house, and if they were pushed for a comment would praise its square, spacious rooms. Mostly Polly's parents lived in the enormous plastic conservatory at the back of the house, which looked out onto the sloping garden and countryside beyond. The house was perched on a high slope of the North Downs, a fact that only became apparent when you looked out of the back of the house. Polly's father was always keen to point out what a good view they had of both the M25 and the M23, which could be seen threading their way through the Wealden land-scape below.

It puzzled Arnold endlessly why the house which, to the man who built it, seemed like the perfect home, to him seemed like a machine designed to suck the life out of people. The lounge was devoted to the watching of televi-sion, where a vast sofa, turning a corner and filling two walls, seemed to mutate and spawn smaller sofas – foot-rests, armrests. The television was of the boxy, old-fashioned type – but was half-hidden in a walnut wardrobe with fold-ing doors that could be closed (but never were) to hide the television completely. There were no books in the house but for a few that had been given as presents and which sat in a shelf specially built for them (*Britain in the Seventies* was one lavishly illustrated title). In the sideboard there was a drawer full of sweet treats, to which children could help themselves as much as they liked, luxuries Polly and her siblings were never allowed when they were young, she always lamented.

It was impossible for Arnold to imagine that his father-in-law had ever strayed. Why was that? He was not moralistic in any obvious way, wasn't a churchgoer, or politically conscious, or culturally knowing, was the same age as Keith Richards, he smoked and drank, yet a strain of old-world puritanism had survived in him. The idea of marriage as a sacred social space, family as a cherished end in itself, prevailed in him in a way that it hadn't for Arnold and the people he grew up with. But then Arnold identified with the post-sixties punk generation (that he had narrowly missed) that wanted to smash the system. If he regarded marriage as sacred now, he was surprised and amazed by the fact, as though he had stumbled on treasure by chance. It was not a deeply held belief. He tried to imagine the horror with which news of his affair, if it ever leaked out, and if it was ever to become something more substantial than it currently was, would be greeted by his father-in-law, and the rest of Polly's family.

Polly's two brothers were at the house. Occasionally it happened this way that the whole of Polly's clan would be gathered for a Sunday, and yet it would have to be this weekend, the one in which Arnold was in thrall to a mistress, that they would have to be there, as if rallying round their sister in a crisis that had yet to erupt, as if to emblazon and embody the very notion of family. The two shaven-headed brothers, Mikey and Buzz (how uncomfortably those names, with their inbuilt and unwelcome familiarity, sat on Arnold's tongue) had both married loud, meaty women who never tired of advising Arnold and Polly on every aspect of their lives. They seemed not to comprehend Arnold's academic career at all and instead regarded the pair – a poet and a paper-maker – as people who had lost their way, or else were pursuing a hopeless dream. Poetry, they rightly recognized, didn't make any money and paper – well, how could Polly hope to compete with the likes of WH Smith? The women had already produced a half dozen babies between them, and were building a solid, slab-like future for them. They made Polly and Arnold feel neglectful and self-indulgent.

The food served on these Sundays was stodgy, claggy, greasy. Polly's mother didn't pour off the fat when she made gravy, so it was pure grease and baked blood with brown food colouring that was poured over their heaped roasts. The meat was home-grown, as Polly's parents had a smallholding that adjoined the garden where they kept some sheep and hens. As far as he could tell they only ate their own meat on Sundays like this, when guests were present, at other times they ate supermarket food like everyone else. Nevertheless they had an inexhaustible pride in their self-sufficiency, and would always invite

Arnold and Polly to agree with them that their meat tasted 'different'.

They often found themselves separated in the afternoons, when the household divided according to seemingly unconscious principles of segregation, with Mikey and Buzz holding court with their father in the conservatory, and the women confined to the lounge. Arnold felt he'd fallen for some sort of trick, to be left defenceless at the mercies of the brothers and their father, and be adrift in a stream of conversation about things of which he knew nothing. They talked about work they'd had done on their cars, each telling the other off for having not got the best deal on whatever it was they'd had done. Arnold knew it was pointless trying to join in this conversation because his own car – they had made it clear – did not entitle him to be taken seriously in any conversation about driving. Instead he nodded and observed, and then imagined that the conversation the men were having was not about driving, but about the shock revelation that he, Arnold, had been having an affair with one of Polly's friends. Their father was disgusted by the news but resigned to it, as though he'd known all along that his poet-son-in-law was not to be trusted. He shook his head in a pitying yet slightly threatening way. Mikey and Buzz were sniggeringly disapproving, and also head-shaking, but more from surprise than pity. They, unlike their father, would never have dreamed it of Arnold, and would have been secretly admiring and full of respect for his prowess, had he not been married to their sister.

The segregation was finally ended when one of the wives entered the conservatory. Holly, Mikey's wife, followed her small daughter into the space and said, 'All right chaps?' addressing all the men as one. Arnold detected a moment's hesitation before she used the term 'chaps', as though she had suddenly become aware of this separation of genders and was struck by its oddness. Her form of address had instantly normalized it, and also suggested it had all been a good and fun thing to do, to let the men and women get on with things among themselves.

By the time they got back home that evening, Arnold felt as though his body had been stuffed but his head eviscerated. He had to get Polly to drive, he was so without life that he couldn't rely upon himself to care enough about things not to crash the car. At night he couldn't sleep properly, he could feel his intestines struggling with the bulk they'd been fed, he could feel the dinner making painfully slow progress through the chicanes of his gut, but he couldn't settle for other reasons. Tomorrow he would see Vera again.

It felt as if it had been in another life that they had embraced, had taken each other so ravenously, yet he had relived every moment as if on a continual loop of memory. He examined the event with the intensity of an art conservator going over an old master, looking at the detail, squinting his eyes at a hairline crack in the pigment. Arnold roved back and forth across his memories, as if to enhance their permanence, but also to make sure everything was there – and each time he went over them he did remember something, recovered a fragment of the experience he hadn't had before – the sensation of her hot breath in his ear, the way her hair got in between his teeth, the dampness of the skin on her tummy, the vocalization she gave when he pinched her nipple with his lips. It had happened in another country, and he had no evidence of it ever having occurred, no photographs, no souvenirs, nothing he could look at to remind him.

Vera might behave as if it had never taken place. At the back of his mind this was what was keeping him awake, how to handle it in the playground tomorrow morning – what were the protocols? What were the right words to use? Nothing could be said directly, it would have to all be inference and suggestion, smiles and non-smiles, everything encoded, and he hated communicating in that way.

As he took Evelyn to school the next morning he felt a coldness inside him, a dread and fear. He was trembling. He had a sense of self-loathing that came from nowhere. He rounded the corner of the old red-brick building and into the playground where all the mothers and the few fathers waited. At first he thought she wasn't there, because the usual spot in the playground where she stood with Irina was empty of her, and then to his horror he realized that she was in a different group of mothers – ones he didn't know so well.

Worse, Evelyn did not make her usual beeline for Irina, and indeed seemed rather reluctant to head in her direction. Had there been a cooling off of their friendship? He could not now drag his daughter to this new group without making it seem as though he was tagging along after Vera, when the natural thing to do would be to stand with the mothers of the old group. He did this, while observing Vera, just a few yards away. It puzzled and worried him. The group she had joined was one of the groups he and Polly sometimes referred to as the locals. It was mainly comprised of mothers who were born and bred in the neighbourhood, many of them having gone to the school themselves as children, knowing each other from those times. They had stood on those precise spots in the playground as kids with their own mothers. They set people like Polly and himself apart as incomers, in a very subtle way that it had taken them several years to recognize.

Their husbands were skilled manual workers – builders and electricians – or else general managers of engineering workshops, or car showrooms, people he had nothing in common with, and who had a completely different world view. When he overheard their conversation it was always of material things – cars, the price of houses, the cost of living. Having spent the Sunday with Polly's family, who were people of the same type, he could not bear the thought of more prattling conversation about nothing. But what was Vera doing there? She would not be interested in talking about those sorts of things, so why had she joined the group? Was it a deliberate manoeuvre to alienate him, to isolate him, to escape from him? He tried not to look concerned or bothered by Vera's change of group. She might have done it, he realized, to avoid being with Polly. She was not to know that he was to deliver Evelyn this morning. She might have assumed he was not coming back, and that Polly was taking Evelyn to school every day from now on. She might have assumed that he was full of regret and didn't want to see her again. But if so she could have given him some sort of signal. She could have met his eye, at least.

When the bell was finally rung and the children gathered themselves into lines and began the slow march into school, the mothers dispersed, being either the busy mothers who rushed off the moment their children were lined up, jangling a bunch of keys in their hands as they rushed to their car, or they were the lingering mothers, who went on chatting in the playground long after the children had gone into their classrooms. Vera was one of these latter, and she hung around in the playground with a few other mothers. This made it difficult for Arnold who, not being in a group, had no reason to linger. He moved as slowly as he could, pretending to be checking messages on his mobile phone, and eventually moved back through the gates, ahead of Vera who was still talking to the other mothers. He got to his car and waited there, observing the mothers from a distance. They dispersed at the gate and Vera began walking towards him, by chance he had parked his car on the route she normally took back home.

It seemed absurd, but he got out of the car as she approached, as if to ambush her. She couldn't avoid looking furtive, glancing over her shoulder to see if anyone could see. What they were doing was terribly conspicuous to anyone with an eyeline – to talk like this surely looked odd. But it seemed safe to assume there was no one around.

'Get back in the car,' she said when she was near enough, 'I'll talk to you through the window.'

He still couldn't read her face – her expression seemed neutral, there was no smile in it, but maybe she was just being cautious.

He did sit back in the car and wound the window down.

'I'm sorry I haven't been able to see you since last Wednesday,' he said, looking up at her with what he imagined must have been sorrowful eyes.

'I wondered what had happened to you.'

'It was just bad timing.'

'Never mind.'

'Is everything OK?'

'Yes, everything's fine. I had a nice chat with Polly on Thursday.'

'What do you mean?'

'It was fine. I felt so strange, talking to her. I was expecting you, but she turned up instead, so I was scared that she had found out. I wondered if she was acting normal, or being normal. Then I realized she didn't know. Even with the fear, I wanted to tell her about what we'd done, but not as a confession, just as a shared experience. I have never felt so strange.'

'I felt the same. I wanted to share the sense of joy I had.'

'But you didn't, of course.'

'No, of course.'

'I mustn't keep you,' she said, 'we shouldn't talk here for too long.'

'Can we see each other again, do you think?'

'We'll have to arrange something.' As if they were organizing a dinner party.

'Soon?'

'Yes, soon.'

'Today?'

'I don't think so. But this week. It's so difficult. There's so little time when I don't have the children.' Arnold had forgotten that she had a younger son who was in nursery only part of the week.

'Are you happy?'

'I am now.'

He wanted to reach out and touch her, any part of her, it didn't matter, just to hold her hand, her arm, to feel connected to her, but even that might be too risky, if they were seen.

'Do you have a mobile phone?' she said.

'Yes.'

'Tell me the number. I'll text you.'

This caused lots of problems. They were both a little unfamiliar with mobile technology and neither Vera nor Arnold knew their numbers off by heart. Arnold's number was somewhere on his phone but it took him a while to find it. He asked for her number so that he could phone her, so that his number would be in her phone's memory, but she didn't have her phone with her. When he told her his, she couldn't remember the simple sequence of numbers and asked him to write it down. So he had to find something to write it down with, and on. Vera didn't have a pen, or any paper. In the door pocket Arnold eventually found an old Bic biro, its central stem of ink nearly drained. And all he had to write on was the back of a carpark ticket. He wrote down the number, scratchily, and handed it to her.

'It's probably best if we don't talk in the playground, from now on,' she said, 'we don't want people to start thinking things.' How burningly beautiful, how painfully thrilling that she had thought this far ahead. What commitment she was demonstrating. Planning and being careful. 'I'll text you later today. Goodbye.'

It was all in her hands, now. The future depended on her making communication. He feared there would be silence from her, but the texts started coming straight away, while he was still driving to work. She explained that she was only free during a narrow window in the early afternoon or morning, depending on when her youngest child was at nursery. The hours were 8.30 till 11.45 on Tuesdays, 1.15 till 2.45 on Wednesdays and Thursdays. Every other hour of her day was accounted for by parenting duties, these were the only slots when she was free. On his present timetable Arnold could only make the Wednesday slot. He asked her where they should meet. And she said, at her house. He asked her if she was sure that was a good idea. She said there was no time to go anywhere else, and where else could they go? Did he imagine they would book a hotel room? Drive out to a lonely spot on the Downs?

But he was worried – what if someone saw me coming out of the house at that time? She said he should use the back entrance. There was a sort of mews-like alleyway at the back of the house, with a gate that led into her garden. It was normally locked, but she would leave it open. There were high walls, trees, no one would see him.

He agreed, but felt sick with fear. To have organized something, to have planned a liaison, rather than just grabbing the moment when it occurred, introduced an element of unbearable tension. He felt weighed down with the burden of his desire.

The next day, Tuesday, it was Polly's turn to deliver Evelyn, so he didn't see Vera. He was glad. He realized that it would be a good idea to stop doing the school run altogether, but that in itself would have seemed odd, although he could have probably come up with some sort of excuse – as it was, on Wednesday he went through the same routine again, of standing apart while Vera retained her position with the locals, and then in the afternoon, at the appointed time, he parked his car near some shops and walked for ten minutes to Vera's road. He found his way into the wide, high-walled alleyway at the end of her street which separated the back gardens of two parallel roads. The alleyway was surprisingly scruffy. At the end a little huddle of overstuffed wheelie bins stood, two had fallen over and spilt their contents, as though they had been felled by the others and were lying bleeding. Arnold had to step over maggoty waste, a half-open and well-filled nappy, food debris. The gardens themselves were hidden behind the high brick walls, though in some gardens these had fallen down and were replaced by splintery wooden fences, or sheets of corrugated iron. The backs of the houses seemed to occupy a much poorer part of the city than the fronts. It seemed incredible that this space could be so neglected. He later learnt from Vera that it was a constant bane of the residents' lives. It took only a day or two to acquire its rubbish and dirt, and no one was prepared for the upkeep.

He was disconcerted that there were no numbers on the garden gates. Vera had told him to count along, but he couldn't remember how far, or what colour she'd said the gate was. He scrolled through his phone looking for the message that had this information, but couldn't find it. He texted her again, but no answer came. In the end he spent some time counting the backs of the houses and tried a green gate that he wasn't fully sure was the gate to Vera's back garden, but when it opened, it seemed there was a good chance, as any other gate was likely to be bolted. But once through there was no way of telling if he was correct, because he had not seen Vera's garden before, and though it wasn't a long garden, it was overgrown enough to make the house itself half-hidden. There was a sprawling holly, and a sycamore that formed a canyon of foliage that led to a small lawn where there was a shed, a plastic swing, a football goal and a scattering of different sized footballs. There was also a rotary washing line strung with a family's clothes, like offerings at a shrine. He thought he recognized the blue T-shirt that Vera had been wearing when they'd made love, hanging there amid the children's clothes and the masculine shirts. Stepping out from the cover of the trees and onto the lawn itself, he saw the house towering. It was rougher brickwork at the back, which made it look slightly less welcoming than the front. With its clinging drains and boiler flue it looked industrial, a little rough, like a Victorian factory. The lingering possibility that he could be in the wrong garden made him approach cautiously, looking desperately for any sign that this was Vera's house – the blue T-shirt itself wasn't quite enough. Every family probably has a blue T-shirt among its washing. He walked onto a mossy patio, past an extension and up to a door through which he could glimpse a narrow, shadowy kitchen. There was nothing about this part of the house that he recognized. It could have been anyone's kitchen. He felt a sudden panic in the certainty that he had come to the wrong house, that he was a trespasser, a burglar, that he might at any moment be discovered, have the police called on him. The notion made him more aware than he had been before, of the wrongness of what he was doing, even if he was at the right address. There was still a chance to abandon this mad project, to turn back to the street and forget the whole thing, and he was on the point of doing that (so he told himself afterwards) when he saw through the window, Vera appear in the kitchen and open the back door for him, and in that moment all those doubts fled from his mind. It was as though his sensible, caring, intelligent self had been completely wiped by the silk cloth of Vera's beauty.

There were many locks and bolts to undo before Vera could open the door for him, but when she did it was clear from her face that she had no doubts or regrets about what they were doing. She had a look of intent, purposeful longing on her face, and a seriousness, the seriousness that was always there, but a seriousness of desire, nothing else.

He stepped into the kitchen and they embraced immediately. There were no overlooking windows, they were safely invisible. The sudden closeness of her, the length of her body against his, aproned to each other, was breathtaking. The pull of her mouth, the sweetness of it, the sourness of it, the metallic bump of her glasses frame against his eyebrow, though she somehow managed to extract herself from the embrace, remembering to relock the back door, and Arnold stood in the kitchen watching her bolt and latch and chain the entrance shut again. They hadn't spoken.

He followed her upstairs. He was feeling less nervous, the sense that he was doing something wrong was now completely swept away in the company of Vera, they together had formed a coalition that was impervious to outside opinions, the only pressure was to maintain secrecy and privacy. They went about their business like children entering a playground, hungry for the delights on offer. And he regarded the prospect of their lovemaking rather like a child might regard the contraptions of a playground, as things that needed careful handling, he felt that he would need support and cooperation.

They had not planned very far. As they went upstairs he could see that she was debating with herself which room to use. They had promised themselves full sex, rather than the intimate touching of their previous encounter, and this meant a far greater commitment to whichever space they chose. They could choose her and her husband's bedroom, but might that not leave a trace that could be discerned by the nine-to-five man? If not, then one of the children's bedrooms, but could they really bear to do it while watched by the stuffed sentinels of their play-cupboards, and all their promising, wonky artwork? She had no spare room. They could perhaps do it in the down-stairs living room, but that gave them no chance at all if there was an interruption. In the end, they opted for the adult bedroom, and unspokenly promised to be as careful as possible not to leave any trace. They had both brought along condoms, and there was a little debate about whose to use. She had wanted him to use his, and he hers. For him to see her proffer the prophylactic seemed such an assertion of intent that it affected him like a gift from the heart.

Then there was the nakedness. She had only desired him, so far, as a fully clothed person. Would she feel the same when she saw what those clothes covered? And what did they cover? Arnold's awareness of his own body had dwindled to the point where he couldn't have identified it if it had washed up headless on a beach somewhere. He was just aware of something that wasn't as strong as it was, that wasn't as compact and as hard as it had been.

It had become soft, podgy, pouchy. He was dismayed to find that, once they had closed the door of the bedroom, they were to undress individually, either side of the bed. He had imagined that they would slowly tear the clothes off each other as they made love, but no, there was an orderliness that had been brought to the process, a clinical aspect. Undressing separately was awful, like preparing for a medical. Vera turned away from him and pulled her T-shirt up over her head, revealing a curved length of back that continued the line of her long neck. The central flute of her spine, barely notched, cut a precise thread all the way down to her lightly downed saddle. But she had become remote and impossible. Arnold could only stand and watch, blind to his own unbuttoning. She lowered her jeans, still with her back to him, as the belt line descended it was as though her body was rising out of a pool of denim. Then she bent forward to finish the manoeuvre, her buttocks tensed in their thin black fabric, her spine suddenly became notched with the tension, for a moment he was looking at something purely physical.

As he undressed he was suddenly overtaken by a desire not to be seen by her, and turned his body and angled it so that she would not get a full view. As she began removing her underwear he felt a longing to slow down the process. The reveal was imminent, in a moment he would have the truth before him and nothing left to his longing imagination, it would all be there, complete and disclosed. She was folding her clothes away carefully. He wondered if this was a deliberate delaying tactic to provide one last extended moment where things could be halted. The line had not yet been crossed. There was still an opportunity to move backwards through time, to retrace their steps, to reclothe themselves and return to the world of separateness.

He had not experienced feelings like this before, how waves of intensest pleasure and joy alternated with crashing waves of sadness and deepest sorrow, it was like being led to the gallows through a ribboned and festooned gallery, by happy children. He felt his own sense of self begin to move and sway within him, as if trying to escape its confines. Then she turned to him in her complete nakedness and it was as though the fabric of all his anxieties and constraints, all his mean little fears and thoughts of self-loathing, had been torn, and through the aperture this incontestable proposition had appeared. The delicate and perfect slightness of her body seemed at the same time capable of crushing everything around it, or of supporting a colossal mass. It seemed to transcend its surrounding, sucking the ordinary darkness of their curtained boudoir and transforming it into light. Her nakedness was also a surprise, and he chided himself for assuming that she, even at thirty-six (a decade younger than Polly), would have the body of a teenager. Her abdomen had the looseness and puckeredness of a childbearer, her body was layered with time, but they were pleasing, silky, delicate layers, beautiful things, inviting touch like a sheet of beautiful paper. But she was quickly hidden as she lifted the covers and slid beneath them, allowing him to achieve full nakedness in a brief moment of privacy, for which he was grateful, before he joined her there.

She allowed him to do everything to her, apart from put his face to her genitals. As soon as his mouth went towards that part of her he felt the gentle yet firm yank of her hands on his head, pulling him away. In fact she seemed little interested in foreplay, and was determined to go as quickly into full intercourse as possible, almost as if she knew nothing else could possibly satisfy her. Arnold didn't want things to happen so quickly, but nevertheless felt pulled along by the stream of her desire. But Arnold was surprised by how difficult he found the situation, not least because he was in her and her husband's bedroom, and in the blend of things, the masculine presence in the room seemed the stronger – the whiff of aftershave on the pillow, the ties draped over the back of the chair, the big black polished shoes standing empty on the floor, the stack of effective management books by the side of the bed whose titles he'd noted – *How to Succeed in Business*, *The Power of Positive Thinking* and Richard Branson's *Screw It Let's Do It*. He wanted to make a pile of these things and set light to them. What, did her husband have ambitions to set himself up in business?

There were traces of religious devotion spread out as well – he had noticed a little Bible, pocket-sized, on the dressing table, a religious pamphlet protruding from under a pile of household documents. On the wall there was a framed sampler that said The Lord is My Shepherd. It looked like an old family heirloom.

He was constantly reminded of his teenage fumblings with girls, the unbearable pressure of being required to get everything right first time. Here the tension was of a different kind of expectation. Both with long-term partners, they had each grown to believe their own lovemaking routines were universal, and so were constantly wrongly anticipating each other's next moves – heads went to the wrong place, cues were misread, elbows clashed, but nevertheless a kind of mutual somatic understanding was reached. He quickly began to understand her preferences, how she liked to be held, where she liked to be touched. He came too quickly, losing a short battle to withhold himself, but gave what he had with a loud gasp and saw beneath him the slight puzzlement on Vera's face when she realized what had happened. Immediately Arnold felt himself compared to the man with the big polished shoes and to be found wanting, in one way at least. A man with that array of ties could probably keep going for hours on end, the nine-to-fiver, the regular timekeeper. But would he have brought such passion to the task? A diamond of redness had appeared between Vera's splayed breasts. The nearness he had just experienced with Vera had transformed how he looked at her, changing her in his eyes into something beautifully familiar.

They said almost nothing to each other. Arnold lay back, breathless, sweaty, gasping for air in the clammy, dark bedroom. It looked suddenly shabby, like a room in a squat, and what they had just done seemed as seedy, yet he couldn't resist when Vera showed signs that she wanted to continue. She was not simply wanting to get him out of bed and back to normal life, but she began working him again, taking the dominant position this time, pushing the bedclothes back and sitting astride him, and Arnold surprised to find himself tumescent again so soon, they managed a second, longer, slower session, Vera's body wonderfully displayed this time.

Then suddenly it was over. A moment after his second, weaker coming, and after a brief rest as they lay embracing each other, she sat up and began dressing. There was no time left, she said. The longer he stayed, the more chance there was that somehow his presence would imprint itself onto the room. Before he left he felt he needed a commitment from her, as they stood in the kitchen, kissing again, by the back door.

He looked her in the face, took in the beauty of it, and said:

'Do you want to do this again?'

She seemed surprised that he had to ask.

'Of course I do,' she said, kissing him smartly and politely.

Nothing was arranged, but he assumed that they would do it again the same time next week, the only mutually convenient time. As he left, Vera was already getting the pushchair ready, to pick up Geoffrey from the nursery.

A sense of well-being stayed with him for the rest of the afternoon. He felt softened-up, blissed-out, born again. He felt lit from within and full of energy. Walking seemed slow and pointless when running was just as easy. He felt supple and invincible. Things around him had an eloquence. Bad architecture seemed beautiful. He could trust nothing to be as ugly as he'd thought it was. Everything sang.

He had one tutorial that afternoon, with a shy and sickening student who was writing a dystopian novel in which humans had become enslaved to a race of giant birds. Though in fact, Arnold was never sure if the birds were giant, or if the human race had been reduced to the size of ants. When he asked the student, he said it hardly mattered. And now Arnold had to agree. For weeks he had struggled to understand this novel, to try and see what the student was getting at. But now it all seemed to make wonderful, writerly sense. Giant goldfinches. The entire human race made to live on a patch of land the size of an average back garden. The bird table towering above them like the watchtower of a concentration camp. Arnold made the student nervous with his lavish praise.

When he arrived home the house was empty but for the kitten, still unnamed, who whined at him with a sort of frenzy in her little voice, after being alone for so long. He had forgotten that it was one of the days for Evelyn to be at Irina's. Vera would have collected her from school, in loco parentis, and taken her to the house he had left only a few hours ago. Polly would be collecting her from there later. The thought chilled him. In less than an hour Polly would be where he had been, in Vera's house, chatting merrily away with the woman he'd made love to that afternoon. He felt he had left a crime scene with evidence all over it. That there were fingerprints of blood all over the walls, his fingerprints. He wanted to go back there and wipe them all off. He hadn't done enough while he was there to ensure he'd covered his tracks. He tried to imagine Vera meeting his daughter after school, tried to picture them walking home together. What would she be feeling? Surely the sense of guilt would overpower her, some wayward emotion would take hold of her, if not then, when Polly called round. It would be like torture for her. And if she didn't crack up, would Polly sense something, or Evelyn, even?

He went upstairs to the bathroom and looked at himself in the mirror. He looked as he'd done that evening when he'd first noticed Vera – sweaty, dishevelled, drunken, or as though he had a bad hangover. He looked closely at his face, checking that it didn't bear some mark. To his astonishment his eyes were wet and his lashes clogged. He had been crying. He had a shower and changed his clothes, realizing that this in itself might give something away, since he never normally showered at this time of day. Polly would wonder why. So he spent some time trying to restore the bathroom to its pre-shower state – hiding away the damp towel in the washing basket, wiping the floor, clearing all the steam from the steamed-up mirror and drying it. Then he'd wondered if he'd just made things worse – he couldn't remove every last trace of his shower, and Polly would only wonder why he had tried to do so.

When Polly and his daughter returned home, he had settled down to some reading in his study and had begun to relax a little. He could tell immediately from the sounds downstairs that things were normal. Evelyn scampered up to her room to get changed, and the water pipes hummed as Polly went straight to the kitchen to begin preparing dinner.

On her way back down Evelyn burst into his room as she often did to report on her day, but he was worried by her face, which was distraught. He had misread the sounds of normality. Evelyn had been crying.

'What's up?' said Arnold, his heart racing. It couldn't possibly be what he dreaded.

'I hate Irina,' she said.

'Oh not again. Why?'

'She's a bitch.'

'Evelyn, I've told you about using that word.' But he could have hugged her for using it, since it took his daughter's grievances so far away from what he'd feared had been their cause.

'But she is one . . .' Evelyn was using that pleading voice, the moaning intonation she produced when she knew she lacked the necessary words to express her feelings '. . . she is so much one . . .'

'What's she done?'

'She wouldn't let me read her mind.'

'Oh God you're not still doing that, are you? I thought Mummy told you not to play with those cards any more.'

'I wasn't using the cards.'

'What were you doing then?'

'I just told her that I could read minds and I asked her to think of something and let me read her mind.'

'And did you?'

'Well she said I got it wrong every time but she was just saying that – I couldn't have got it wrong every time.'

'And of course there was no way of knowing if she was telling the truth.'

'Of course there was, I could read in her mind that she was lying. She was thinking about a parrot, but she said she was thinking about a koala bear.'

'Listen, Evelyn . . .'

'And then she was thinking about an owl but said she was thinking about a balloon.'

'Evelyn . . .'

'It was so unfair, she just didn't want to admit I was right.'

'Evelyn – you don't actually think – I mean, you don't really believe you can read minds, do you?'

'Yes, of course.'

'Because no one can. It's not physically possible.'

'Who says?'

'It just can't be done. If it could be done, someone would have proved it by now, and no one has.'

'Then let me prove it. Think of something.'

'No, Evelyn.'

'Just think of something!' she shouted with impatience, and closed her eyes in concentration. Arnold was tempted to test her, but as soon as he paused long enough for a thought to enter his head, he saw Vera's naked body spread before him, glossy with his spittle. The image had been in his head all afternoon, almost as though it was permanently fixed to the pinboard of his mind. He shook with the effort of trying to wipe the image from his brain, in terror that there was the slightest chance that Evelyn possessed the gift she claimed. But then here was the saddest proof of all that his daughter was not psychic, for she could see nothing of that seared image and instead was chuckling at something much pleasanter she'd seen.

'You're thinking about Emily,' she said.

'Emily? Who's Emily?'

Evelyn gave a cackling laugh. 'Emily? Don't you know who Emily is?'

'No, I don't.'

'She's downstairs. She's the kitten. I thought of a name for her. Didn't you know?'

'No, I didn't.'

'And were you thinking about her?'

'No, I wasn't.'

'You were!' Evelyn gave the long moan again, her body twisted with frustration.

'I wasn't, I was thinking about something else.'

'What were you thinking of?'

'I was thinking about Mummy.'

This seemed to satisfy Evelyn a little, as though her mother and the kitten were the same sort of thing. They went downstairs together to find them.

# 5

It wasn't exactly triumph that Arnold felt when he went downstairs to live out the rest of the evening as a perfectly normal, regular evening of eating and chatting and television, but a sense close to that – that he and Vera had done it, they had done it and got away with it. No one had been harmed, physically or mentally, and life was carrying on as normal. It was true that they had planted something in their lives that could, at any time, burst into flames, but if they handled everything as calmly and as carefully as they had that first day, then there seemed no reason the current of things couldn't continue indefinitely.

It was almost as if without any planning at all that he and Vera slipped into their adulterous routine. Amateurs who had discovered a talent for something they'd never dreamed of before, their lovemaking session of that afternoon was repeated the following Wednesday, and then after the agony of the Easter break when it was impossible to arrange anything – and during which Arnold had been particularly anxious about the reawakening of Vera's religious conscience – on through the summer term, each time with the same sense of excitement and discovery as on that first afternoon. It became timetabled into their lives as much as the classes Arnold taught or the lectures he gave. A weekly encounter, an appointment not to be missed. They left him feeling flushed, exhausted and tremblingly happy. The feeling would last well into the evening, to be replaced by a crushing wave of despair brought on by a realization of what he was doing and the new power he had to destroy the happiness of his family.

He wondered if Vera felt the same way but felt afraid to ask, in case she did. Yet she showed no sign that she did. In every other respect their feelings and their outlooks seemed to run parallel – but not their sense of guilt and shame. It unnerved him a little. As someone with religious faith, surely she would have felt more strongly the wrongness of what they were doing. And because he regarded her as someone with a stronger moral outlook than himself (indeed he regarded her with something approaching awe in this respect), he took some comfort from her apparent ease with their transgression.

At times he felt that what they were doing was a thing of such concentrated wrongness that it existed beyond the range of conventional perceptions. It was such an unlikely thing that people wouldn't have seen it even if they had dropped some clue. It made him feel that their affair inhabited its own world, an invisible structure, a palace of glass that soared above the other buildings, but which people walked right past, or through, without noticing. Polly could walk past it and not see it, she could walk through it, walk right through the middle of it, and not feel the touch of its walls.

In counterpoint to this, Arnold was dismayed to find that the real building he lived in, his house of red bricks and Victorian stained glass, of chessboard-tiled floors and toy-filled bedrooms, had become smaller, darker and colder. He felt this most strongly on the days when he'd made love to Vera in their invisible palace, though in the ensuing days it lost some of its dankness and littleness, and he could begin to find attraction in its lighting, its pictures, and its ever-growing population of sewn and stitched things that continued to emanate from the little machine that had started it all.

He could not look at his wife properly. She seemed to have drifted out of focus, or only to exist in his peripheral vision. Sometimes he would try and correct this, and would find himself staring at her for long periods, while she was unawares. His relationship with Polly granted him the privilege to look at her, yet when she noticed, she found his gaze unsettling.

'What are you looking at?' It was the first time, in over an hour, she had looked up from her work at the sewing machine.

'Nothing.'

'Why do you keep staring at me?'

'I like looking at you.'

Polly gave a little laugh, as if to say she wasn't fooled. 'No really, why do you keep looking at me? Is there something wrong with me?'

About her husband Vera said very little, though she did once tell Arnold that he had not 'paid court' to her since the day of their marriage. He liked the way she used that term, 'paid court'. He also liked the fact that she didn't understand why it amused him that she used it.

Arnold supposed that he himself did pay court to her. As their affair continued they had grown increasingly secure in each other's company. Inhibitions about their respective bodies had disappeared; they gave each other permission to range freely across their neighbouring territories of skin, and would spend long minutes charting new discoveries there, of moles and scars and veins that were to them like archaeological treasures. They teased each other's bodies for new ways of raising pleasure, experimenting and improvising. They spoke very little. Their lovemaking was like a dumb-show. Afterwards they would lie together in silence almost as if in celebration of the fact that they did not need to talk, concentrating all their thoughts on the abstract realms of bliss. To speak would have felt like an intrusion. Instead the only accepted form of expression was smiles, touches, sighs, giggles. The few times Arnold did try to talk, she hushed him quiet, smilingly laying a finger on his lips, as if urging him not to break the precious spell.

At first he found this conversational absence a relief. Their relationship was freed from the pressure of language. But as the weeks went on, he began to worry that their affair existed only for the slaking of Vera's sexual thirst. Eventually that thirst would be satisfied, she would have had her fill, she would be rehydrated – and what then? He didn't even know what they had in common, if anything. And every time they made love the same ties hung on the back of the chair, the same polished shoes stood on the floor. At times he thought he could hear them pacing restlessly up and down while they were in bed. He could hear the toes tapping with impatience, waiting for them to be done . . .

Why was she doing this to her husband? Had the man in the big shoes mistreated her? Arnold wanted to know. Were they just bored with each other, or was it something more than boredom? He wanted to find out about her. He wanted to talk to her about her parents, what country they had come from. He wanted to know about her childhood, her first boyfriend, her finding of God. He wanted to know what she and God thought about what they were doing. He wanted reassurance from her. He wanted to know, from a religious woman, that what they were doing together was, in some way, explainable. But for all he knew she had given up on God, had lost her faith. The thought troubled him, as though at some higher level their affair might no longer be sanctioned. At the same time he didn't want to awaken in her a sense of guilt, or shame that might have slumbered on otherwise. He didn't want her to be like him, full of fear and trepidation.

Arnold could not quite believe what had happened to him. He was not someone upon whom the world rushed to bestow favours of love, in fact he had begun to feel, in his more recent years, quite the opposite. In this sense he had become disappointed with life. Beyond his marriage it seemed that people had very little regard for him, his company was not sought as an end in itself, his own friends were few, and could not tolerate too frequent contact with him. He guessed it was because he had an innate ability to put people on edge, to make them feel awkward, to appear cross when he was anything but, to seem impatient when he wasn't. At times brittle, defensive and cranky, he realized he was not easy company. The urgency of Vera's passion for him seemed all the more surprising, therefore. She didn't misread his mood, as so many people did, but seemed to perceive it with astonishing accuracy. Polly was the only other person who was consistently able to do this. Furthermore, Vera seemed anxious to experience him as intensely as possible. He had some sort of quality that she desired strongly. It was not his looks, as these were ordinary, and his character, as he understood it, lacked charm, yet there was something attractive about him, and to have this confirmed by someone other than Polly, that there should be two people in the world of seven billion who desired him, doubled the previous figure and so doubled his sense of self-worth and confidence. He became terrified of continuing the affair with Vera, and he became terrified, equally, of losing her.

Sometimes he tried making the suggestion that instead of using their weekly assignation to make love in her house, they could go somewhere else, but not to make love, just to have lunch, or a drink, and to talk. Always her answer was the same.

'There is no time. We would have to go somewhere very far away, to avoid the risk of being seen together, and we haven't got time for that. And besides, we can talk now. We can talk any time.'

'But you always hush me when I try to talk.'

'Oh, it's just because we have something so special, so different, that we risk spoiling it by talking about ordinary things. Once we start talking, we start realizing how complicated everything is. Without talking, it is just you and me, our bodies, our selves, and nothing else.'

It seemed at first that Vera couldn't quite grasp this need of his to experience her mentally as well as physically. Yet she claimed to be a spiritual person, worshipper of an ethereal deity, believer in Cartesian dualism, of spirit that detached from the body and floated away in death. With Arnold she seemed to value nothing but his body. He could see that she was beginning to understand that this worried him. She agreed that they should talk more, but thought that they would have to go somewhere away from home to do it. It would seem absurd to go through all the subterfuge of his creeping in through the back door, just to have a conversation. Then one day she said to him,

'You are right. We should do other things as well. I will meet you in town one day. There's a cafe no one we know goes to. We could meet there.'

# 6

It was called The Market Café, although the cattle market it had once served had moved, twenty years before, to a location outside the city. A bus station had been built where they had once auctioned heifers and swine, and the customers of the Market Café now were mostly bus drivers and their forlorn passengers. Arnold and Vera looked out of place. Vera had dressed differently, as though she was in disguise, reverting to a charity-shop student-chic that would have been her normal garb in the days when there was still a cattle market over the road. She had on a woolly, rainbow-coloured beret, and wellingtons, for no reason that Arnold could think of. She drew very little attention from the men in the cafe, yet Arnold couldn't think why they weren't staring at her.

To his amazement she ordered a mixed grill. He had thought she was vegetarian, but then realized he had no reason to think this, other than it would have suited her.

'I'm hungry,' she said, as if reading his thoughts. She removed her beret and let golden strands fall beautifully about her face. It seemed strange, but he felt he had her much more in his possession now than when she was naked beneath him in her and her husband's double bed. Here, though clothed, she was before him and for him in her entirety, sitting across the table from him, a miniature Manhattan of condiments between them, and the laminated menu from which they'd ordered.

He wanted to take stock of her beauty. In their relationship so far, in its rush of emotions, in its hastiness and secrecy, he hadn't been able to take his time to appreciate what she was. Her face was little, trim and perfectly balanced. It bore so few signs of ageing, and yet she was unmistakably a woman of her years. For the first time he saw traces of otherness in her, of a different line of descent, the Slavic, eastern races noticeable in her eyes and cheekbones. He kept forgetting she had a Russian mother and father, or was it grandparents? In her voice there was nothing more pinpointable than southern English. He felt he knew nothing about her.

At the same time, no matter how much he appreciated her physical presence, he was bothered by the feeling that this wasn't all of her. That the whole of her was something beyond her flesh and blood, rainbow-wool-and-wellington-booted-here-and-nowness. He thought something as ungraspable as mist was a part of her, that could detach itself and drift away.

When the food came, he was horrified by her serving. Bacon, sausages, a chop, black pudding, kidneys. So much muscle on the plate, her meal looked more likely to eat her than the other way round. It pained him to imagine all that protein attacking her body, when she seemed made of purer things.

'What's the point of coming to a place like this if you can't have the full eating experience?' she said.

Arnold was disappointed.

'I didn't think we chose this place because of its food.'

Vera looked slightly less attractive when eating. Her face lost its symmetry, and she kept having to extract unchewable things from her mouth. She kept blowing her nose, an action that gave her hamster cheeks and eyes. He had given up an afternoon of sex with her for this.

He had not ordered any food, wrong-footed into believing that Vera wouldn't be hungry, and he didn't want to be the only one eating. By the time she ordered he'd already committed himself to having nothing, just a mug of tea. And now he was hungry. He didn't believe she would finish it. All that grease and tissue going into that slight, pure body must surely cause some sort of chemical insurgency.

'You are eating like someone who's been held hostage.'

Vera said nothing but went on sawing away at the meat, placing it delicately in her mouth, then chewing, with difficulty. She seemed to be forcing it down, the long neck rippling with each swallow. She offered him a piece of offal on the end of her fork. He politely refused. She smiled at him.

'Why won't you eat anything?'

'I'm not hungry. And like I said, I didn't think we came here to eat.'

'No. But then you're not doing anything else, at the moment.'

'I am doing something.'

'What are you doing?'

'Looking at you.'

'Looking at me stuffing my face.'

'I like looking at you.'

Vera smiled again, but didn't return the compliment. She seemed to be taking little notice of him.

'So what did you want us to talk about?' she said.

'I just wanted us to know a little more about each other.'

'In my limited experience, the more people know about each other, the more complicated everything gets. But go on.'

'For instance – where were you born?'

'Siberia. A little town called Bratsk. A few buildings and a hydro-electric dam. That's all there is.'

'You came to this country as a child?'

'A teenager.'

'Your English is wonderful.'

'Thank you.'

'Why did your family come here?'

'My father was a scientist. He had wanted to defect to the West for years. He was always in trouble with the authorities. That's why we ended up in Bratsk. As soon as the Soviet Union collapsed, he came here. Brought us all with him. He's dead now.'

'Did you have a happy childhood?'

Vera leaned back and sighed heavily. 'This isn't a conversation, it's an interrogation.'

'OK, I'm sorry. It's just that you have a really interesting background. And you never talk about it.'

'Backgrounds are complicated, like I said.'

'Mine isn't . . .'

She didn't pick up the cue to ask him about his, and they were silent for a while. Arnold looked out of the window at the double-deckers nudging into the parking bays, the exhausted-looking passengers lining up at their doors. He watched as ten, fifteen, twenty or more people disappeared into the gaping mouth of the bus. Then marvelled at how they seemed to filter themselves, some going upstairs, others remaining on the lower deck.

'Vera, I must ask you – does it trouble you that I am a heathen?'

Her answer shocked him.

'Yes, a little bit.'

He didn't know what to say. He had been expecting the opposite response. Then she said, 'Though that is an interesting word you use to describe yourself. The heathens had their gods.'

'I was trying to be funny. I'm an atheist really. Is that worse?'

'Yes, because there's no hope for you.'

He laughed. There was the faintest sparkle of irony in her voice. He wasn't sure that she was serious.

'You know I will never believe in God, for as long as I live?'

'I wonder how you can know that.'

'All I'm saying is – if you are thinking of asking me to come along to your church . . .'

'I wouldn't do that.'

She looked troubled, and turned her face downwards towards her empty plate. She had finished her food, all that was left on the plate was the chop bone, curled like a bass clef, picked clean.

He wondered if he'd offended her.

'It must be difficult for you, with what's happening between us. All I've done is been a bastard, but you've sinned.'

He felt a little more confident now that he could say things like this. After a long silence she said, 'I suppose I have faith in Him that there is a purpose to all of this.'

'Surely your Church regards marriage as sacred.'

'I don't know, Arnold. The Christian God is a God of love. Perhaps it is love that is the sacred thing.'

He thought that was a beautiful thing to say, and stayed quiet, so the words would hang in the air for as long as possible. Then, after another long silence, and very quietly, 'Yes, perhaps it is.'

Before they could meet again, the sewing evening intervened. Arnold would normally have done his vanishing act even before the women arrived, but this week he decided to remain as a presence. He hung around as the women entered and chatted, as the bowls of olives and nuts were put out and the drinks distributed. He sat at the dining table while the women filled the lounge, unfolding their stitched fabrics, showing them to each other. One woman was making bridesmaids' dresses for a friend's daughter's wedding. Peach silk with puffed shoulders and a square neckline. Another was making a set of dungarees profligate with pockets. Arnold intruded on a conversation with praise for someone's needlework. The comments were taken in good, if puzzled spirit by the needleworker, though he sensed he was testing the patience of this group by lingering as he did. It slowly became evident that Vera wasn't attending this evening.

'Isn't it time for you to retire discreetly?' asked the woman with the highlighted hair, who always seemed to resent Arnold's presence more strongly than the others.

He wanted to ask where Vera was but remained silent. He looked at the group now, in the absence of Vera, and it seemed a tawdry thing, a coven of seamstresses, fiddling with hooks and catches. A fussy little posse of haberdashers unpicking and plucking at things. They bared their teeth to break a line of button thread or to loosen an overtightened stitch. He suddenly felt an urge to bear down on this little gathering as though it was an illegal sit-in or protest, to shake a can of pepper spray and let them have it full in their painted faces, spray it so hard their hair flew. He wanted to march through them and trample their delicate lacework, wield a batten and crack some skulls, rip their frocks. Make them get the hell out of his house. Shocked by the violence of his vision, and the sense of delight in it that he tried to fight back, he left the room unnoticed, and went to his study, not bothering to listen in.

# 7

As the weeks had gone on, to avoid arousing suspicion, Arnold and Vera saw as little of each other as they could, aside from their weekly lovemaking sessions at her house. He had managed to reduce by small degrees his ferrying role, and so was only occasionally in the playground, and if he was, he stood apart from Vera. They communicated by text only, and these were kept brief and cryptic, so that if either's phone fell into the wrong hands, nothing obviously incriminating would be evident.

It made the weekly meetings all the more important and longed for. This approaching Wednesday would be the last before the half term, and Arnold balked at the thought of even a week's absence from Vera.

He was in his office at work, a space he shared with six other members of staff, though there were rarely more than two in the room at the same time, and had just returned from giving a plenary lecture on form in poetry. He took out his mobile phone as he sat at his desk and read the latest message from Vera, 'look fwd 2 poetry workshop, 2day 1.15'. They had taken to using the language of creative writing as a code. He was about to text back 'have got new poems 2 show you', when he received a phone call from Polly.

'Sorry to bother you sweetie but do you think you could come over to the shop?'

'Is something wrong?' He should have said immediately that he had a lecture, but she seemed to know that he hadn't. He wondered if she had already spoken to the departmental secretary to check his availability.

'Well, something rather odd's happening here. There's a young man outside the shop, wearing a suit made of paper, and he's causing a disturbance. I've called the police, but all they can do is ask him to move on. But then he comes back. He's not actually doing anything illegal.'

'Did you say he was wearing a suit made of paper . . . ?'

'Yes. I think he's someone we – or you – turned down for the press. I don't really understand why he's so upset. He was hanging around yesterday and the day before. But now he's actually trying to stop people coming into the shop.'

'And what do you want me to do about it?'

'He has mentioned you, by name. He seems to bear a grudge? I think you may have written some harsh comments on his rejection slip, or on his manuscript. He doesn't make a lot of sense when I try and talk to him.'

'So you want me to come over and apologize to him? Is that what you're asking?'

'Maybe if you just talked to him. It's you he wants to see, I think.'

'Now? Right now?'

'I'm losing custom, Arnold. He is turning people away, they are afraid to come in the shop. As I said, the police can't do anything. He keeps coming back.'

It was something Arnold had long dreaded happening. The Papyrus Press had, over the five years of its operation, been surprisingly successful. Some well-respected but mostly forgotten poets had had their names revived through their efforts. They had discovered some brilliant unknowns who had gone on to publish with major imprints. At the same time, they had attracted a fair number of the desperate and the unhinged. He had twice received letters from solicitors accusing him of publishing their client's poems under someone else's name, and a policeman turned up at the shop once, a little apologetically informing a puzzled Polly that he was enquiring after some poems that had been reported missing. They were obliged to investigate, he told her. But so far, no rejected poet had themselves turned up at the shop to complain about their treatment by the Papyrus Press. Some innate sense of dignity and modesty prevented even the most desperate from doing that. He was glad, because the last thing he wanted was to confront some of the people behind the worst of the poetry they were sent.

Even as he gathered up his papers and left the office he was working out his timings. If he was quick and could find a good parking space he could deal with this incident at Papyrus and still have time to get across town to Vera's house. He texted her, warning her that the poetry workshop might be a little late. Those precious minutes. Each one mattered. A minute with Vera's body was worth an hour in the real world. She texted him back with the words he'd used to Polly – is there something wrong? Nothing wrong, just a hiccup.

Polly's shop was in the old quarter of town, not far from the cathedral, in a pedestrianized Elizabethan street with boutique shops, mostly selling arts and crafts, vintage clothes or fine foods. It was an area popular with street performers; there had been a recent trend for living statues, people dressed as monuments and standing still, as if paralysed, for hours on end, so the protestor dressed in paper didn't look particularly out of place, though he did look striking. A tall, youngish man, thin and wispy. The paper was curled around his torso and limbs in sections and plates Sellotaped together, with elaborately hinged joints, like a suit of armour. It had few creases or tears, he looked immaculate and fresh, a blank sheet straight from the writing cabinet, new and tempting. He looked both powerful and fragile at the same time. The bright white paper made his skin look grey in comparison, his lips too red, his teeth yellowy. But he was handsome, exquisite, even. He was giving out leaflets. A few passers-by had stopped to watch, thinking him to be a street entertainer.

When Arnold came closer he saw that the paper the boy was dressed in wasn't blank but had been written on, in tight, narrow handwriting too small to read. It looked as though he was covered in poems.

Whenever anyone approached the shop the young man stepped in front of them and made an attempt to block their way. If the person insisted on going in the shop he would let them pass, but he was clearly deterring some, who backed off, not wanting a public confrontation with someone who appeared to be mad. Arnold could see the problem. The man was surely doing something illegal, the police should have acted.

He went forward and made his own attempt to enter the shop. The young man barred his way, as he would anyone else, and held out a leaflet.

'Would you like something to read, sir?'

Arnold took the leaflet and glanced at it. It was something handwritten and photocopied, in small script, hardly decipherable. The man went on. 'It's all there, sir. Free to you. But the people in there refused to publish it.'

Arnold didn't say anything and tried moving around the young man and gain entrance to the shop. The man shifted sideways and continued to block him.

'Are you trying to stop me entering this shop?'

'No,' the young man said, a little shocked by Arnold's tone, and stepped neatly aside.

Arnold passed through. There were some people in the shop and Polly was busy with them. She had not seen Arnold's confrontation with the paper boy and he was disappointed by this. He browsed the tables where paper was laid out in reams of different colours and textures, some of it so thick and rough it was more like some sort of fabric. He looked again at the leaflet the boy had given him. Tiny handwriting; neurotic, cramped, shrunken. He realized that it was a poem, but not just one poem, several poems, some written at right angles to fit into every inch of space on the leaflet, a mosaic of text. But none of it was readable.

'There you are,' said Polly, having dealt with the customer, and speaking to him as if he'd been hiding. 'Haven't you seen him yet?'

'Of course I've seen him. He was blocking the door.'

'Well did you say anything to him?'

'I just asked him to move aside, and he did.'

'He's got no right to stand outside my door turning customers away.'

'He looks pretty harmless.'

'To you, maybe, but you're a man.'

'The police can't do anything?'

'They tell him to move on, and so he moves on. Then he comes back.'

'He's a wisp of a thing. Looks like he could get blown away.'

Another customer was trying to get into the shop, the boy was blocking her path, pushing his leaflets onto her, talking into her face. She gave up and went away.

'Look what he's doing. It can't go on like this. You've got to talk to him.'

'What am I supposed to say to him?'

'I don't know. Offer to have another look at his poems, perhaps?'

'And then what? Publish them?'

'Maybe. It depends.'

'We're not going to be bullied into publishing some lunatic's poetry. And if we reject him again, he'll just come back and carry on doing what he's doing now.'

'Perhaps if you reject him in a more sympathetic way than you did last time, he might calm down.'

'How did I reject him last time?'

'I don't know. Why don't you ask him?'

'Do you know what his name is?'

'It's on these leaflets, look . . .'

He looked at the leaflet. The writing of the poems themselves was too small to decipher, but the name was larger, in block capitals. *MARTIN GUERRE.*

'Obviously that can't be his real name,' said Polly.

The name triggered something in Arnold's memory. Among the forty or fifty submissions they received every month, this name, if nothing else, had enabled the poet to stand out from the rest.

'I think I remember him,' said Arnold, 'but I can't remember his poems, or what I wrote on them.'

A customer had made it past the poet and into the shop, and Polly attended to her, leaving Arnold to think.

He was at a loss for how to approach the man. When he rehearsed in his mind what he should say, he found himself taking the role of a nightclub bouncer, or hefty security guard, pushing the young poet firmly out of the way, locking him into a half-nelson when he offered resistance. Well, that was surely not the way, yet what else? The admonishing headmaster, telling the young poet not to be silly? Then, as he approached the door and the young man beyond it, dressed in a suit of his poems, he realized there was only one way to deal with him, and that was to read him.

'Some of these lines are quite beautiful, but you might have used a bigger hand,' he said, bending to peer at the boy's paper torso, on which were written dozens of sonnets. The boy made no reply, and looked a little uncomfortable with the close attention. Arnold was evidently the first person to attempt reading what was written on the paper suit. 'Why did you write them in such small lettering?'

The boy shrugged. 'It's just my normal handwriting.'

'But you wanted to make a display of them, in public.'

'No. I just wanted to wear them.'

Arnold straightened himself. He was touched by what felt like a very pure form of honesty in what the boy had said. 'You are angry with us for turning down the poems you sent us. I'm sorry. We . . .'

'I'm not angry.'

'OK. But you're not happy . . .'

'Why do you keep saying what I'm feeling?'

'I'm just trying to apologize to you.'

The boy laughed, but with what seemed genuine humour.

'I'm trying to say I'm sorry if we upset you, I may have written some comments . . .'

The boy's expression suddenly became serious, as

though stunned by a sudden moment of revelation. 'Are you Arnold Proctor?'

'Yes, I run the press here . . .'

'I loved you.'

'Oh.' The comment completely silenced Arnold.

'Your poems are beautiful.'

'You've read my book?'

'It's in the college library. I keep taking it out. I'm the only one.'

'You're at the university?'

'The art school.'

A moment of silence, again Arnold felt wrong-footed. If the boy had been at the university he could have found common ground, but the art school was unknown territory to him. He wasn't even sure he knew there was an art school in the city.

'You had no right to write those things on my poems.'

'Were they very bad, the things I wrote?'

'It doesn't matter what they were, you had no right to write on them. I sent them to you as a poet, not as a student. I know how to write poems.'

'Are you sure about that?'

'Yes.'

'Such confidence. Where does it come from?'

The boy didn't say anything for a moment, and then, 'If you are true to your feelings, then the poems will write themselves.'

Arnold hadn't the heart to challenge this assertion, even though it seemed to stab at him, personally.

'Can we have a talk, somewhere more private?'

Arnold had gently begun guiding the boy away from the shop, placing a hand on his papered elbow and turning him around. He was light and fragile beneath the paper, hardly a sense of a body there at all. He offered no resistance to being manoeuvred, and in fact yielded too readily to Arnold's guidance. It felt to Arnold as though he was stealing a child.

'I don't want any tea,' the boy said, as they walked along the High Street, Arnold's hand still on the boy's papered elbow. Beneath his hand he could feel warmth within the paper. It was an unnerving sensation, like feeling a gift-wrapped present that contained something alive. 'I only drink coffee. Fair-trade coffee.'

Arnold knew of a place, five minutes down the High Street, left near the cathedral, that had been open only a few weeks, a place that served coffee with an earnestness that he thought the boy might appreciate. It sold specially imported coffee directly from growers. The tables were rough wooden desks. The boy's appearance drew looks of surprise from the other customers, and some laughter. A table of young women kept turning and sniggering. The waitress recommended Rwandan red bourbon, which arrived at their table in pretty blue cups. The boy looked awkward, embarrassed. Sitting opposite each other, Arnold could examine him closely. He was extraordinarily beautiful, like a martyr in a Renaissance painting. At the same time he looked as though he had been thrust into an adult body before he was ready for it, not knowing what to do with his facial hair, which grew both long and short about his jowls. There was an electrical sensitivity to his face, the lips occasionally fluttered, the eyes sparked, glowed and dimmed repeatedly. Now and then he took deep breaths, as if trying to contain an emotion that was overspilling.

'I loved the Papyrus Press,' he said, almost the first words he's spoken since they left the shop.

Arnold didn't say anything but smiled at what he took to be a sort of compliment. The boy went on, 'They publish books using their own paper, hand-made by the woman in there. She produces special paper for each book.'

Arnold chose not to remind him that he knew this already, as husband of the paper-maker and editor of the press. The boy had this curious ability to detach himself from commonly accepted knowledge. 'My poems are all about paper. They would fit in so well.'

He lifted the cup of black coffee to his lips, frowning. When he took a sip, he shuddered, grimaced.

'That's disgusting.'

'What's the matter? Too strong?'

'It's got no sugar in it.'

'They said we had to have it without sugar.'

'I can't drink coffee without sugar.'

'That's the way we're supposed to drink it, the woman said.'

'So we have to do what she says?'

Arnold saw that he would have to try and get some sugar – he called to the waitress, 'Could we have some sugar? Please?'

'It does corrupt the flavour – we do recommend . . .'

'I understand that, but at the same time, we would like some sugar.'

'Of course.' Now it was the waitress who looked a little hurt, behind her smile. She returned, after what seemed too long a pause, with a little bowl of brown sugar cubes.

The boy looked at them sulkily. Arnold suspected he was going to ask for white sugar. Instead he picked one up and put it in his coffee, performing the action clumsily so that the coffee splashed over the edge of his cup and dripped down the side.

'So what sort of things do you paint?'

The boy shook his head slightly, as if unable to believe the stupidity of his question.

'I don't paint things.'

'You're a sculptor?'

The boy sat back and blew air from his lips exasperatedly.

'I just make things with paper. Paper is the important thing.'

'That paper suit looks like a work of art to me.'

The boy flexed his arms and contemplated the smooth working of paper hinges.

'My girlfriend did it for me. She's in the fashion department.'

Arnold felt a strong sense of relief when he discovered that the boy had a girlfriend.

The boy drank his coffee again, he didn't grimace this time, but still wasn't satisfied.

'It needs milk,' he said, in a strangely cold little voice.

'It's fine without. You've got sugar . . .'

'It needs milk. I can't drink it without milk.'

Arnold didn't think to wonder why it was incumbent upon him to make the request for milk. The boy who'd staged a one-person street protest should have been quite capable of making the demand, but he was deliberately placing the onus on him as a sort of authority figure. You've brought me here, he seemed to be saying, so you sort out my coffee. Arnold called the waitress over again.

'I'm sorry to bother you again, could we have some milk for this young man's coffee . . .'

'Milk?'

'Yes, please.'

The waitress couldn't hide her disappointment, as she nodded and turned away. The boy called after her:

'Warm milk.'

'I'm sorry?'

'I'd like warm milk – hot milk, please.'

The waitress looked back at Arnold, as if she needed confirmation of this request, then back at the boy, then at the barista behind the bar, before walking off.

'They bring a little jug of freezing milk, the coffee will be turned stone cold. It's already cooled down a lot. Wasn't exactly scalding when it arrived.'

So now the boy was some sort of coffee connoisseur, thought Arnold, as he persisted with his own milkless cup.

'So what do your parents think about it?'

'About what?'

'About you and art school. Do they approve?'

'They don't understand what I'm doing. They understand if they think I am learning how to design things. But I keep telling them I'm not doing that. I don't want to design things.'

'What do your parents do?'

'What's the point of talking about them?'

'I'm just interested.'

'Well I'm not.'

'No?'

The boy shrugged, and then made an effort to explain, 'My mother's just – she's just a mother. The guy she lives with – I don't really know what he does to be honest.'

'What about your father?'

'He pissed off when I was ten. I've stopped thinking about him.'

Just a little while ago, Arnold was thinking, the young man before him had been a child. He tried to imagine the child he had been, in a toy-rich world, unconcerned about the publishing of poems, doted on, then sent into turmoil by the parental split-up. He wondered how much that episode had been responsible for the fragility of the thing that sat before him now, how easily it had replaced the perkiness and enthusiasm of the child with a talent for drawing with this thing of pain and nerves.

He felt a sudden urge to feed the boy. The thinness of him, visible beneath the paper shell, was shocking. He was as thin as a letter.

'Do you want something to eat, Martin?'

'I don't think they do food here.'

'There were some cakes on the counter.'

The boy shook his head in a slightly embarrassed way, as though Arnold had mentioned something he shouldn't have. Martin spoke as if to cover this embarrassment. 'I don't need any advice about how to live my life.'

'I wasn't going to offer you any.'

'And I don't need any advice about how to write poems.'

'The same, I wasn't going to give you any.'

'Then what's the point of us talking?'

'I wanted you to send me your poems again. Send me the manuscript. I want to have another look.'

'Are you serious? After what you wrote on them, do you seriously think I would entrust them to you again?'

'I wouldn't blame you if you didn't.'

He noticed a subtle change in Martin's demeanour. The brittleness had softened slightly. He had dropped his guard, despite his defiant words. Arnold had unashamedly touched the most sensitive part of him.

'I've got better things to do with them,' the boy said.

'I don't doubt that. All I'm asking for is the chance to read them again. I'm not saying I am going to publish them, we publish very little anyway. But I am only asking because I think I may have made a big mistake the first time I read them. And reading you – the poems you are wearing, even though your handwriting is terribly small, I can see there are some very beautiful things there.'

Arnold, who hadn't thought about her for well over an hour, suddenly realized that, had this boy not intervened, he would, at this moment, be fucking Vera in her husband's bed. He felt a surge of guilt, the origin of which was the innocent presence of Martin, the boy. Arnold kept thinking of him as a boy but he was a young man, out in the world, away from his parents. Yet he had a childishness to him that was so easy to probe and manipulate, heartbreakingly so. A pureness of conscience that made Arnold wince when he considered the state of his own conscience.

'I don't know,' the boy said. 'I feel like you're just going to trick me, or something.'

Arnold moved his chair in readiness for departing. 'Will you think about it?' The boy gave a very small nod, barely more than a twitch of the head. 'Do you want me to give you a lift anywhere? What about I take you to your college?'

'No, I don't want to go there, not today.'

'Home then?'

Martin agreed, in a dazed, blurry kind of way. He didn't seem to know what had hit him. Even his paper suit was beginning to tear.

They walked out of the cafe together and then to the multi-storey where Arnold's car was parked. He drove him out to the western quarter, where all the grand houses had been converted into student bedsits and house-shares, the

odd world that he had once inhabited, though in a different city, with kebab shops on every corner, charity shops
everywhere, second-hand record shops. It was a part of
town he rarely visited, to avoid the extra-mural encounters
that could turn into out-of-hours tutorials. He had once
gone in a pub round about here, when he was new to the
city and to the job, a pub which had seemed charmingly
peaceful and relaxed at first, but by the time he had finished his first pint he was surrounded by students, many
of them his own, and they all thought it amazing and
funny that their lecturer was in the pub that they regarded
as their territory. He had tried his best to be friendly, and
they worked hard at catching him off guard, and tried to
get him drunk, and even offered him drugs, and in the end
he had to do his best to make an inconspicuous exit. Now,
driving under the boy's direction, he felt a strange sense
of envy, for the old ground of studenthood, with its easy
come easy go atmosphere. He parked outside a shabby
Edwardian terrace.

'You could give me your poems now, if you like,' said
Arnold. 'Are they in there? Do you have them?'

The boy hesitated. 'I don't know. I need to think about
it. What to do with them. You hurt me very bad. I don't
know if I should give them to you again.'

'But,' Arnold tried to moderate his tone, he was becoming a little frustrated, 'in that case why were you picketing
the shop? It looked to me like you were demanding to be
reconsidered.'

'No, I was just trying to draw attention to an injustice.'

'But you do realize, don't you, that you can't just demand to be published, it doesn't work like that.'

'My poems have to be published, it's vital. And they should have been published by Papyrus. They are the only publishers who understand paper. And Papyrus can only publish them if they love them, like I loved yours.'

The conversation went on like this for a little while as they sat in the car. He managed, in the end, to extract from Martin a commitment to send Arnold his poems. Arnold for his part said he couldn't promise anything, but that he would give them more time and consideration than perhaps he had done previously. In the meantime, he asked Martin to end his one-person protest outside Papyrus.

The boy was out of the car now, his paper costume disintegrating, a loop of card that had clad an arm came unstuck and blew back in through the car window. The big sheet of cartridge that wrapped his torso had split. There was just bare skin beneath. The boy bent down to speak through the window.

'You can't make me do anything. I don't have to do what you say.' He uttered these words in such a tight voice it was like an act of ventriloquism, his lips hardly moving. He turned and walked to the house, a rambling building with overgrown privet almost blocking the path. He didn't go in by the front door but disappeared round the side.

Arnold looked at his watch. If he drove back to Vera's now, he would have about thirty minutes before she would have to leave to pick up her littlest. They would not have time to make love, but he could spend at least a few minutes in her company, talking. But the traffic was bad and the minutes ticked away in his car. He gave up and went home.

# 8

There followed the week of half term during which Arnold and Vera both spent time at home with their children. Arnold felt a new phase was beginning in his relationship with his lover. His longing for Vera had been somehow diverted by his encounter with the boy in paper. When he thought about her, when he thought about her body, his thoughts were drawn away by the image of Martin Guerre as a wounded bird, his paper garments like white quills. He felt the boy to be a pinpoint of moral energy. When he looked again at his own poems, which now filled several cardboard folders, he felt almost ashamed of them. The hours he'd spent, folded up at his desk, scratching those lines out, then feeling too afraid to think of publishing them. It was unimaginable that he would ever think of wearing them like the boy had done, parade them down the street, hand them out to passers-by. Was it simply a lack of critical self-awareness that enabled the boy to make such bold moves with his poems? Or was it that he was somehow more deeply connected to the things he made, more deeply invested in them? He was like some of the young writers he taught, who thought the literary qualities of their writing was not the important thing. The important thing was that their poems existed at all. You couldn't criticize a poem when it was an event of flesh and blood occupying physical space and time. All you could do was feel it. Energy. That was what he envied the boy, and others like him. His own creative life had fallen into little fragments, widely separated. There was no one to bolster him, no one to tell him to carry on, to keep going, to value the subtleties of thought and feeling and language that he had once felt he could master. Now all that mattered in poetry was the self, the physical self standing on a stage or in the street. The word made flesh.

He thought of Vera in her house, round the other side of the park and beyond the local shops, looking after her own children. What thoughts was she having? With a reading week at the university coinciding with half term they were both housebound spouses, taking the burden of childcare while their other halves worked. Was she suffering? He needed to talk to her, he needed to fuck her, if just to break out of this spell the boy had cast.

Polly reported that Martin Guerre had dropped his one-man protest outside her shop. 'Whatever you said to him, it seems to have worked. What did you actually say to him? You didn't threaten him, did you?'

'Of course I didn't threaten him. I just got him to talk, that's all. He was obviously troubled about something, and taking it out on you. He's got his parents on his back, and he was upset about his poetry. So I praised his poems. That seemed to cure him.'

'Excellent. Now you just need someone to praise yours, and we'll all be happy. Oh, that reminds me. Although he has stopped protesting, he did pop in yesterday, while I was out, and left this for you. Tamsin said it was urgent. Where is it?' She looked among her work things which she kept in an alcove beside the kitchen, before finding the large padded envelope.

Arnold felt both delight and dread. Delight that he had somehow managed to reach through to the boy's vanities, dread that he would now have to read his stuff.

'You know what it is?'

'I asked him to resubmit his poems.'

'Oh no, Arnold. This is what started the whole thing off. If you reject him again, he'll come back worse than before. Do you realize this means we'll have to publish him. I'm not having that boy standing outside my shop again, bullying my customers.'

'OK, so we'll publish him.'

'And if we publish him we'll have to deal with him. You know what it's like, he'll be on the phone all the time asking about why we haven't got his book reviewed in the *Observer*. And it'll harm our reputation if we publish rubbish. On top of that we'd be doing a disservice to the boy – risking him being exposed to mockery and bad reviews . . .'

'I seem to remember you were the one who suggested publishing him last week.'

'That wasn't a serious suggestion. I'd rather we broke any connection with him at all. Publishing him would tie him to us for ever.'

'Maybe it's not rubbish. And maybe he'll quieten down if he thinks we're taking his writing seriously. Who knows? I don't think we have a choice.'

Arnold took the unopened and unnervingly heavy envelope up to his office, and left it there.

During the holiday he saw Vera twice. On the first occasion they both attended a children's party that had an adult offshoot, where the parents sat around in a separate room to chat. He noticed Vera deliberately manoeuvre herself so that she didn't have to sit next to Polly, and he noticed, with relief, how Polly thought nothing of this. Vera avoided his eyes with such efficiency he almost felt as if she were deleting him from her field of vision. At the same time, her concentrated avoidance was a visible token of their closeness. He cherished the way she refused to meet his eyes, even on the few occasions when he held the room's attention with a remark or anecdote.

He wished Polly hadn't started talking about the boy in the paper suit, but it was a story that fascinated everyone, and the conversation kept returning to the subject, and Arnold had to add his own details.

'It sounds to me like he could be seriously disturbed,' said someone.

'Bring him to a sewing evening, we'll stitch something together for him to wear.'

'People like that can be so unpredictable, how do you know what he'll do next?'

'Oh, he has clothes to wear, I don't think he was dressed in paper because that's all he had.'

'He's not dangerous, no, far from it. I think he is a simple, harmless soul.'

'You are so sweet, Arnold.'

'You should adopt him, the boy in paper. Take him in.'

'I think we've got enough on our plate.'

He noticed Vera look at him when he said this, the only moment in the whole afternoon that she did so.

Later in the holiday he found himself tasked with retrieving Evelyn from an afternoon spent with some other children at Vera's house. He had doubts about whether he should really do this, and wondered if he should try and find a way out of it, thinking it might be a bad idea to rerun the circumstances of their first sexual encounter. And when he went there, he was in a very different mood, with the feeling that he was stepping into a trap. He saw himself as if from the outside, from a distance, or watching himself in a film. And when he went there he found everything as it had been that other time – the strewn living room with left-over food turning cold on the table. In the playroom the children were again in the grip of the television, ready and waiting to be betrayed. But this time he and Vera did not steal up the staircases to make hurried love, instead they behaved like a tired married couple.

'I'm so looking forward to when this week's over,' Vera said as she handed him a mug of tea, 'aren't you?'

The tone of voice in which she said this suggested she was just tired of having the children at home all day, not that she was longing for the return of their trysts.

'Ye-es,' he said, cautiously.

'You don't sound that sure.'

'I've been wondering if we need to rethink things.'

'I didn't realize we had thought things in the first place.'

Realizing the conversation was going to deal with these personal matters, they moved into the front room, well away from the children, and continued their conversation in whispers.

'Well, perhaps we should have. Being in love, if that's what we are, has given us a special kind of power that neither of us wanted.'

Vera nodded, but more to make him explain himself.

'The power to hurt the people who love us.'

'That power is always with us . . .'

'Not this kind of power. We are armed to the teeth. I feel like I have been given charge of a huge animal that is peaceful most of the time, but that at any moment could turn savage and start eating people.'

'I don't know why you think we should ever have to hurt people.'

He didn't know what to say to this. Did she not understand? Or did she understand more than he realized? Had she some plan that would mean their lives could go on unaffected by their relationship? That what they were doing could be somehow contained, for ever.

'I think we both need to understand what we are doing, and how it might affect other people.'

She seemed disappointed. He felt suddenly that he'd failed her in some crucial way. She did her best to disguise her feelings, but they surfaced in the form of visible concentration. She was staring hard at his mouth, then his eyes, then his mouth, as though actually trying to read the words he was speaking, so intent was she in extracting any hidden meanings in them. It unsettled him. He had been hoping for some form of assent, agreement, sympathy. Surely she was worried as well, about where their relationship might lead. Two families destroyed, for the sake of something purely sensual.

'Let's talk about it after the holiday,' she said in her low, quiet voice, her serious voice. And almost immediately Arnold was back in the sensual realm, desiring her, just because of the movement of her lips, the beadwork beauty of them, the glimpse of a richly pink interior they gave as she spoke, the plush tongue. It made him want to venture into her, and he had to resist strongly. The blind power she had to reach instantly into his primal desires, just by the slightest movement of her facial muscles. How could he ever hope to escape, or to maintain a reasoned viewpoint on their situation? He felt an overwhelming sense that when the time came to draw the line he would be unable to free himself from the grip of her beauty. The sacrifice would go on and on. His passion for her was relentless in the sacrifices it made, he would chop down tree after tree until there were no trees left on the island, he would shoot every seabird until there were no seabirds left, and no meat to cook, he would strip an island's resources bare, in order to preserve what they had. It maintained itself above all other considerations, values, wants. Why not just give in now and save the agonies that lay in store, say goodbye to his family and his life?

So the meeting on the first Wednesday after the half term was to be a test of his resolve. He had determined that he would ask for an end to their relationship. He would be staring into the fire of her beauty, and would have to not flinch. He worried about it for several days. It was not something he'd ever had to do before and he couldn't quite work out a formula of words. When he arrived, creeping as usual like a criminal through the back gate and the shrubs of her unkempt garden, she seemed to have made a special effort with her appearance, wearing a pretty yellow dress. He had never seen her in anything other than jeans before. It was heartbreaking.

'All I am saying,' he said, once they were settled at the table, 'is that we should perhaps have a break . . .'

'We've already had a break, it's been three weeks since we last fucked.'

Her use of that word, blunt and uncharacteristic, sent such a thrill of pleasure through his body that he couldn't gather his thoughts for a response, and she carried on.

'What you mean is that you want to end it completely. So why don't you just say it?'

'I'm not saying that . . .'

'Even if you aren't, what is the point of having this break?'

'So we can think carefully about where we go from here. Look, I don't want to lose my family, and I don't think you want to lose yours. If Polly found out about us I don't think I would last more than five minutes before I found myself homeless. The longer we continue our relationship, the more chance she has of finding out.'

Vera didn't seem impressed by any of these comments. 'Was it the boy dressed in paper who changed things?'

'Yes, in some ways it was. I saw how he was damaged by his parents – his father left home when he was ten. You can see the pain of it written all over his face, no matter how bravely he tries to cover it up. I keep thinking of Evelyn. I find it very hard to handle the fact that I possess knowledge that would destroy her.' The look on Vera's face made him have another go at phrasing his thoughts. 'Not "destroy", then, but "damage". Damage badly. She would survive, of course. We all would. But we would all be badly wounded. It wouldn't make a difference if I was unhappy with Polly, and I have tried everything I can think of to examine that question, of how happy I am with her, and though I am more excited by you, I am not unhappy with her, so I can't justify to myself breaking things up for that reason.'

'That is good of you, Arnold. And it makes me feel bad,

but on the other hand, if what we do goes no further, that we simply keep it to this once weekly meeting, then we could maintain this for as long as we needed to.'

Her words chilled him. He had not expected resistance to his plan, even though this was a mild, reasoned, considered form of resistance. He was expecting to have his plan agreed to immediately. It puzzled him.

'But you see, the longer it continues, the more chance there is that eventually we will be discovered, that someone will see me coming out of here, or will see us together somewhere, or we will accidentally leave some clue, or Polly will smell you on my clothes – something like that will happen in the end . . .'

'Not if we're careful . . .'

'But careful for how long, a year? Two years? Five years? The rest of our lives?'

'Why not? I've heard of people who've done things like that.'

'For five years? Imagine what Polly would think if she found out we'd been sleeping together for five years . . .'

'We can't predict how people will react. Why should it be any worse a reaction than if it had been for five weeks?'

'Because of the depth of the deceit. Because of the depth of our commitment to the deceit, to maintain it for that long, it proves that we had years to think about how wrong what we were doing was, but went on doing it anyway.'

'I think you are worrying too much, Arnold. Our love for each other should be allowed to exist – if it grows, then we have to look after it, if it dies out, then we can go back to how we were, but we would be disrespectful to it if we killed it now, it would be too cruel.'

'I'm not saying we end it. All I'm asking for is time.'

She smiled at this. 'It's the one thing we haven't got. Just these few minutes once a week. Don't you feel the preciousness of it? For me, it feels like my whole life is compressed into those two hours. I am not sure I would be able to survive properly without them. But – if that is what you want, then you can have your moratorium. Starting from next week? Yes?'

She was suggesting that, if their period of abstinence was about to start, they should use the present moment for one last session of lovemaking. The Shrove Tuesday of their sexual Lent. He agreed. And he was surprised, after the soberness of their conversation, at how swimmingly aroused he felt. The mood changed instantly from one of courtroom sombreness to one of dreamy sensuality. It was like someone had thrown a switch to dim the lights and ignite the candles. The longing that suddenly rose in his body was a physical sensation like the pain of hunger, but without specific location, it seemed not to belong to the genitals, but was spread more evenly throughout his abdomen, a pain that moved all the way up to his heart, a kind of dyspepsia, though not acid in its origins. They had not made love for three weeks, and he had thought, in that time, that he had slowly built a form or resistance to the tremendous power of her beauty, that he had inoculated himself against it, but in the bedroom, all the barriers melted away. And she was emboldened and enhanced, as though anticipating he might have put up defences. She had dressed herself in beautiful underwear. It was a shock, and he had never thought of himself as someone likely to be aroused by something so tacky, but Vera wore it and had produced a wonderful edition of herself. The notion that she had committed herself so strongly to his arousal, by investing in this material, and wearing it, when it could have been of little benefit to her, overwhelmed him with a sense of gratitude, that she had transformed her entire body into a sort of gift, and was presenting it to him. She was the last person he imagined would find sexy underwear appealing, it was another of the little sacrifices she was making, another tract of undergrowth slashed and burned, another clearing constructed in the forest, another turret added to the invisible palace.

She attached little pieces of jewellery to herself, sparkling things to her earlobes, faceted little crystals, she said they were her grandmother's, that she had never worn them before because they hurt her ears and that she would have to take them off soon, but the effect on her was startling. Again he was not someone who cared much about jewellery, Polly's was of the wooden-bead type, nothing that flashed and dazzled like this, casting rainbow light on Vera's wonderful neck, round which another piece of work hung, making her something that was easy to worship, indeed he felt a weakness in his knees at that moment, at the spectacle of her, little pieces of compressed quartz, yet they seemed to bathe her in a rejuvenating light, smoothing her skin so she seemed younger by a decade. He approached her like a fool with his hands out, blinded by the glare of her body, attracted to it like a moth, as stupidly.

Later, spent, utterly drained, he realized this couldn't possibly be the last occasion on which this could happen. Still stroking him, she held him transfixed in a continuous palm embrace, her hand swam through his body as though he was a pool, lifting him, parting him, stirring him, so that he couldn't think, or rather he was thinking in a way that he hadn't thought before. He thought in a way that was closer to the way he thought in dreams, seeing things in terms of pictures and stories, and setting himself against a situation where he has to push a large obstacle out of the way. He supposed they were on a raft in a huge ocean, but a raft that was utterly secure, unsinkable, stocked with an inexhaustible supply of food and water. Vera rose above him, naked now, but for the necklace, she straddled him, though he was soft and helpless, indeed he was in a certain amount of mild pain. Her breasts moved in front of his face and he felt the befuddled sense of being stared at by them, they were still shiny from where he'd sucked. She knocked them playfully against his nose, one after the other. Beneath them her wetness met his own wetness, and they stirred against each other, she pestled him slowly, until miraculously he found himself rigid again, as though he had risen out of his own pain, fresh and ready.

He had arrived here determined to end things, but now

he was more deeply connected to Vera than before, he was of a piece with her, their very skins seemed stitched together. And the worries he'd had now seemed trivial. Why should their spouses find out about them, and if they did, so what? Families split up every day. It is more the norm than not, to split up. Who now stays married for life? The world is full of stepchildren and second husbands, and everyone seems to manage.

And so their affair resumed its previous course and direction – a straight, regular routine that appeared to be leading nowhere. It was as though they were building the dead straight track across the outback, sleeper by sleeper through the flat desert, rails winched into position, screwed down, mile after mile, all that energy and ingenuity going into building one dead straight track, but nowhere at the end of it, no station, no destination in sight. This continued to bother him.

# 9

For the remainder of the summer term Geoffrey, Vera's youngest child, was in the nursery school for three full days a week. That was eighteen hours, spread over three days, when Vera would be free of all responsibility for her children. 'If circumstances were normal,' she said, 'I would now be thinking of trying to pick up the pieces of my academic career, perhaps some part-time lecturing, or even some research. But now that I have whole days free, I just want to spend them with you.' How the sentiment filled Arnold, it was such an exquisite thing to express, this longing of hers, for him. Her words smothered him sweetly, he danced with them for hours and hours after he had parted from her. She was sacrificing her scholarship for him, putting aside her wonderful mind, putting her brain on hold so that she could devote herself to the pleasure of his proximity. She was dumb with love. She was plebeian, illiterate, doltish and village-idiotic with it. And so was he.

Arnold had more time now as well. Teaching had finished, the exam season was over and he was required to be on campus much less. With their newfound time-richness they decided to venture beyond their world to somewhere they could be together on neutral ground. They were thirty minutes' drive from the coast and they decided to meet in one of the fishing towns. Here they could disappear together among the sightseeing crowds who came for the sands and the piers and the amusement parks, who kept an old, ridiculous economy going by purchasing tacky souvenirs and silly experiences – trampolines arrayed on the beach like a little industry devoted to testing the durability of children, donkey rides that seemed to do the same, the shoreline telescopes that swallowed twenty pence pieces only to give a little wheezing noise and a view of blurred blueness in return. Vera and Arnold delighted in these things as if they were children again.

Sometimes Vera was able to arrange childcare so that she didn't have to be home until late in the afternoon. They used this time to experiment with hotels, booking a room as early in the day as they could – giving them a few hours together in which they could live as they'd never lived before, in a state of true privacy, in their own space, completely cut off from their other lives.

In these neutral zones Vera was able to free herself of that inhibition he had noticed in her since she had started talking about her beliefs and her past. In fact, she seemed more free than before, and had developed a love of self-display, of stripping naked and parading her body, striding around the room. Sometimes she would stand on a chair, holding her breasts, or lifting her arms to the ceiling as if she was a supporting column, her armpits yawning with hair. There seemed no reason for doing this other than to present herself, to celebrate her body. She encouraged Arnold to do the same, and they would some-times dance naked together on top of the bed, a precarious and static waltz or tango that would have the struts beneath the mattress straining. They would collapse gig-gling onto the bed, to bounce prone like trampolinists making an exit. This was almost as gratifying as the sex that followed, which would also be more open, not con-fined to the bed and its covers, but would be conducted in the room itself, using all its space and apparatus.

Afterwards Vera would leave to drive back on her own, and Arnold would sometimes stay on for longer, until the early evening, for no other reason than he felt a parsi-monious need to get his money's worth from the room, before letting it go, unoccupied for the night they had booked for themselves, the little shred of time that they so longed to fill, but were unable. Soon, Vera said, soon I'll be able to arrange something, make some excuse to be away for the night, and we can sleep together like two real people in a real hotel.

It was Polly who reminded Arnold about the existence of Martin Guerre. She reported that he had come into the shop again, agitated and wispy, to ask after his poems.

'It's only been a few weeks,' said Arnold.

'He seemed to think that was long enough, that you

should give his poems priority. There are heaps of other manuscripts, I keep telling you. They are building up.'

The reputation of the Papyrus Press was continuing to grow, and the hopeful poets continued to send him their work. Arnold's usual routine was, once a fortnight, to visit the shop and inspect the manuscripts, which were piled in a corner of the workshop, still in their envelopes, though carefully kept apart from the stacks of waste paper that were Papyrus's raw material. Here he would carry out his preliminary filtering operation, rejecting anything hand-written, anything on coloured paper, anything on scented paper and anything that contained a photograph of the author. He would retain anything by a poet with a known name, and of the rest a quick reading of the first two or three poems would tell him if the manuscript as a whole was worth reading. This process would usually reduce the pile by about ninety per cent, giving him a handful of manuscripts to take home to be read at leisure, the rest to be returned, using their own self-addressed envelopes, by one of Polly's staff.

By this process a second pile accumulated in Arnold's study at home, because it took him longer than a fort-night to find the time to read the manuscripts with enough close attention to be able to make a decision about them. The pile in Arnold's office could sometimes grow so tall it had to be divided into two piles, and some-times his heart sank when he finally got round to reading a manuscript and found that the covering letter was dated six months ago. That was when the follow-up letters would arrive, via Polly's shop, politely enquiring after the whereabouts of the poems. One paranoid writer had insisted that the Papyrus Press existed solely to provide a free supply of paper pulp for the workshop, which Arnold had actually considered as a viable option for manuscripts that arrived without return postage.

So it shouldn't have been unexpected that Martin Guerre would visit the shop in pursuit of his poems, though Arnold was a little put out that he should be so impatient, thinking that his offer to look at them at all should have been enough to quieten the boy for at least a few months. But he was already reapplying the pressure, the insistence on being seen and understood. So that evening after eating with his family, playing his usual role of tired adversary in his daughter's arguments and games, he went to his study and opened the envelope that was from Martin Guerre.

It was a big thick padded envelope that when opened revealed not a manuscript but a shallow box of marbled cardboard with a deep purple ribbon around it. This was precisely the kind of presentational preciousness that would normally have Arnold rejecting a manuscript out of hand. But this was Martin Guerre's manuscript. He had more or less committed himself to publishing whatever rubbish it contained. There was a letter on top of the box.

*Dear Arnold Proctor,*

*I am enclosing some poems that you haven't seen before, that I have been writing. I feel these poems express my true*

*feelings, and I have the courage to show them to you now, after your encouraging talk. As you will see, the poems in this collection tell a story. I would like you to consider them for publication with the Papyrus Press.*
*Yours sincerely*
   *Martin Guerre.*

*P.S. I have been re-reading your collection 'Macroscopia'. It is truly a major work of genius, and has been very inspiring for me.*

He pulled the bow and lifted the lid of the box. There was tissue paper within, and in the centre of the creased layer, a half-open rosebud, bright pink fading to brown, and very dead-looking. Arnold lifted it off as if it was an old fishbone. Then opening the layers of tissue paper, he came to the manuscript itself. On the cover was a drawing in pen and ink, of a lonely, bearded figure, wispy and awkward, holding in his hand a heart, coloured red, matching in shape the red hole in his chest. There were no words on this cover page, no title, no author name. On the next page, hand lettered in the same washy ink, the title page

*The Paper Lovers*
*By*
*Martin Guerre*

Martin Guerre's short manuscript told the story of the unrequited love of a young man for an older woman. In most of the poems these characters were described as if they were made of paper. It became quite clear to Arnold that these two characters represented Martin Guerre himself, and Polly, Arnold's wife. She was described in great physical detail – her paper glasses, her paper hair, her paper lips. It was well observed. One poem seemed to describe lovemaking between the paper figures – 'I take your paper breast, it crumples in my hand . . .'

In nearly every poem the Martin figure suffered some sort of torture appropriate to his material – he was torn, burned, creased, crumpled and, at the end, snipped to shreds with scissors. The Polly figure, his paper lover, remained intact and pure. It was not clear whether she wielded the scissors, but she was the cause of his suffering. The scene that troubled Arnold the most, however, was one of explicit lovemaking that described in detail the paper topography of the female body, in ways that were quite startling. Arnold felt something stir in him. Anger and effrontery, he thought, though perhaps a strange form of arousal as well. To have his wife's beauty described by another man made the beauty live again in his mind. It was as though by verification it had been made more vivid and intense. At the same time – who the hell did he think he was? It wasn't as though he was a harmlessly charming young teenager. Martin Guerre was a fully grown man staking a claim on another man's wife. That had been the thing all along. He was infatuated with Polly. In love with her, in whatever stupid and shapeless form of love the boy dealt.

He said quietly to himself, 'You little devil.'

———

The poetry itself had some good qualities. If published it could hold its own against some of the other pamphlets they'd published. The phrasing could be awkward, but the imagery was startlingly original. And there was an undeniable emotional power to the collection. Arnold admired it, yet could hardly bear to read it. The poems by turn evoked feelings of revulsion and awe, fascination and hatred. The boy's poetry described a desire he was not entitled to. Arnold could see the irony and the justice that was being meted out to him. Yet he could not publish this stuff, and have himself and Polly ridiculed. What would people think of them, editing such a volume, allowing it to be printed under the name of their press? Anyone who knew them would recognize Polly the Paper-maker in Martin's poems.

Arnold realized he would have to show the poems to Polly straight away. After Evelyn had gone to bed he presented them to her, just as she'd settled down on the couch in front of the TV. She groaned.

'Do I have to?'

'I think you should, they are all about you.'

She sat up on the couch, a look of amusement on her face. 'Well in that case . . .'

'I don't think he's a psycho or anything but I think you should know what his feelings and intentions might be . . .'

Polly read them with far more speed than Arnold had, and he wondered if she could really have taken them in.

'Oh, Arnold. These are harmless. They are quite fun, but harmless.'

'You think so? You think it's fun when he describes the structure of your clitoris?'

'Well, first of all you are making the obvious mistake of identifying the characters in these poems with real people. Why should these paper figures be anything other than fictional characters? He is describing the clitoris of a woman made of paper. I am made of flesh and blood.'

'That is not how the boy's mind works. He is a truth-teller. That's his thing. He writes about his true feelings, that's what he's always talking about.'

'And the other mistake you are making is assuming his infatuation is with the woman in these poems. Any idiot could see it is not the woman he is in love with.'

'What is it then?'

'It's paper.'

Arnold pondered her observation. She elaborated, 'He has fetishized it. He must be the only writer I can think of who finds origami erotic. Oh God, my shop, for him, must be like a sex shop, a sleazy emporium of rubber gear, or something. No wonder he kept coming back.'

'I must admit I find that poem about lovemaking as a form of paper-folding very original. Nevertheless, it's you he's folding and unfolding. There's no doubt about it.'

'Oh I don't know. If he was a different type of person I might be worried – but he's Martin Guerre. He's harmless, like his poems.'

'Are you sure? You seemed worried about him once.'

'That was when he was stopping people coming into my shop. And anyway, if you want to worry about someone, it should be him. These poems seem to enact a kind of death wish.'

'You mean the scissors, at the end?'

'Yes. If you want to take things literally, these poems enact Martin Guerre's suicide.'

'Perhaps I should talk to him.'

They were silent for a moment. Then Polly said, 'Do you know you sounded quite cross when you came downstairs?'

'Did I?'

'Yes. You had a sort of accusatory tone in your voice. Almost as if you were blaming me.'

'I don't think so, you're imagining it.'

'You're not jealous, are you? Jealous of the little thin-as-a-cornstalk poet?' She nuzzled him teasingly, pushing her face into his neck.

# 10

They were walking along the harbour front in their chosen fishing town when, without any warning, Vera asked Arnold about his past. Her interest in him was so unexpected and sudden he wondered if she had suffered some sort of mental collapse. She had asked him about his parents, and he told her they had both died when he was in his twenties.

'I'm so sorry,' she said.

'There's no need to be. They were old when they had me, so I always knew they would die while I was still young.'

'What did they do?'

'My father was a bookseller. He had a shop in Highgate. My mother was a musician and music teacher.'

'What did she play?'

'The flute.'

A seagull landed on the harbour wall, just in front of them. It touched down with the same lack of gravity as a puppet on strings. They were startled by its size, its brilliant whiteness, and by the stern, frowning face. A breeze lifted some of its feathers. As though realizing it had landed too close to the human couple, it took off again almost immediately.

'The only time I ever have any thoughts about life after death is when things like that happen.'

'Things like what?'

'That seagull. It was my mother.'

'So you are a heathen after all.'

'Any animal out of place, that strays into the exclusively human realm, I think it's her. An owl trapped in a church nave, once. A dog who sat by the lamp post across the road and watched our house all night. That's the nearest I get to seeing the dead.'

Vera, who had her arm through his, pulled herself close to him.

They were wandering towards the fish market, walking without any strong sense of purpose; no one did in the fishing town, apart from the fishermen sometimes. The fish market occupied one side of the harbour in a series of large open barn-like structures of black corrugated steel. The market itself had finished much earlier in the day, but the fishmongers were still there, behind their long, chilled displays of crushed ice.

'When the first cosmonauts went into space, my mother said they saw angels out of their windows. She believed the Communist Party suppressed the reports.'

They were in the market now, walking the salty floors of cement, looking at the stacked plastic crates where unsold fish were beginning to rot. Men in gory aprons and galoshes were sweeping heads and tails into bins, others were hosing down the stainless-steel tables. Arnold and Vera wandered among the displays where, on long counters of snow, the whole or splayed bodies of fish were on show. There were crabs and lobsters, monstrous and red. Dogfish as doey-eyed as puppies.

'Do you like fish?' Arnold said, eyeing the displays with slight revulsion.

'Do you mean to eat, or to look at?'

'To think about.'

The question caused Vera to ponder deeply. She looked at the fish.

'I don't know about them. They seem to come from another world, when you see them like this.'

It was as though they were in a museum of the fish. People ambled around with no apparent intent to buy anything, and instead gawped at tanks of live eels, or watched the gutting of bream and bass. Arnold and Vera felt a greater freedom to talk than usual. With no prompting, Vera began talking about her family.

'My father had a terrible argument with his own father – my grandfather. He had been an active member of the League of Militant Godless. Have you heard of them? They were a group dedicated to destroying religious faith in the Soviet Union. They tried to do this by confronting religious believers with irrefutable scientific truths. Of course I wasn't even born when this was happening, but my mother told me stories that she heard from her own mother, about how they would conduct parades through her village, at Easter and Christmas, the holiest times, and they would carry effigies of Jesus or the Virgin Mary dressed in clown costumes, along with pagan images and Egyptian gods, to show that they were no better, that Mary was just Isis in another form. Or even worse, they dug up the bodies of local patron saints to show that they were decomposing, just like the bodies of ordinary mortals . . .'

Arnold was not listening very carefully to what Vera was saying, because he had just been knocked almost senseless by the thought that he had spotted someone he knew among the crowds in the fish market. He grabbed Vera and started steering her away. The person he had seen was not in the fish market itself, but on the quay outside, standing close to the edge and peering down into the waters; a black-clad figure, tall and thin with loose curly hair. Arnold had never seen Martin Guerre in anything other than a paper suit, but still he felt convinced the figure was him.

'What's wrong,' said Vera, 'why are you pushing me?'

'I've seen someone I know.'

He felt Vera stiffen as he said the words.

'Where?'

'By the quayside. If he turns round, he'll see us. Don't look, in case he does.'

'Do I know him?'

'No.'

By now Arnold had steered Vera to the back of the

market, deep within the structure, and far enough away from the figure that was still gazing into the water. The problem now was that they were trapped, if Martin Guerre should turn around and enter the market. There was no telling which direction he might head, once he had finished contemplating the water.

'Who is it?' said Vera, turning now so that she could see the figure.

'Just a student.'

'Are you sure it's him? You can tell from behind?'

'No, I'm not sure. But I've a strong feeling. Why is he standing there? Why doesn't he go?'

'The best thing would be to split up,' said Vera. 'If he hasn't seen us together yet, and doesn't know who I am, then I can walk away on my own and meet you at the hotel later.'

'Yes, I hadn't thought of that. What is he doing?'

The figure had taken his coat off and had just dropped it on the ground behind him. He then climbed onto one of the stone bollards that lined the quayside.

'He's going to jump in,' said Arnold, suddenly panicked, moving forwards through the holiday crowd, 'he's going to kill himself . . .'

He was hurrying now, suddenly, against all his own expectations, acting quickly.

It wasn't just what Polly had said about the latent death wish evident in the poems, for the last few weeks Arnold hadn't been able to get the boy out of his mind, and had become convinced that he was, in one way or another, going to cause him great trouble. He was going to – Arnold didn't know – do something stupid, reckless, ridiculous. And since reading and rereading *The Paper Lovers*, he felt more than ever that there was something brewing with Martin, that he was a danger to himself. He could be thought of as that kind of person. He was pure and innocent and straightforward. He was the sort of person who might die for a principle. And the way he was poised on the bollard. Preparing himself for death, he had stretched out his arms like wings, as though he was going to take flight in just the way the seagull had, without even having to think about it. Arnold was running now, terrified that he wouldn't reach the boy in time.

Afterwards he wondered how he could have been so deeply in the grip of the boy's poems, that he accosted a complete stranger, a thin, attenuated practiser of tai chi, who had no intention of throwing himself into the deep waters of the harbour, but was merely exercising his living body. It was Arnold's intervention that had put him in danger, throwing him off balance and sending him plummeting over the side. Not before he had turned and shown Arnold a most un-Martin-like face. It would only have been suicide for a non-swimmer with weights in his pockets. The tai-chi practiser disappeared with a ripping, pluming splash but bobbed up to the surface within seconds, spitting sea water and shaking the salt from his eyes as he breast-stroked to the nearby ladder. And he had been so understanding. He was, in fact, a great advert for the tempering powers of tai chi, for he showed not the slightest ill will towards Arnold, but instead said he quite understood. He had understandably mistaken him for someone about to throw themselves to their death. Even as he stood there dripping, the man smiled, and shook hands with Arnold, patting him wetly on the shoulder.

The incident had drawn a small crowd, though to Arnold it seemed vast. From his previous position of anonymity within the town he was propelled to sudden celebrity. It felt as though the entire population was looking at him. He feared that Vera was too close, and they would be seen together as a couple. But she moved away quickly and was soon lost to his sight. They didn't rendezvous at the hotel as planned, but went their separate ways to their separate homes.

# 11

From his position on the bed, Arnold could see the sewing machine. Was it identical to Polly's? He had never looked closely enough to check. But this afternoon, as he lay in bed, the sunlight was coming in through the nearly closed curtains and falling on the machine so that it was half lit up. He devoted all his attention to it for a few minutes. It was as white and as clean as royal icing, its smooth body punctuated by circular handles and levers that had no obvious function. There were ungraduated dials, buttons with no labels. Sockets that would take a cable of some sort, but which were presently empty. There was a ventilation grille in the form of a starburst. It seemed for a moment to be designed as though for an initiated cabal who had no need of instruction. He saw it as someone from the distant future might see it, as a beautiful object for sunlight to fall upon, but nothing else.

He suddenly noticed the bed was empty. He must have fallen asleep for a while. He looked around the room. Vera was at the foot of the bed, naked, but positioned in such a way that she looked like a little girl saying her bedtime prayers. Suddenly he wondered if that was what she was doing, though when she moved it seemed she was merely looking for the clothing she had discarded earlier. They had made love, but disappointingly. It was a week after the incident at the fishing town.

'That thing you told me about your grandfather – you never finished it.'

Vera looked puzzled at first, then remembered.

'Oh, the League of the Militant Godless. Yes, I did my Ph.D. on them.'

'And were they effective? Did parading the image of Christ around in a clown's outfit persuade anyone to abandon their faith?'

Vera was sitting on the edge of the bed, side-on to him, pulling on her jeans. It was a view of her body he loved, her breasts in profile, one nipple peeping out from behind the other.

'Well, as my mother said, you'd think they'd never heard of the crucifixion. The whole Christian faith is based on the humiliation and torture of its central figure.'

Arnold smiled, and enjoyed the remaining spectacle of Vera's dressing, which compensated a little for the disappointments of their earlier lovemaking. It had been the first time they had failed to achieve the fullest pleasure in each other. Instead it was as though they had run out of energy, or had lost confidence in themselves.

Vera spoke without turning to face him.

'It was the boy made of paper, wasn't it?' she said.

'What was?'

'Last week. By the fish market.'

'He wasn't made of paper – but yes, I thought it was him.'

Vera was silent for a few moments and then said, 'It's almost like he's in the room. I can hear you thinking about him.'

Arnold wondered for a moment if she meant it literally. He tried to laugh at the remark. 'You are right. He keeps popping into my thoughts. I feel partly responsible. Whenever I think about him I think that he is going to come to some sort of tragic end. I didn't think people like him really existed any more.'

'What do you mean?'

'I don't know. People as beautiful as him. There is something unapproachably beautiful about him. You can't bear to touch him.'

Now fully clothed, Vera moved back on the bed, but sat upright against the headboard, whereas Arnold was still lying flat.

'You are worried that he may come to harm?'

Arnold wanted to talk to Vera about Martin Guerre, but realized that he couldn't do so without exposing his own feelings of guilt and betrayal. He himself didn't fully understand why he was so troubled by the boy. He tried to explain it to himself as a natural concern for a vulnerable young man. At the university he was occasionally put in the absurd position of dispensing pastoral care to milksop first years. He had objected at first, saying that he was foremost an academic, and that the role of pastoral care should be assigned to people who actually cared. The chorus of disapproving gasps and tuts this raised in the meeting caused him to clarify his point. He had meant people trained in the strategies of caring. Now, to his surprise, he found that he was caring about the welfare of someone for no obvious reason other than that he felt an ambiguous sense that he was the cause and origin of his anguish, and not just because he had written some unkind comments on his poetry. He had done that many times before, after all, and no one had poisoned themselves as a result, as far as he knew. Arnold had hurt Martin in a deeper way.

'I admired you,' said Vera.

'Admired me?'

'Yes. You pushed a man into the sea. For some reason, I found that impressive.'

'Personally, I have never been so ashamed of myself. I could have killed him. My own stupid clumsiness could have killed him.'

'I wanted to laugh. Did you notice, a lot of the people on the quayside thought you were playing a joke on a friend? They thought you were some sort of prankster, and they were laughing.'

Arnold remembered, and was now worried that they would never be able to return to the town, the place that had become their own.

'I can't get out of my mind the idea that he will do something terrible. I've only met him once, and I have no obligations to him. All he has done is sent me his poems.'

'He must be a very unhappy young man. It's touching that you are so concerned about him.'

'It's not that so much – it's more the feeling that he is beyond reach. I don't even know why I think that, but there's a remoteness about him, and a fragility. He seems breakable, like china.'

'Or paper . . .' Vera smiled. 'There is something that you could do for him, Arnold. That you and I could do for him, together.'

There was a note in her voice, a slight tremor, that served as a warning. Arnold sat up a little and turned to her.

'What do you mean? What could we do for him?'

'We could pray for him.'

He looked at her for a moment, trying to gauge the seriousness of what she had said. He was wondering if she had meant it as a joke. He lay back again. He didn't know what to say. For the first time in her company he felt embarrassed. It was a terrible feeling.

'Is that what you were doing just now? Praying?'

'When?'

'I saw you kneeling at the end of the bed.'

'No, I was just trying to find my bra.'

'Ah. Well. You know, even if I believed in God, I'd find it

impossible to believe that he would grant me personal favours if I prayed to him.'

'That's not what I mean. That's not what prayer is.'

Arnold was silent for a few moments, not wanting to allow the conversation to follow this line too far. Vera spoke again.

'I've struggled with it since I met you, Arnold. I gave up praying. I didn't feel the need. But now I find that I miss it very badly. It's not about asking favours of God. That would be ridiculous. It's about finding strength and support. We wouldn't be asking God to help the boy made of paper, but praying for strength so that we could help him . . .'

Arnold suddenly sat up.

'I'm not going to pray, Vera. Please, don't ask me to.'

He could see her face filling with disappointment. He began dressing. Vera fell silent and sank back into the bed. He didn't look at her but could hear the quietest sounds of weeping coming from her. They confused and annoyed him. When he was dressed he made for the door and thought for a second that he was going to leave without saying a word or giving her a glance, but at the last moment he paused and turned. She was still lying against the pillows and was looking straight ahead of her. She had stopped crying but her face was red and damp. He realized he had hurt her badly by his reaction.

'I'm sorry, Vera,' he said, 'it was a shock for me, that's all, hearing you talk like that. I'm not against people praying . . .'

Her answer was to sink down into the bed and turn away from him. He left quietly.

Arnold hadn't mentioned the fact that the real source of his anxiety lay in his decision not to publish Martin's poems. If only he hadn't put me in this position, he thought to himself. If only he had written poems about having sex with someone other than Polly. Arnold had an idea that he could offer to publish some of Martin's other poetry, something on a different theme. But he felt he had to say this to him personally.

Martin Guerre had left no contact details, there were none on his manuscript, not even a return envelope – he was not expecting to have it returned. The only thing Arnold knew about him was the house he had dropped him off at, after their coffee together. The tall shabby house in the student zone. He went there one afternoon after work, picking his way through the littered path round the side of the house to a door that led directly into the kitchen. The door itself was open, and a couple of students were inside, a male and female, sitting at a messy dining table, staring together at something on a laptop. Arnold tapped on the door as he entered their space, they barely acknowledged his arrival. This was a house where people came and went without much ceremony.

'I'm looking for Martin.'

'Who?'

'Martin. Martin Guerre.'

'Don't know who you mean.'

Of course, Arnold forgot it was a nom de plume. 'A tall man, wispy and thin, with long dark hair.'

'He means Ryan.' Said the girl, 'Are you one of his lecturers?'

'Actually, I'm his publisher.'

The two students looked at each other conspiratorially and smiled. They were beautiful in a similar way to Martin.

'He's in the other room, on the settee. You can go through.'

A little cautiously Arnold passed through the kitchen and into a hallway that led to the front door. To the left was a doorway to a large silent living room. There was a television that was not on, and the curtains were drawn, making the room quite dark. Not until he was fully in the room did he notice a figure sitting on the couch, as if watching the television, and though it gave him a momentary shock and feeling of coldness, he quickly recognized that this figure, though life-sized and fully human in form, was some sort of mannequin or dummy. He was about to leave the room, thinking the students were trying to play some sort of stupid joke on him, when he turned to find they had followed him in. They were both laughing.

'Did you find him?' the girl said.

'Yes, very funny. Is he in the house at all?'

'That is him, we weren't having a joke with you. Go and have a look.'

'It's really cool,' the boy said, 'he's made lots of them.'

'Right,' said Arnold, 'it's some sort of sculpture of his, is it?'

'It's not just a sculpture, it's a full body cast, of him-self.'

They had moved into the room and towards the figure on the couch. Now Arnold could appreciate the quality of the work. The white mottled texture, the naturalistic shape and proportion. Then he suddenly realized.

'It's made of paper – isn't it?'

'Yeah, papier mâché, whatever. He makes it from his torn-up poems. He tears up his poems, turns them into pulp. Then takes casts. He's done about three here. There's one in his bedroom.'

'He started off doing casts of smaller things. A kettle. A coffee-maker. Then he took a cast of a television. He makes ordinary things look spooky. Then he started on himself.'

'If you look closely,' said the girl, 'you can see words, little bits of his poems . . .'

Arnold did look closely and could see them. The ghost of Martin Guerre, sitting on a sofa, made of his own poetry. He saw the word 'heart'. Then 'melancholy'. Then 'rebarbative'.

'That's why we thought you was one of his tutors. He doesn't seem to go in much now, but he's doing loads of work here, at home. One did call round the other day. He thought Ryan was doing some good work. But he said he needed to do it in college, not home. I think Ryan sort of said something like it was easier for him to do this sort of work at home – where he could use the bathroom and so on . . . I don't know.'

The ghost of Martin Guerre was almost too much for Arnold to understand in a single sighting. It heartened him that the boy was regarded so warmly by these house-mates of his, and that he was putting in what must have been many hours of work in making what was a very striking sculptural project, albeit without the support of his college. But the hollow man sitting on the couch was unnerving and disquieting to such an extent that he wished he had never seen it.

After they'd had their joke the students directed Arnold to a pub where they thought it most likely that Ryan, as they called him, was currently to be found.

It was a pub Arnold knew as a student haunt, the same one that he had once found himself trapped in, as a newbie lecturer, by eager students, and he had misgivings about going there. Being only late afternoon, however, the pub was not crowded, and Arnold spotted the boy almost immediately, sitting at a table with a girl and two others. The girl, he supposed, was the girlfriend he had men-tioned, since she was dressed as a fashion student might be – outlandishly in something golden and high-collared. It seemed Martin didn't immediately recognize Arnold, and instead looked at him with incomprehension.

'Hello,' said Arnold. 'I've come to talk to you about your poems.'

The boy stood up, leaving the others at the table, who had taken little notice of Arnold.

'What did you want to say about them?' He saw the anxiety move across Martin's face like a jolt of electricity, it was as though Arnold had pliers in his hand, and was about to apply them to the boy's flesh. To settle him down Arnold couldn't help but blurt –

'They are beautiful.'

Martin's face became coloured-in, just as if a child had set about him with crayons. His eyes watered.

'My god,' he said. He seemed close to collapse. He put a hand on the bar to steady himself. 'This is so . . . so . . . amazing. You don't know what it means to me.'

Arnold cursed himself for laying the ground so poorly. He would have to just come out with it, be cruel.

'But I don't think I can publish the ones you sent me.'

'But you just said . . .'

'I can't publish those poems. They are too . . . It's not about the quality of the poems, it's their subject.'

'You're talking about censorship?'

'If you want to know the truth, I find them personally offensive.'

Arnold regretted what he had said, but held to his guns. The boy's eyes were dampening, he became tongue-tied and was completely at a loss for how to respond. Arnold talked quickly.

'I'd be happy to consider any new poems you have, on a different subject. Or any older poems, for that matter.'

The boy shook his head. 'I won't be writing any more poems. And I've destroyed all my other work. These are the only poems I want to have published. They say everything I want to say.'

Arnold thought of the mannequins, composed of Martin Guerre's collected works.

'Don't you think that would be a terrible waste of your talent as a poet? Your poems are getting better by the day. These poems are so much better than the first collection you sent me. If you carry on you are going to write something truly wonderful. You just need to keep going.'

The boy was almost laughing now. 'Poetry is like water,' he said, 'there is only so much to go round. If you use it up, the well runs dry. There's no more. I'm not going to write poems just for the sake of it. If I haven't got anything to say I'm not going to force them out. That's why I admire you. Admired you. You wrote one book, one brilliant book, and then stopped.'

Arnold had never had his failure to produce a second book praised before.

'I admired your purity,' the boy went on, 'your truthfulness. I would like to believe my poetry is as honest and pure. You only write poems when you have something to say. I wanted to be like you.'

Martin returned to the table with his friends, leaving Arnold to make his way home, where *The Paper Lovers* still waited for him on his desk.

# 12

They had arranged to meet, as usual, at Vera's house, Arnold taking the back-door route through the under-growth and past the rotary washing line and the aluminium goalposts, but from the moment he arrived at the door to the kitchen, to be met by Vera, he could see that something terrible had happened. She greeted him wordlessly, and her face was white and puffy, her eyes damp.

He thought she must still be upset after their last encounter and the things he'd said about prayer. He made to put his arms around her and give her a conciliatory hug but she backed away and walked straight through to the lounge-diner. There her husband was waiting, standing with his arms folded, having just got up from one of the dining chairs, over the back of which his jacket was hang-ing. He was wearing his working clothes, the business suit, white shirt, a purply brown tie. One of the other dining chairs was out of position, and Arnold imagined that they had been sitting talking face to face across the corner of the table, for most of the morning. She must have called him home from work.

No one said anything. Arnold turned from Angus to Vera, but she had lowered her gaze and wouldn't meet his eye. She looked small and folded-up. He turned back to Angus, who was looking him in the eye, with an expression that was hard to read at first, but which Arnold decided was one of concern. Serious concern. Arnold guessed from the way these two were behaving that Vera had voluntarily confessed everything to her husband, and that they had become reunited.

Arnold wanted most of all to ask Vera why she had done this, but he already realized that the Vera he was confronted with now was a different one from the woman he'd known. Her sense of self had shifted, or returned, to where it had been. Perhaps it was the conversations about her faith, about prayer, or the knowledge of the damaged boy made of paper, or something Arnold didn't even know about, but a curtain had come down on the part of her that he had loved. Under the gaze of her husband he couldn't say anything to her. His gaze burnt through any bond between them, separated them completely.

'I'm sorry, Angus,' he said. 'I don't know how much Vera has told you. I take full responsibility.'

Angus gave no response at first. Then, as if having been reset, he took a step forward, holding out his hand.

'I want to help you, Arnold,' he said.

'Help me?'

'Yes, I want to help you. This is going to be a very difficult time for all of us.'

Arnold took the hand that was proffered, and shook it, conscious that his grip was the weaker, and that his own hand shrank within the encompassing grasp of Angus's meaty fist. Arnold turned to Vera again. Already she looked physically different, he could almost imagine that her flesh was changing before his eyes, as though a numbing acid had been thrown in her face.

Angus was a large, physically powerful man. He had a stocky build, a beard full and tawny, a slightly balding crown and glasses. He could, if he had wished, have flattened Arnold with a single blow from the fist that had, instead, shaken his hand.

'Perhaps I should just go,' said Arnold.

Angus looked disappointed.

'Just go?'

'You and Vera need time to talk.'

'You think you can just walk away from this and everything will be like it was?'

There was no threat in Angus's voice, but instead a kind of incredulity, a disbelief.

'Whatever you need to do is between you. Unless you have some plan in mind to take revenge, then I don't have any role here . . .'

'You have a very important role to play here, Arnold. You and Polly.'

'Polly?'

'Your wife.'

'I know who she is. Polly mustn't know anything about this.'

'Do you think that is fair?'

It was Vera who made this remark, the first words she had spoken.

'Probably not, but what's fairness got to do with it? If we were worried about fairness, this wouldn't have happened in the first place.'

'She has a right to know. I have a right to ask for her forgiveness.'

There was a moment of silence while Arnold tried to process this turn in the conversation. He had come up against something that was completely alien to him, a religious moral imperative in action.

'Are you saying I should confess to her?'

'I am asking you if you think she has a right to know.'

'She has a right to know, but I have a right to try and save my marriage.'

'Your marriage is already damaged, Arnold,' said Angus, 'you must be able to see that. The only way you can save it is by adopting a strategy of truthfulness.'

Arnold was conscious that he was shaking his head mechanically, while he tried to form words. 'No, no. This is mad. You've got to let me handle Polly my own way.'

'By continuing the lies?' said Vera.

'If necessary.'

'Believe me, Arnold,' said Angus, 'truthfulness is the best strategy. What you need is Polly's forgiveness. You have mine. Vera has it as well. Now you and Vera need

Polly's forgiveness. If you are truthful, absolutely truthful, she will forgive you, Arnold, believe me.'

'It is the most loving thing you can do at this moment, Arnold.'

He began to realize that this is what the two of them must have been discussing all morning, the need to involve Polly, the need to persuade Arnold to involve her. Angus had probably put it to Vera as an ultimatum, he had bullied her into submission. He realized he knew nothing about their marriage.

'Thank you for your opinion, Angus, and you too Vera, but I believe I am the best judge of Polly's character and I know how she will react if she discovers the truth. I also have my daughter to think about. Or do you think I have to involve her as well, ask for her forgiveness? Can't you see this is ridiculous?'

The two were silent, though not in a way that suggested he had stumped them. They were simply waiting for him to say something else.

'Maybe I will tell her one day,' he said, 'but not now. And not in the near future. When Evelyn is grown up – I don't know.'

Arnold began to leave.

'Would it help you if we told her?'

It was Vera who said this. Arnold stopped and turned. Then Angus spoke.

'It would really be no trouble for us. Or we could be there with you when you tell her, to give you both strength.'

Unable to control himself, Arnold gave in to a short fit of laughter. 'You really mean that, don't you? You actually think it would be a simple thing. What do you think will happen when I tell Polly, that heavenly light will shine down on us? That angels will appear? That choirs will sing . . . ?'

'We just want to help you, Arnold. Out of love for both you and Polly.'

'Let me tell you what would happen if I told her myself. She would throw me out of the house. She might well become physically violent. She might even try to kill me. I am quite serious. I have seen her lose her temper. What I have done would be such a betrayal I could never be forgiven. She would divorce me at the earliest opportunity and do her best to deny me access to my daughter while suing me for the biggest alimony settlement she could possibly obtain. I would be financially and emotionally ruined. I might never recover. I would probably end up an alcoholic even if I hadn't found a quicker way of killing myself before then. I don't care what you say about truth or sincerity, this is a question of survival. Nothing else matters. Polly does not need to know anything about this. She doesn't ever need to know. Do you two understand me?'

He had made again to leave, and by the front door this time, but as he made his way down the hall, he felt a pang of anxiety that he hadn't done enough to convince the newly strong husband and wife of the importance of not telling Polly anything about the affair. Their silence seemed to follow him down the hall. He turned to meet it, and retraced his steps. Back in the dining room, the husband and wife had not moved a muscle. Both of them were looking at him, expectantly.

'Would you like me to beg?' he said.

They didn't reply.

'Look at me, I'm begging you. Don't tell Polly. You have got no right to interfere with my marriage.'

'You have interfered with mine,' said Angus, quietly.

Arnold had no answer, and turned to Vera, as if expecting her to express her share of the guilt, to take some of the weight of wrongdoing off his shoulders. But it now seemed she belonged to the new world order of strong marriages, that have been strengthened by the cycle of betrayal and forgiveness. Already he was looking at her and desperately trying to understand how he had once loved this damp, hollow little creature. So sudden, the loss of her glamour, her power to fascinate. Worldliness was re-inhabiting her. Her glances now were full of moral purpose and scrutiny. When he caught her look, it was analytical, judicial. She was seeing him now as something separate from herself. Matter out of place.

'How did you do it?' he said. 'How did you do it, both of you?'

'We haven't yet, Arnold,' said Angus, 'but we've begun the process. It will take time. We can help you. You greatly underestimate Polly if you think she doesn't have forgiveness in her heart. You paint an unflattering portrait of her as a vengeful bully. I may not know her as well as you, but

I know she is not like that. If you told Polly, we could, together, begin the process of reconnecting our hearts.'

Angus was talking, but Arnold was looking at Vera, still. He was waiting for her to speak, to add to what her husband (how difficult to even think that word) was saying. She wiped the end of her nose with a piece of tissue, but didn't speak. Angus continued.

'The process of reconnection can only begin once the fact of disconnection is acknowledged. You can't mend a broken vase if you deny it's broken in the first place.'

'That has nothing to do with me and Polly. You have acknowledged your disconnection, as you call it, but Polly and I, we were never out of love. Nothing was broken.'

'Don't fool yourself, Arnold. You couldn't do what you've done to someone you love.'

'I didn't fall out of love, it's just that I thought I'd found a love that was greater. Thought. Now I see it was an illusion. A trick.'

Now Vera spoke. 'It would help us, Arnold, if you shared in the process of renewal with Polly. It would give us strength. It would give us energy and resolve. We could help each other. Angus and I know you don't have faith, but even so, prayer alone is not enough. For us. We need the support of people we love. You and Polly. If the four of us shared the burden, we would gain strength, all four of us.'

'You're proposing some sort of . . . therapy group, for the four of us?'

They laughed, the newly reunited married couple, the

nine-to-fiver and the quiet woman. And their laughter was so out of place, so out of tune with the mood and atmosphere in the room, it was as though a hole had been rent in the ceiling and some unwelcome blinding light had poured in.

'Not a therapy group, Arnold, oh no, no, no. Nothing so glamorous. But you could call it a group of strength through prayer. A way of being close to Him.'

Him? It took Arnold a moment to realize who they meant, then that recognition of the religious use of the pronoun.

'A prayer group, then. You want us to join your church?'

They didn't say anything but both looked at him with such expectation in their faces, such big yesses in their eyes, that they didn't need to.

'Well, that is something that is not going to happen. I mean, Vera knows how I feel about praying, but Polly is even more strongly averse to that sort of thing. I would be happy to go along with it if you felt it would help you – but Polly. She is really – how can I put this? She is not merely an atheist, she is quite anti-religious.'

'What we envisage wouldn't have to happen in a church, and wouldn't even have to involve consciously praying. It would merely involve talking, and reflecting. Thinking deeply, and being close, in a special way.'

Slowly Arnold became aware of another peculiar turn the conversation was taking, and a sudden fear crept into his body, that Angus was proposing, in simple terms, some sort of wife-swapping party. Arnold had had an affair with his wife, now he was expecting to be able to do the same in return. Was that really it? Was that really what Angus was hoping? That Vera was some sort of debt that he could repay with Polly. Polly could be persuaded, through conversation, music, drink and regret, that the only way to pay Arnold back for his despicable actions was to have sex with Angus. It would fit in with what he realized now was his long-standing but half-forgotten view of the religious mind, that it was a cover for something deeply corrupt and unsavoury. Was Angus now going to come out with the words, 'You know, Arnold, I have always been attracted to Polly, and I believe the feeling is mutual.' He looked closely at Angus, the orange hair now going grey, the tawny beard doing the same. 'You know Arnold, you and I, we are men of the world. In primitive times we would have been at the head of our respective tribes. We can sort this out in a man-to-man way. If you want to screw Vera, I must be allowed to fuck Polly.'

Arnold now felt it imperative that he get out of there before Angus had any opportunity to utter those words, or any to a similar effect. He turned again towards the door. 'I'm going to go now. I need time to think things through. You are probably right, it is best if I tell Polly everything, clear the air and start anew – she will, undoubtedly, do some of those things I mentioned earlier, but the storm will pass, and perhaps we'll be able to start afresh, but I must have time to think it through.'

They thought with the careful consideration of bank managers assessing a loan, and they looked at each other.

Arnold thought he saw a glance of assent pass between them.

'You can take some time, Arnold,' said Angus, 'but it must be soon. What you and Vera have done is corrosive. It continues to eat away at the heart, even now that you have ended things. It must happen within days. Before the end of the week.'

# 13

Having at least been given the promise of time, though not very much, Arnold left the house. The world outside felt very still. By some fluke the usually busy street was empty of traffic and people. He could have walked in the centre of the road if he wanted. He wondered for a moment if something had happened, that the road had been closed off for some reason. But then an ordinary little hatchback appeared round a corner and the world resumed its usual motion. Arnold felt he was in the space between one disaster and another – between the fury of Angus and the fury of Polly, which he thought would be far more difficult to weather. The possibility that Polly would accept his confession in the way that Angus had accepted Vera's was impossibly remote.

When he got back to his car he decided to drive into the city. Polly would still be at the shop and he felt a sudden need to see her, to check up on her, just to reaffirm for himself who she was, and if she was still the same person he believed her to be. He couldn't trust his own thoughts and feelings any more. It seemed that anything might pop into his head, any thought at all, or anything that might claim to be a memory, and assume legitimacy, requiring to be acted upon. The breakdown of the affair with Vera had disrupted the new reality that had been settling around him, the invisible palace had been razed and now he had to go back to the old reality and see if it could be lived in as before.

He parked as usual and walked along the pedestrian-ized medieval street with its tourist shops towards Papyrus, a hundred different types of paper, hand-made, recycled. What was he going to say to her? He went in. There was no sign of Polly. There was her young assistant in the shop. He had forgotten her name.

'Is Polly around?'

'She's gone to the wholesalers,' said the assistant, 'to pick up some bags and cellophane.'

'Right. Can you pass a message on? Tell her I won't be home tonight? Tell her something's come up. I've got an engagement I'd overlooked . . .' He was making it up as he went along, and not very well, though he was aware that the young assistant was naive and unsuspecting, and would believe anything he said. 'A poetry reading. In Birmingham. I'd forgotten all about it . . .'

It suddenly seemed a stroke of luck that Polly wasn't in the shop, that he hadn't had a chance to see her. It was impossible for him to go home that evening. He needed a night away from both Polly and Vera, to give him time to think things through, to come up with a plan. Perhaps it was one of those thoughts that he feared popping into his mind that he couldn't ignore, a dangerous, risky whim. Nevertheless, there it was, in his head, the idea that he had to spend a night away from home. He began walking back to his car, knowing he wouldn't change his mind.

He lived in an English city that was ordinary in every way except for the fact that it happened to have one of the world's finest Gothic cathedrals in the middle of it, towering above everything else. When he'd first moved there he'd been fascinated by it, from a purely aesthetic and historical point of view. He'd loved to take a few minutes out of his life to contemplate its beauties and wonders, chiefly the stained glass, some of the most beautiful in the world, every window slowly yielding its bright narratives for him, of suffering among the ancients. He would stop and admire a piece of carving, and be lost for half an hour. He took great pleasure in the slow process of learning more about the building with every visit. All that ended when they began charging an entrance fee. It wasn't that he couldn't afford it, but that it took away the spontaneity and brevity of those visits. Paying a fee meant a feeling of pressure to spend a long time in there, make it a proper visit. He couldn't just walk through, in idle contemplation, as he'd done before.

Now, as he passed it on the way back to the car, it seemed like a solid expression of the agony of time. All that carving by hand, stone upon stone, the masons chipping away for centuries to raise this accretion of geological sediment. He could only think of pain when he looked at it, of bleeding thumbs, the broken necks of those who'd fallen from its heights, as many must have during all those years of construction. And of the stone itself, chiselled out, undercut and bevelled, those actions so anathematic to flesh. Yet something of that pain was now in his own body. He could feel the cut of fine blades, hammered home. The idea came into his mind that his own flesh and the flesh of the cathedral were entwined in some way.

There was one way to get into the cathedral without paying, and that was if a visitor was intending to pray. Occasionally Arnold had wondered if this would be a good way of gaining access to the place he had loved, but then wondered what would happen – what were the protocols? Did you tell the person in the ticket office that you were here to pray, to worship? And if so, did they do any follow-up checks? Did someone come up behind you to check you were kneeling down, and if you weren't were you tactfully but firmly escorted off the premises? He thought it unlikely, but he never tried it, because somehow the burden of pretending to worship was just as troubling, if not more so, than the burden of shelling out for a ticket. It killed the experience he was looking for, the idle contemplation of carved stone and stained glass that he had loved.

There were tours up the tower. He could go up there and throw himself off – that would be a message that would ring home to Angus and Vera. Their precious religiosity used as an instrument of suicide. Too obvious. Too melodramatic. If he was to kill himself, it would have to be done with appropriate understatement.

It was a depressingly commercialized entrance – turnstiles, a ticket desk. He went up to the woman at the desk and said,

'I have come here to worship.'

The woman smiled, and said, 'Of course.' He wondered for a moment if he would be given some sort of ticket or pass, something to denote him as a worshipper among the tourists, some sort of badge or stamp? But of course, it didn't work like that. We are not in a football stadium or a cinema, there are no ticket inspectors or store detectives. His declaration of an intent to worship was to be taken on trust – but then why doesn't everyone do it, and get in free? Because not everyone is so lax and morally bankrupt as you, Arnold, who can tell a bare-faced lie to a Christian woman, can make fun of their faith while simultaneously benefitting from it, can use its facilities for nothing and feel justified in doing so. Vainly he felt disappointed that he didn't have some sort of badge or sash that identified him as a person of faith; like Hancock's blood donor he felt a need to display his righteousness.

Even though he felt unfollowed, and had no intention of worshipping, even if he knew how such a thing was done, he thought he should make a show of piety in case the woman at the ticket office was watching him covertly, even though for all she knew he might be the sort of person who worshipped while ambling around and looking at stained glass. But even so, he found a seat among the many hundreds of empty chairs, and sat, feeling unable to delve so deeply into his subterfuge to kneel. The cathedral soared on all sides around him in great plumes of stone whose lines and curves gave one the sense of great energy, that there was something pulsing through all this solid stuff like blood through arteries.

He tried to imagine a conversation with Vera.

I went to the cathedral and I did it. I prayed.

Well done.

I prayed in order to seek answers from God.

Answers to what?

To what I should do about Polly.

And what did God say?

He said I should keep quiet about it.

Really?

Yes, he said I should act as if nothing has happened, and keep up the pretence for the rest of my married life. He said if I told her the truth she would never forgive me, she would throw me out and I would never see my daughter again. That option results in the unhappiness of three people. The prior option resulted in the unhappiness of only one, me, and that was only mild compared to how I am feeling now.

This was how he would justify his silence to Vera when the time came.

But what about me? she would say. I have also betrayed Polly, as her friend. Do you expect me to be complicit in your deception? Angus won't forgive me unless I confront Polly with what I've done and seek forgiveness from her.

When he came out of the cathedral he felt a little calmer, and the process of emerging from the ancient shadows of the interior into the brightly lit gaudiness of the tourist city was one that was charged lightly with a sense of renewal. If he had the desire to so do he could construe a way in which this could be thought of as a religious experience. It was the same experience he used to have whenever he visited the cathedral in its free entrance days, and the same experience whenever he visited any ancient church. But this was because they were beautiful places, not because of the presence or proximity of the divine.

He was glad he had made the instant decision to stay away for the night. He could have gone anywhere that evening, he could have gone anywhere in the country within a few hours' drive, but instead he went to a cheap Wayfarer Inn on the outskirts of his own town, a bleak, shabby place on the bypass, next to a newly built industrial estate and a petrol station. He did this because he didn't want to be distracted by pleasant or charming surroundings. The drab, corporate blandness of the hotel's little world was perfect for thinking about things. And there was no danger of his feeling guilty that he was treating himself or having his own little holiday. This night away from home had a purely functional purpose.

He was with the company reps, the lorry drivers, the

families with too many children. The hard bed, the welcome tray with its past their sell-by date biscuits. The little paper stockings of revolting coffee. The view from the window was of grey units, still empty. The Wayfarer had no restaurant and didn't do breakfast. There was a Happy Eater on the other side of the roundabout, behind the Texaco petrol station, the receptionist told him. He could walk there in five minutes. They recommended it for breakfast as well.

Arnold felt strongly compelled to ask the receptionist if she was interested in sleeping with him. He felt the sudden realization of his own badness as an adulterer, and wanted to test a new theory of himself, that he was the sort of man who could sleep with any woman he chose. There was a lecturer at work, his former head of department, who claimed he had routinely asked any woman he met, at a party or other social function, to sleep with him. The majority said no, but even if only one in twenty said yes, that still meant he was sleeping with a different woman perhaps once a month. The extraordinary thing, Arnold thought, was that this man seemed totally unbothered by the nineteen rejections he received in order to get the one acceptance. Lacking any physical attractiveness or social charm didn't seem to matter; if you were prepared to ask enough women, the law of averages would see you through to a night of sex, eventually. The knowledge of this man's sex life, something he liked to recount as an amusing aside at gatherings in the pub, deeply disappointed Arnold, in a way that made him wonder if he was actually, to his surprise, quite prudish. Perhaps it was jealousy, of a rival in the rutting stakes, who, possessed of no sexual attraction at all as far as Arnold could tell – but then who was he to discern that sort of thing in a man? – and who in fact seemed the least sexualized individual he could imagine (to the extent that if Arnold was asked to design a person least likely to appeal to the opposite sex, he would come up with something very like Professor Jim Stodmarsh), had still been far more successful than him.

The receptionist was pretty, though in a way that suggested they had completely different views about life. She was artificially tanned, heavily mascaraed, bleach haired, her fingernails lacquered and curled like eggshells. She seemed to have gone to great lengths to conceal anything natural about herself, had expended long hours in nail bars and tanning salons – such work to create this sheen. She probably referred to her breasts as 'boobs'. He imagined doing a Stodmarsh, what words would he use? He imagined the professor's pass would be as bluntly to the point as it was possible to be. Would you like to sleep with me tonight? And then he imagined the response. He might be reported. There was probably a camera watching them, that would capture the slap around the face he would get.

He thought about what she would be like in his room, if he was successful, the sprayed body glowing like teak, the cosmetic film covering her face. Neither Polly nor Vera ever wore make-up. He had not made love to a heavily made-up woman almost for as long as he could remember.

Would she strip the paint off her face in preparation? And then what would she look like? A completely different woman, like in that poem by Swift, *Corinna, Pride of Drury Lane, for whom no shepherd sighs in vain*. But nothing happened. As he stood watching the woman take his booking, she barely looked at him, didn't even offer him the bland corporate smile he might have expected. It wouldn't have put Stodmarsh off, but Arnold could no more approach this woman than he could have touched a tarantula. He went to his room feeling relief and a certain amount of reassurance, that he was not a casual philanderer of the Stodmarsh sort. But what if the woman had flirted with him? What if she had signalled a willingness? What would he have done then?

Hardly possible to believe it happened. Shameful. Absolutely shameful. Suddenly Vera seemed like an indulgent habit of monstrous proportions. He had behaved like a heroin addict who'd stripped everything out of their house to pay for drugs. What was the difference? He'd stripped the trust of his family as surely as if he'd gutted his house. He tried making himself a cup of tea, with a teabag that dangled from a string like a rogue on a scaffold, but once the kettle had boiled he forgot about it, and it went cold again. He looked out of his hotel-room window. An expanse of car park with five cars and a white van parked in it. Beyond that the looming sheds of the freshly built industrial units. But it looked like another planet. He had to ask himself, what was there out there that he knew about? What were those buildings anyway? He was stranded as far away from his own life as he could be. There seemed no way to get back to it.

He needed to phone Polly. It would seem odd if he didn't phone, spending his first night away in ages, and without any warning. She would probably phone him, and he didn't want to be phoned and caught unprepared for a conversation. He decided to phone while he was in control of the situation. She answered straight away.

'Hello. Did you get my message?'

'Yes, I got your message. What's the matter with you? How could you forget something like that?' The voice didn't betray a scrap of suspicion in her voice.

'Quite easily, it's only a little event.'

'But it's not as if you do poetry readings every week, is it? I thought this would have had a massive flag-up in your diary.'

'Well, that's just it. It's become such a rare thing that I didn't even bother checking my diary.'

'OK, so you've just driven off to stay overnight, and you didn't even come home to pack anything.'

'I didn't have time. I had to drive straight from town, or I'd have been late. You can't be late for your own reading.'

'What about underwear?'

'I bought some in town.'

'Where will you be staying?'

'They've booked somewhere for me. I don't know where.'

In the whole saga of his affair with Vera, he had never

lied to his wife so directly, so elaborately. And this was not even in the service of spending a night with Vera. He was using up all his lying capacity for a night alone in a dismal hotel less than three miles from his house.

'OK, call me later, after the reading. Or text me.'

'OK.'

And that was how the conversation ended. Neither he nor Polly liked telephones and tended to end conversations as quickly as they could. Now he wondered if this was to be the last conversation he would have with her as an equal partner in marriage. If the next time he saw her he was to confess everything, her voice would be very different. There wouldn't be the calm certainty in it that there was just now, the loving trustfulness. He had known her lose her temper, he had known her in a state of anger and he knew what sort of voice came from her then. But he imagined the loss of trustfulness would produce something very different, something more than anger. He spent most of the night trying to imagine it, the voice Polly would produce in reaction to the revelation. He was never able to conjure a satisfactory sound in his mind, and as his mostly sleepless night progressed, he felt more and more strongly how impossible it would be for him to tell Polly about his affair.

He looked at his mobile phone. The texts he'd exchanged with Vera were all still there, contained in speech bubbles, blue for him, green for her, as though two off-stage cartoon characters were talking across a void of theatrical space. Eight hundred and fifty-nine texts they'd sent each other. The affair had lasted just four months. They had texted several times a day. That was some sort of measurement. Some sort of gauge of their relationship. A sudden cascade of words cast across the radio waves. Badly spelt. Badly punctuated. Abrupt and crude. He scrolled back through the conversations and saw his affair with Vera run suddenly in reverse. He pictured his affair as if in a rewound film, him walking backwards into the house, a little hunched as if to keep his body profile low among the rambling shrubs of that little back yard, entering the house backwards, climbing the stairs backwards, entering the bedroom backwards where Vera was already naked in the bed, sweatily damp, red-faced, red-chested, raw-looking, clammy, exhausted, and he undressed, his own dampness and clamminess increasing as the clothes are removed though he doesn't drop them but carefully lays them on the floor, as though they are delicate things that can be broken. He watches the scene in his mind as if through the peephole of a what-the-butler-saw machine, the memories flickering backwards in black and white, him suddenly collapsing onto the side of the bed, from which a space for him has been thrown open by Vera, and he lies down, covers himself, suddenly exhausted, breathlessly staring upwards as though a great weight has fallen on him, as though he has been drenched, as though he's been under a waterfall, then slowly, exhaustedly, he moves on top of Vera with nothing in his loins, clamps himself to her, then with sudden energy and violence his body retracts what it had put inside her, sips up the spilt seed, and then suddenly everything is energy and movement, the helplessly rhythmic movements, and as they continue, the clamminess recedes, their hair is gradually straightened, they comb each other's straight with their fingers, they carefully suck their own saliva from each other's mouths, repossess what each had given the other, Arnold uses his mouth to carefully straighten a strand of her hair, he deftly and skilfully puts back the violet bra that jumps into his hand, then blindly he finds her T-shirt and pulls it down over her, instantly pulling the wrinkled fabric flat, the same with her other clothes, everything goes back on, and she does the same to him, they dress each other, and then spend ages caressing the creases out of each other's clothes until the fabric is flat and smooth. Everything is straightened, tucked in, how patiently and attentively they look to smoothing out every last imperfection in each other, Vera uses her lips to remove the redness that has appeared on his neck (a blush, not lipstick). They walk backwards down the stairs and through to the kitchen door, Arnold walks back out of the house, backwards down the garden, as if he can't bear to take his eyes off the house, as if he dare not turn his back, and is gone.

Twelve times the speed of life, that's how fast he'd lived in that time. It was as though six years had passed, and the invisible palace had outgrown the whole neighbourhood. And as he watched it spool back, he could still picture every second of it, every second crushed into his fist, into the phone, into the texts, and then suddenly he's in the room again, the room where it first happened, when the smell of her had knocked him back, the scent of her that he realized now, when he said to her one day, your perfume is so beautiful so gorgeous, and she'd said to him – I don't wear perfume, Arnold. You should know that. I hate perfume. It brings me out in spots. It burns my skin. He didn't believe her. He can still hardly believe it. The scent had been so strong, yet it was just her, her body, he was sensitive to something in her chemical make-up, he was sniffing her essence, right down into the hereditary material. And now it was gone.

# 14

He winged a day of teaching, and arrived home at the normal time. All through the day and the night before he had been playing out different scenarios in his mind – the one in which he confessed everything to Polly and suffered her rage, and the one in which he told her nothing and somehow dealt with Vera and Angus instead. How well could he anticipate Polly's response? Was there a possibility that, after rage, there might come some sort of acceptance? His first and only affair. Might she give him a second chance? Yes, there was a possibility, that after much agony and attrition and perhaps a temporary separation of a few days or a few weeks, he might be allowed his second chance. If so, what was the likelihood? What were the odds? It seemed absurd to him that it should all come down to a gambling question. He was aware that he was ignoring the moral imperative, that there was a right and a wrong way to proceed. The right thing to do was to confess all to Polly, the wrong thing was to hide the truth from her for as long as she lived. Yet here he was, calculating the best odds for his own survival.

Thinking of himself. That's certainly how Angus and Vera would view his practical reasoning. That he was putting himself first. But he remained unconvinced that the moral imperative should trump the pragmatic one, the utilitarian one, the one that would result in the largest amount of happiness for the largest number of people, and there was no doubt in his mind that keeping quiet, keeping everything secret, would result in more happiness for more people than telling the truth. And who were Vera and Angus to say that the resulting happiness wouldn't be true happiness, that it would be false, tainted, corrupt? Happiness was happiness.

Yet they would have to be managed. He had left them with an understanding that he would confess to Polly. They had threatened to tell her if he didn't. That was the impression they gave him, at least. He had a responsibility to her and to them to tell the truth. He worried that they had already told her. Perhaps Polly and Vera had met at the school gates and Vera had felt compelled to confess, as she had done to Angus. He texted Polly several times during the day and felt cold with fear when there was no reply. It was only a temporary coldness however, because the reply eventually came, mundanely carefree and trustingly warm in its response. She didn't know anything.

Polly was getting the dinner on the table. He discerned a multitude of ways in which nothing had changed. There was the same light coming from the light bulbs, the same cuboid space defined by the four walls of the lounge-diner, the same ceiling separating them from the upstairs worlds.

The furniture had retained its ability to stay still. There was one thing about the room that surprised him, not because of its newness but because he had not noticed it before, and that was how much of it was under the sway and influence of the sewing machine, which still sat on its coffee table near the bay window, a spot that could be regarded as pride of place, bathed in light from the window, overseeing everything and being seen by every-thing in the room. But apart from that, the space was draped and stacked with the folded product of that machine, the fabric creations, the throws and pillowcases, and clothes and cushion covers that Polly and her sewing-machine friends had created over the months. It was not that these things had suddenly been produced while he was away and put on display – rather that they had always been there, only strengthening and thickening their occu-pation of the house's living space, to the extent that it now resembled a clothing or fabric emporium, or one of those trendy market stalls that sells hippyish garments and drapery, batik scarves and shawls and capes and pon-chos and snoods with jewellery and fragments of mirror sewn in so that the wearer sparkles like a glitter ball.

They had been busy, the sewing maidens, they had been busy and enthusiastic. That could be sensed merely from the presence of all this material.

They ate their dinner with the usual messy talkative-ness. Arnold and Polly had worked hard at making mealtimes social occasions where conversation flowed. It had not always been easy, their daughter had sometimes to be prised from wherever she was and cemented into her place at the table, and meals could pass in a frowny silence where the cheerful comments of the parents went unanswered. But this evening was not one of those, and both Polly and Evelyn were keen to ask him questions about Birmingham and his poetry reading. It seemed his unexpected absence the previous night had excited them in some way – not with interest in what he had done so much, but the unplanned change to their routine had put them on edge and made them anxious, which expressed itself as a form of nervous energy.

'It's absurd. It's Britain's second biggest city and I've never been there,' said Polly.

'Have I been there?' said Evelyn. No one answered her.

'What was it like, Birmingham?'

It amazed Arnold that they had believed his lie so easily. This was the evening he had earmarked for telling Polly the truth, yet he began it by telling her the most detailed and layered lies he had ever told her.

'I didn't have much chance to look around . . .'

'Where was the reading?'

'It was in a sort of old church that had been converted. I can't remember what it was called now . . .'

He had never been to Birmingham either. Britain's second biggest city, and he'd never been there.

By the end of the conversation he had constructed an elaborate and entirely imaginary Birmingham, at once precisely detailed enough to be convincing, and vague enough that it couldn't be checked or verified online. He was aware of the pointlessness of all this lying if he was going to tell Polly the truth later on that evening, when Evelyn was in bed.

After dinner there were various chores to do. Evelyn was dragged to the kitchen to help with the washing up, Arnold stole a few minutes in his study, where the poems of Martin Guerre were still sitting on his desk. He cursed himself for not having taken them with him when he went to see the boy in the pub. Now their presence seemed an insurmountable problem, even though all he had to do was put them in the post. But something about Martin's attitude to them, his claimed loss of interest in them, made it difficult to think about returning them now. He wondered if he should just destroy them and forget all about Martin Guerre and his dodgy poetry. At least if Polly and I split up, he thought, I won't have to worry any more about indignant poets. The Papyrus Press would fold.

Later, it was his turn to read to Evelyn. He went upstairs to her bedroom, which had been carefully decorated according to her specific and precise demands. She didn't want murals, but she wanted each wall painted two different colours, divided horizontally in half. They were bright and clashing, but Arnold had done as he was told. Her room was so bright it hurt the eyes, and his daughter so pretty it hurt his eyes as well. Even when she scowled, as she was doing now. It was a mock-scowl, because he was late, and she had been waiting for him. She pointed out that there was a spider in the room, but it was so small he couldn't actually see it. She became annoyed with him for not being able to see it, even when she was pointing directly at it, and it was just a few inches in front of him. When he did finally see it he laughed, because it was barely bigger than a little fingernail. But it was still a spider, size didn't have much to do with it, as far as Evelyn was concerned. He passed a finger through the spider's invisible thread and took up its slack, and became bound to it. It seemed to Evelyn that he held the creature by some magnetic force, that it was attracted to his fingertip, and she was repelled, rucking her face in disgust. The spider's face bore a similar expression, Arnold imagined, looking at it closely, bringing it up to his eyes to see what moved there in the little speck of energy. A cross face, disgruntled, scowling, staring. He put it out of the window.

He began reading a book about American teenagers. He had dreamed of reading his daughter the beautifully written classics that he had loved as a child, but she found the Alice books baffling, and *The Wind in the Willows* boring. It broke his heart, but she insisted he read her books she had chosen. Teen novels set in Los Angeles, in which over-pampered girls competed to lose their virginity. They had a strong moral undertone, according to Polly, though he couldn't quite see it himself. But he was grateful that Evelyn had wanted him to read at all, and was interested enough to have even developed a literary taste, no matter that it seemed almost deliberately to be as far removed from his own as possible. He read the story of the 8th Street Girls, doing the voices in shrill LA accents that always drove Evelyn to laughter.

'Daddy, do you like my laugh?' she said, interrupting him mid-sentence.

Arnold pretended to give the question careful consideration, weighing up the pros and cons before answering, 'Yes, it's a very good laugh.'

'What's good about it?'

'It's just a very good laugh. It's funny.'

'Because I don't like Irina's laugh.'

'Don't you?'

'No. It really gets on my nerves.'

'Why? How does she laugh?'

'She's just got this really annoying laugh, like she throws her head back and makes this sort of clicking sound, and her neck folds up.'

'I can see that might be annoying, but if she's happy . . .'

'Laugh,' she said. It was a command.

'Not now.'

'I want to hear your laugh. Laugh.'

'I can't just laugh.'

'Yes you can.'

'You laugh first.'

'No. You've got to laugh first. I want to see how you laugh.'

'You know how I laugh.'

'I can't remember.'

'Say something funny.'

'I can't. Do you like Mummy's laugh?'

'Of course I do.'

'My friend Caley has a stupid laugh. She hoots like an owl. It's so embarrassing.'

'Do you like any of your friends' laughs?'

'Not really. But I feel bad because Susie said she likes my laugh. She said I've got the best laugh in the school. But I don't like hers, she's got a silly laugh. She sounds like a mouse squeaking.'

They talked for a while about laughing, Arnold giving her a little lecture on the varieties of laughter, that while we can say that someone has a particular type of laugh, most people have a repertoire of laughs for different situations – the sarcastic laugh, the incredulous laugh, the knowing laugh, the hysterical laugh and so on. Evelyn seemed satisfied with this, and Arnold was allowed to go on reading about the 8th Street Girls, and then he went downstairs, neither of them having laughed out loud for each other.

It was a slow terrifying descent for Arnold, because he was entering the phase of the evening that he and Polly set aside for themselves. Usually they spent this time on their own separate tasks – Arnold working in his study, Polly in her own corner of the living room which had become her office, and sometimes they would watch something on TV together, or listen to music. If Arnold was to tell her about his affair with Vera, then this would be the time to do it. He had an inkling of what it might feel like to walk to the scaffold. He would be ending the life he had known, sacrificing his life with his family. It seemed mad, to do this. He was aware that telling Polly the truth was going against every instinct he had about how to live his life. Now that the affair was over it had rapidly dwindled to something of insignificance for him. A few days ago he would have struggled to choose between his family and Vera, but not now. Now a sanity had returned to him, a steadiness of gaze and purpose, a greater knowledge of himself and others. He believed he understood the damage he had done and how best to handle it. It was completely outrageous that he was being put in this position by Angus, that he was being threatened. And then the thought – what if Polly found out from Angus rather than him, would that not be far, far worse? He had to tell her, and before Angus had a chance.

He had spent some of the time in the hotel the previous night rehearsing this moment, if it should come to it. The form of words he should use, the tone of voice. At one point he thought he had found it, the perfect form of words that gave him the best chance of a response that wasn't instantly apocalyptic. Now he couldn't remember a single thing about that rehearsal, not a single word, not a single intonation.

When he entered the living room he found that Polly was standing in the middle of it, completely transformed. She had changed her clothes and was wearing something he had never seen before, a sort of patchwork trouser suit in brightly contrasting hues. She looked like a clown or Pierrot or Harlequin, but without looking ridiculous. The garments were of such complexity he couldn't take them in at once, but just noticed a general pattern of colour and texture, of irregular patches of brightness and of seams and broderie in twisting twirling shapes. It was as though a stained-glass window had come to life – like one of those windows in the cathedral, the clothes seemed to move and swirl, as if they were alive. And out of this swirl of living patterns and colour there was Polly's face looking at him with a broad smile, a look of triumph that was beautiful in the same way that the clothes were beautiful.

She had put herself on display for him. She had, while he was reading to Evelyn, gone to the hurried trouble of changing her clothes, ready for his return to the living room. He vaguely understood that these were clothes she had made, that she had been working on for months. The clothes were so extraordinary that it was as though Polly had instantly planted herself in his mind, replacing the now almost forgotten Vera. He reached out to touch the clothes, as if unable to believe they were real, but they were, and felt as exquisite as they looked – some of the patches were velvety, some were silky, there were bits of mirror that were hard and smooth, there were sequins and gemstones. She was smiling in the midst of all this colour, and she asked him what he thought, and he didn't quite know what to say that didn't sound stupid, or banal, so instead he just carried on feeling her new clothes, and this turned into a kind of intense lovemaking that took place in the living room, more intense than anything that they had done that year.

# 15

In the events of that week, crowded as they were with his imaginary journey to Birmingham and his sense of reconciliation with Polly, Arnold began to put to the back of his mind the promise he had made to Angus and Vera, that he would tell Polly everything by the end of the week. In only a matter of days that shocking confrontation with Angus had receded into the past. When he thought about Angus and Vera, they seemed small, unfrightening things. He imagined that they, like him, would feel, as the days passed, that the initial sense of betrayal and anger can quickly dissipate, so that we wonder why we felt so strongly about something that only a few hours beforehand we might have given our lives for. Vera was already something that he could only puzzle over – the quiet, colourless woman who had once held his attention so that he forgot the brilliant spectrum of his own wife's personality and form. She too must wonder what she had seen in him, the quiet, faithless poet, a feeble, invertebrate thing next to the pious, bearded bear of her husband. They surely must see that time alone was enough to heal their wounds, there was no need for prayer groups or therapy groups or sessions of primal screaming or whatever they had in mind. And so he regarded the end of the week as no kind of deadline. He didn't expect anything to happen.

And then on Friday evening, just before dinner, Polly mentioned in a casual way that she had met Angus in the school playground that morning, and that she had a message to pass on. The cold fear Arnold felt the moment Angus's name was mentioned was softened a little when it became apparent from her tone of voice and manner that Polly was still innocent of any knowledge of his wrongdoing.

'Angus?'

'Yes, Vera's husband. I didn't know you were friends with him, but anyway, he asked for you to phone him.'

'Does he often do the school run?'

'I've never seen him there before. It was very unusual. Vera wasn't there, I suppose she was sick, I forgot to ask, I was so surprised. He must have taken the time off work.'

'Why does he want me to call him?'

'He said you'd know what it was about. Something about Sunday?'

So Angus had refused, so far, to disappear. The confidence that Arnold had slowly built up over the last twenty-four hours vanished instantly, and he felt a sense of cold dread for the rest of the evening. He wondered when he would find an opportunity to phone, and how to explain the conversation to Polly, if she overheard any part of it. He stumbled through the routines of the evening. They watched a bit of the news on TV, and he laughed at something a political commentator said. Polly asked him what he was laughing at, and he became irritated, because he couldn't find a way of explaining the joke, which made him realize he didn't fully understand it himself. And he became tetchy at having his own vanity and ignorance exposed.

'Men don't like to admit to their ignorance, do they?' Polly said. 'You start so many sentences with the words "I'm sure . . ." I could find it quite annoying if I thought about it too much. "I'm sure everything will be all right. I'm sure your lump is benign. I'm sure the environmental crisis will sort itself out."' She never talked like that normally, she was never so detailed in her criticisms of him. She never went to such lengths to identify and illustrate them. 'You are always sure about things, aren't you?'

Arnold didn't say anything.

'Daddy's not sure,' said Evelyn.

'I need to do some work upstairs,' said Arnold, lifting himself up, with difficulty (he felt unaccountably tired) from the couch and moving towards the door.

'What about phoning Angus?'

'I'll phone him from my study.'

When he did phone later, sure that Polly was still downstairs and out of earshot (though she would have had to stand with her ear to his study door to catch anything), it was Vera who answered.

'Hello, Vera, it's me.'

'Oh, hello,' there was a slight panic in her voice, as though she wanted to get off the line as quickly as possible, 'Angus – it's . . .' She evidently couldn't say Arnold's name. But her voice was quickly replaced by her husband's.

'Hello, Arnold, thank you for calling.'

'Polly said you wanted me to.'

'Yes. I wanted to hear about your plans.'

'What do you mean, "plans"?'

A moment's pause, as if Angus couldn't believe he was being asked the question.

'It's quite obvious that you haven't told Polly yet.'

'No, I haven't told her.'

'Only you said you would tell her by the end of this week, and today's Friday, so . . .'

'Listen, Angus, I realize I've done a terrible thing, and I apologize most profoundly – you have every right to be angry with me, but you mustn't think you have the right to interfere in my family and how I handle my relationship with my wife.'

Another pause.

'Let me explain something to you, Arnold. What you have done is more than terrible, and what I feel is much more than anger. You seem to think you are free to pick up your life where you left off, as though nothing had happened. We do not have that privilege. The damage has been done and the healing process cannot take place without your help. I am not threatening you in any way, but if you don't undertake to help us in this process, I will have no recourse but to turn to Polly for help. I could come round this evening . . .'

'No, no. Angus, please. Listen . . .'

'Do you want to know what I was doing this afternoon? I was searching through the internet for poisons. Not to give to you, or Vera, or anyone else. I was looking for poisons for myself. Something I could drink that would act quickly and painlessly and stop the pain for ever. And then I only felt all the more terrible for even having those thoughts. I got down on my knees and prayed. Right there in the office, at my desk. People around me asked what was wrong. I told them a relative was sick. Another lie. Then I felt bad for lying.'

'Angus, I don't know what to say.'

There was a lengthy pause on the line. Then Angus's voice again, slightly more reasoned.

'There is another way forward, Arnold. The reason you are unable to tell Polly the truth is because you don't have the strength. The courage. This is not your fault. I don't blame you. But there is a way of gaining that courage and strength, and that is to come to our church.'

Arnold couldn't help letting out a breath of laughter, that he drew back almost immediately. He shook his head to himself, in disbelief. This is what the nine-to-five man had wanted all along, he said to himself, this is what they both wanted, to save his soul.

'Really, Angus?'

'It is only through following that path that you might

begin to understand the importance of forgiveness, and why you and Vera need it from Polly.'

'Angus. I'm not a believer. I've told you. It would be pointless.'

'That is precisely why it would help you – and us – if you came. If you refuse, then I am afraid I really will have to involve Polly. I can't see any other way these issues can be resolved.'

Arnold paused, made dumb by the shock of Angus's demand. He wanted to ask him what he was supposed to tell Polly. Was this another secret he had to keep from her?

'I'm not sure, Angus. I'm not sure – it's just another way that Polly might find out. I would have to explain going to church to her.'

'That's not my problem . . .'

'It is if you are asking me to do something so out of character that it will arouse suspicion.'

'Well, you have until Sunday to make up your mind, but I will expect to see you at church.'

He gave the address and the time they were to meet, and then put the phone down, allowing Arnold no further say in the matter.

If Evelyn would allow them, Arnold and Polly usually spent Sundays slowly and lazily, not getting up till nine or ten, and spending the rest of the day reading, eating and going for walks. But Arnold had to be at Angus and Vera's church by nine fifteen. He would have to get up early on a Sunday, and explain why. He spent most of the

Saturday trying to think of a plausible reason for going somewhere on Sunday morning. His first idea was to say he was playing golf with Angus, since that was something he understood regular men liked to do on Sundays. The problem was that he had not shown the slightest interest in golf in his life until then. Fishing? Football? Flying lessons? The problem with all of these kinds of lies was that they would need Angus and Vera's corroboration, and he rather doubted they would be keen to back him up. Then there were the children. How could little Irina and her siblings be expected to join in any subterfuge; they would be more likely to ask Evelyn why she hadn't come to church with her father. He realized he would have to tell Polly the truth, and tried to imagine her response.

'Are you insane? Church? Why are you going to church?'

In fact, her response was quite different. Silence, at first, as though she had not heard. She lifted her face from the paper she was reading, looked at him quizzically, noticed that he had a half-smile on his face, as if he was joking, realized he wasn't, wrinkled her nose slightly and said, 'What for?' As if she already knew the last thing he could be going there for was to worship.

And then he found the only answer he could give convincingly.

'Research.'

'Research?'

'Yes.'

'So you're writing poems about church?'

'A novel, actually.'

'I thought you said you hated novels.'

'I never said that.'

'You said that novels weren't real literature. That the form was dead, killed off by the corporatization of modern publishing, reduced to a mere commodity, subservient to the market. Those were your actual words. I've remembered them.'

'Well, maybe I said that once, now it just so happens that I thought I'd try my hand at one.'

'Have you actually started it?'

'No.'

'What's it about?'

'I'm not sure yet. All I know is that one of the characters goes to church.'

'Why?'

'Oh for God's sake, why all the questions . . . ?'

'I'm just interested.'

'But you know how it is – if you try explaining too much too soon, the whole thing can slip out of your grasp . . .'

'How would you know, you've never written a novel before?'

'Perhaps I have, for all you know. Look – can we just leave it, I don't want to go to church, but I need to find out what it's like. I've never been, apart from weddings and funerals.'

'Can't you just ask Angus and Vera, ask them what they do in there?'

'It's not the same. And actually, I have asked them, and it's not enough. I have to see it.'

'So you're leaving us? Leaving us alone on a Sunday morning so you can go to church? When will you be back?'

'Not long, I don't think they last very long, church services, about an hour? You see? I don't even know that . . .'

It seemed to be working, this strategy. He didn't actually feel like he was lying, because as a writer he could regard anything he did as research, even having the affair with Vera, in an extreme way, since he would undoubtedly be using some of that experience in his writing, in one way or another. As long as he maintained the playful tone of the thing, as long as he didn't get cross or tetchy, which was in fact very hard because he found the lying very stressful, then Polly showed every sign of accepting this turn of events.

'Fine, go to your house of God. Just tell me one thing – are you going to be a detached observer or are you going to – you know – join in?'

'I'll play it by ear,' Arnold said, 'I'm hoping I can observe things from a distance, but if I have to join in, then I suppose I will.'

And so, on Sunday morning, Arnold went to church.

*Part Two*

At the back of her workshop Polly stored the raw materials for paper-making. Bundles of recyclable paper tied up with string and stacked according to thickness and colour. Newsprint was the easiest to come by, but the ink made it difficult to work with if one wanted to achieve anything other than a dirty grey hue in the finished product. In other bundles were the rarer papers, the pure white sheets of packaging or the coloured tissue papers that she had once had to scavenge for at the backs of shops. These days she had arrangements with various stores around the town to take their used paper, and had more than she needed. The cycle of paper production was slow and she always accumulated the raw material at a faster rate than she could process it, yet she couldn't bear not to take in paper that was available. She hoarded it like those old people who had started to feature in prurient TV documentaries, who stuff their houses until they can hardly get in the door. One day, she realized, there would be no more space.

The slowness of the production process had been one of the biggest early obstacles to the shop's profitability.

The pulp had to sit for hours in the tanks, slowly disintegrating. Then it could only be turned into paper one sheet at a time, lifted out of the vat on a mesh, pressed and dried. The only way to speed up production was to increase the number of tanks, but space was limited. Even so, she had six large tanks of paper pulp in constant operation, six stagnant pools of plant fibre where the water did its work silently and wouldn't be hurried.

Before seeing the demonstration in the Welsh slate caverns, Polly had never realized how simple the process of paper-making was, nor how magical. Dipping the mesh into the tank of pulp and lifting it out, it was almost as if the paper had made itself, sitting within the rectangular frame like a lawn under virgin snow, as though the complete leaf had been there in the water all along, waiting for her to find it. She came away from the caverns with a feeling that she had been given secret knowledge (which made no sense, given that there were daily public demonstrations), and after that it all seemed to happen so fast – from practising at home, taking courses, impressing friends and eventually starting her own business, she still hadn't quite taken in all that she had achieved.

Her mornings were usually spent in the workshop turning the pulp that had been soaking overnight into leaves of fresh new paper. Few customers called before noon, so the shop itself could be tended by an assistant. When custom picked up towards midday and early afternoon, Polly would dry her hands and come into the shop itself, while Tamsin or another assistant would attend to minor tasks in the workshop. The day ended with the preparation of new pulp, which meant the tearing up, by hand, of hundreds of sheets of paper from the stacked bales at the back of the shop, and stirring them into the water, along with the dyes (and any other additives) to soak overnight. Anyone who was available would take part in the tearing of the raw paper, and it had become a kind of ritual at the end of the day, a festive occasion, almost party-like in its atmosphere. Tearing, rather than cutting, was essential, to break up the fibres in the paper, and the smaller the pieces that resulted, the better. If there was enough time the paper would be torn almost to fluff before being sprinkled into the pulp tanks. The noise of paper being torn could at times be deafeningly loud.

In contrast the mornings were silent, contemplative. A space in her life that resisted all outside pressures, leaving just her and the pulp tanks and the leaves of paper that she lifted from them, one by one. As they dried in their frames on the bench she sometimes revisited the thought that first came into her head when they started up the Papyrus Press, that her business was making the blank pages for others to write on. They were all around her, the clean slates, empty and inviting, books in embryo, yet she had never thought to write, or draw, or paint on them herself. She wasn't creative in that sense, and sometimes felt disappointed, or even surprised by that fact, since she believed herself to be someone who experienced the world as thoroughly and as intensely as any of the writers and artists she knew. She could see the world vividly and clearly, but she didn't feel the need to report on this experience. A tree is enough of a thing in itself, she thought, why try adding another one in paint or words that can never be as good as the original? She'd tried this idea on Arnold once, and he dismissed it quite quickly, saying – if she remembered rightly – that art wasn't simply reproduction. The painted tree is a thing in its own right, as miraculous, in its own way, as the tree itself. She wasn't sure she agreed. It depended who painted it, she supposed. But the fact of producing paper at all, let alone the high-quality artisan paper she made, with its embedded rose petals and sweetly scented mulberry leaves, its natural dyes of varying subtle shades, was something that delighted and amazed her. When one day one her customers said to her, 'You know, I'd like to buy one of your sheets of paper and just hang it on my wall. It's such a beautiful thing to look at,' she felt a sense of fulfilment that she supposed was something close to that of artistic achievement.

She had studied English at university and, even though she had done well, was left with a nagging feeling of guilt whenever she derived pleasure from reading. This was dispelled when she took a job in publishing, where she was allowed to enjoy novels again, as things that enthralled and enchanted. She was a junior in the publicity department when she met Arnold at a literary party. They immediately bonded, even though she had nothing to do with the publishing of his poetry, and indeed hadn't long been aware that he was one of their authors.

She and Arnold had lived together in London for a

while, but she was quite happy to give up her job when he got the post at the university, perceiving that she was unlikely ever to progress from publicity into editing. Besides, she was on maternity leave by that time, and had been doubtful about ever going back. Evelyn had been a handful as a baby, but in the town they'd moved to she soon found a circle of friends, other young mothers, who proved very supportive. She had been so involved in this new circle, and in the raising of her daughter and in the setting up and running of her business, that she had to confess she hadn't taken much notice of Arnold in the last few years. She assumed everything was OK at the university, even though he didn't talk much about it. With the larger house they were able to buy in moving away from London, he had space to make a study, and no longer had to use a corner of the living room to write. The fact that he had, since the success of his first book of poems, made only slow progress towards a second did not seem to cause him much anxiety. He was a slow writer. He would remind her that Philip Larkin only produced a slim volume once every ten years.

No one was insensitive enough to remark that, alongside Arnold's failure to produce a second book, had been their joint failure to produce a second child. They had been trying now for many years but for some reason – a reason they had refused so far to investigate medically – the second child remained unconceived. It would have been nice for there to have been a boy to add to the family, to balance in gender Evelyn's bright presence and bring symmetry to the household. But both Polly and Arnold seemed wordlessly to agree the moment had passed. Time was now against their family ever growing.

Their work together on the Papyrus Press had been a point of intersection in their lives that otherwise followed different courses. They did their best to have their dinners and evenings together as much as possible, and concentrated their home lives into that space. And even though Arnold led his own life, teaching and publishing and editing and trying to write, she didn't feel that his life was in any way inaccessible to her, had she wanted access. It was a life she understood and could comprehend. But the moment he stepped across the threshold of a church, he had entered somewhere she could not understand, nor have access to.

She recalled the first Sunday of what he had started calling his 'fieldwork', when he was up early and showering and putting on smart clothes, as though he was setting off for a job interview. She had accepted his reasoning, albeit reluctantly, that he needed to do research, even though he had never written a novel, as far as she knew, nor expressed any serious desire to write one, before now. And when she asked him about this novel he became withdrawn and defensive, saying he would risk damaging the creative flow if he started talking about it too much, becoming quite annoyed sometimes, saying she didn't understand the creative process, which made her quietly angry and upset. He had never said anything like that to her before.

To cover her hurt she tried to make light of the event. 'Is that your version of a Sunday best?' she said when he came into the bedroom to say goodbye. She had stayed in bed while he was getting ready, propped up on some pillows, reading, as if determined to live her own Sunday as normally as possible. 'You look so smart. God will approve.'

'It's not God I'm worried about,' he said, bending to kiss her, 'it's the Christians.'

'Bring back some wine,' she called to him as he left, 'or fishes. For lunch.'

He was gone for four hours. She and Evelyn spent a puzzled morning not quite sure of how to handle the space in their lives that Arnold had left vacant. They were due to attend a picnic in the park in the afternoon, organized by the mothers of some of Evelyn's friends. She hadn't thought that she would have needed to remind Arnold to be back in time for that, because she assumed he would only be gone for an hour or so. When he did finally return she felt angry with him again and it turned into one of those days that starts off badly and never recovers. They got to the picnic late. She walked there and told Arnold to take the car and buy some picnic food, their contribution to the event, and meet them there. He did so, but arrived with such junk – jam tarts, sausage rolls, bottles of pink pop – that she could hardly bear to put them out with the dishes of hummus and cherry tomatoes, and noted the looks of bemusement, or barely concealed horror, on the faces of some of the mothers.

He wouldn't say much about going to church, but she could see it had effected some change in him. He was quiet, surly, shocked. When she asked him, he said it was boring. She asked him what sort of church it was, what the building was like. He said it was a modern building, like a house. In fact it had been a guest house at one time. There was a large conference room at the back that was used for worship. He said it was uninspiring, a little bit depressing. Nevertheless, it was a very useful experience for what he was writing about.

'Such dedication,' she said. 'What a thing to put yourself through for the sake of your art. I could almost admire you for it. In fact I do admire you. Despite the mess you've made of our lives this morning.'

They spent the rest of the afternoon peaceably enough, enjoying what was left of the picnic, playing with the children. In the evening she felt as though she had run out of the energy needed to restrain her feelings. She thought she could smell something on him.

'You smell of religion,' she said to him.

He looked a little taken aback.

'What do you mean?'

'You have a smell on you, a religious smell. Candle smoke. Flowers.'

'They didn't have any candles there. It wasn't that sort of place.'

'Did they say Hallelujah?'

Arnold laughed, but didn't reply.

'Come on, tell me more. Did they babble in tongues? Drink the blood of Christ?'

'It was very boring. Just people talking. One of the preachers, he talked for an hour or so. All about the book of Corinthians. It was like listening to a lecture on English literature by someone who'd never read a book before. He said he went to a sales conference in Cincinnati, and thought this was what heaven might be like. So it was depressing, drab. But useful.'

'Did they wear funny clothes, the preachers? Regalia? White double breasted suits?'

'No, they wore just ordinary clothes, grey suits, like sales reps. They had name tags.'

'Do you think they'll wear name tags in heaven?'

Arnold laughed. 'Almost certainly. It must be a very confusing place.'

Now Polly laughed, pleased that Arnold had opened up a little. She wondered why she had worried so much. After all, if he had gone to a meeting of neo-Nazis for research purposes she wouldn't have been worried that he might come back with fascist views. But then, he was too intelligent to be swayed by such obviously flawed ideology. Religion didn't work like that. Intelligent people were susceptible too, she supposed. She might, in her less considered moments, think religion was for the lame-minded, but otherwise she had to concede that it wasn't so simple. The problem was that Arnold's behaviour was encouraging her to examine her own prejudices, and as far as religion was concerned, she was normally happy for these to remain unexamined. By conceding that reason-able, intelligent people could find something in religion, she was making herself vulnerable to its seduction.

'Well,' she said, 'I suppose you can at least thank God you'll never have to go to one of those places again. You've suffered enough.'

He didn't reply but left her remark hanging. She didn't feel wholly satisfied. Arnold had said the things she would have expected him to say, but otherwise she sensed he was holding back. If it had been the neo-Nazis, he would have been full of stories about them, of their vileness, their stu-pidity, their crop-headed aggressiveness. He would have been full of contempt for them. But the worst he could say of the Christians was that they were boring. She so longed for him to say something rude about them. She offered him one more chance.

'Such poor fools,' she sighed, 'to believe in fairy tales.'

He seemed not to hear her.

When, the following Sunday, he went through the same routine of rising early, showering and dressing in present-able clothes she had to think for a moment before she realized what he was doing. She had assumed the visit to the church would be a one-off.

'You're going again?'

'Of course. I only scratched the surface last week. I need to get a sense of the people there, what goes on in their heads.'

'Surely there can't be much . . .'

He laughed, but it was another dutiful laugh, she thought, delivered to express loyalty to herself. And having let him go to church last week, she didn't have strong grounds to object now. But by the third Sunday, she felt she had to make a stand.

'Arnold, I don't like you going to church.'

He laughed. 'I'm not going to church. I'm just going to a building that happens to be a church, as an outside, detached, atheist observer.'

'Where did you get that awful tie from?' she said, as he adjusted a brown and purple length of fabric round his neck, 'and your hair. Have you put something in it?'

'Just doing my best to blend in. You have to think of this as a sort of undercover operation. I have to look the part.'

But he looked wrong in a tie, to Polly. He looked as though he'd been lassoed. And the gunk he'd put in his hair. He would have to wash that out when he came home. It was bad enough that he was behaving like a Christian, she didn't want him to look like one as well.

'I don't know why you can't just interview people. I'm sure they would be willing to talk to you. Why do you have to actually go and join in?'

He shrugged, as if it was both too simple and too complicated to explain. 'It's not the same,' he said, 'and I'm not "joining in". I'm a detached observer, like I said.'

It annoyed her that he found her objections amusing, as though she was being the silly little girl frightened by the big bad wolf of religion. He cuddled her in a fatherly way as she sat in bed, kissing the top of her head and telling her not to be 'daft', in such a patronizing tone that as he turned his back she made a gesture that he couldn't see, the middle finger raised in both hands, jerking them aggressively up and down while biting her top teeth over her lower lip, screaming silently as she did it, which came out as a little puff of anger at the conclusion of the gesture, which he didn't hear.

Sunday mornings were now a new and different space in the week. To make sense of them and to make a claim on them, she devised things for her and Evelyn to do on their own. Since the one thing that Evelyn was sure to appreciate and never refuse an opportunity to do was going round the big department stores in the city centre, they did that. They indulged themselves in the material and the mercantile in a celebration of everything that Polly supposed was as far removed from the piousness of the religious mind as possible. They ate in fast-food outlets, and lingered over make-up counters trying lipsticks and perfumes. She had always felt uncomfortable before in pandering to Evelyn's need to indulge in what she and her young friends called 'girly stuff'. When she had been their age it was the slashed leather jackets and porch ghoul mascara of Siouxsie Sioux that had inspired her, not this plasticky world of pop princesses and squeaky clean boys. But now she took it up with relish, the pair of them returning home sometimes after Arnold had returned from church, bright with sugary energy and glittery purchases, their breath sweet with carbonated drinks. Though it only seemed to please Arnold that they had found things to do in his absence.

He went regularly to the church all through the summer, taking a break only when they went on their fortnight's holiday to the Languedoc. There, he seemed restless and agitated, complaining about the heat and the fact that their house didn't have a swimming pool. He was like a smoker who'd given up smoking, though Arnold had given up smoking before Polly even knew him. She thought it was because they were on their own, when usually they holidayed with friends who had young children, so that Evelyn would be occupied, and would give him some time each day to read and write. Though he never did much reading or writing on holiday, and it puzzled her that he had always looked on the summer holiday as an opportunity to catch up on those things, when everyone else could see that they must be the worst possible times to seek the necessary seclusion and concentration, when all around him people were having fun and asking him to do things.

And this time the matter of religion penetrated even as far as this crumbling farmhouse in its grove of olive trees. She had overheard a discussion he was having with Evelyn. She had asked him about the cavemen, and if they would ever get into heaven. What about the people who built Stonehenge?

'Heaven is not like a club where you have to know the

password to get in. I think they'll allow anyone in who's lived a good life.'

'That's not what Irina said. She said the cavemen wouldn't be allowed in because they are descendants of Adam, who disobeyed God. But I think it's so unfair. If God made human beings, why did he wait until two thousand years ago before he let people into heaven? Why didn't he come down earlier, in the Stone Age, or the Bronze Age, at least?'

'Well, we are the lucky ones then. A bit like the fast lane at Alton Towers, where you can get quick entry to the ride, while all the cavemen have to wait in the queue.'

Polly had listened to this conversation from downstairs, wondering if she should intervene. She realized that they had never had the conversation with Evelyn that they thought they would have, when they had to explain what happens after death. She remembered an incident when Evelyn was much younger, perhaps just three or four years old. She had begun crying uncontrollably because she had convinced herself that she and Arnold were going to die and leave her on her own. And they had both struggled to deal with the situation, Evelyn had been completely inconsolable for an hour or more, she almost seemed to cry the humanness out of herself, becoming something more like a riled gamebird or distressed tree monkey. She had been touched in a profound way by it, because it seemed to mark the emergence of Evelyn's own independent consciousness, an awareness that her parents were not only separate individuals but ones susceptible to damage, to change, or that could be lost altogether, that the world was not the safe protective nest in which she had existed so far, but that there was a darkness beyond the nest that extended for ever. It was her own sudden awareness of her dependence.

They had reassured Evelyn that, although people do die, her parents were likely to be around until she herself was an old lady. There was no need to worry. The words themselves had no effect, and Evelyn's anxiety could only be worked out by what seemed like an almost metabolic process, carrying on until she had run out of tears. They had ended up singing nursery rhymes together, and their gentle sweet rhythms seemed to finally draw the fear of death from her thoughts, and she returned to the safe shores of childhood. But where had it come from? That was when they realized they would at some point have to talk about death, and decide what to say. But they never had agreed, and now, without any consultation, he seemed to be telling her there was a heaven.

After Evelyn had gone to bed, she spoke to him about it as they sat on the terrace with a bottle of wine beneath a Van Gogh sky.

'Did you listen to yourself? Did you hear yourself speak?'

'I had to say something, and just because you are explaining the religious point of view, doesn't mean you subscribe to that view.'

'You said "we are the lucky ones", "we'll get into heaven".'

'I was joking.'

'How can you joke about it – do you want our daughter to grow up thinking heaven is a real place?'

'She knows it's not a place,' said Arnold.

'What disturbs me more is that Evelyn is now starting to think of you as someone who knows about religion. She sees you go off to church every Sunday. She asked me the other day why we don't go as well.'

'But she knows why I'm going there, doesn't she?'

'I'm not sure she really understands.' And Polly thought she could add, 'and who does?' but didn't. And religion wasn't mentioned for the rest of the holiday.

There was something she remembered from her student days – perhaps it was George Eliot, who claimed that she gained all the knowledge she needed to write about French Protestant youth in a single glimpse she'd had through an open Parisian doorway into the home of a pasteur. Some of the Protestants were seated at a table round a finished meal. When added to her existing stock of knowledge about France, Protestantism and youth, the glimpse was enough to furnish an entire world in her imagination. So it was a shock, on returning from France, to find that Arnold, on the first Sunday back in England, resumed his routine of going to church. And more than that, he had begun going to midweek meetings as well. Not at church, but in people's homes. They were informal discussion groups, he said. He had been invited, and so he thought he should go. He said the chance it gave him of seeing more deeply into the lives of the people he was researching would be invaluable. He would see them in their own homes.

'Arnold, how long is this going to go on for?'

'Oh you know, when I feel I know enough.'

She tried countering with the George Eliot example. He knew it well. It was quoted in Henry James's *The Art of Fiction*, something he used regularly in his teaching. In fact, she now suspected he was probably the one who told her about it. 'We can't all be George Eliot,' was his riposte.

'Do the people there know you're just doing research?'

'Yes – though they may have forgotten.'

'What about Vera and Angus – have they forgotten?'

'I think they might have,' he chuckled. 'They think I've been saved. I don't really want to remind them.'

'Do you think that's fair, deceiving people like that?'

'I'm not deceiving them. I'm just being polite. If someone tells you they believe they are going to heaven, it's very rude to contradict them.'

'They think you're going to heaven, do they? You've booked your place already.'

'From what I can gather it's quite hard to avoid going to heaven. There's almost no talk at all about the other place.'

'Well, I won't be going to heaven – so you won't see me there.'

'I won't see anyone there, because I'm not going either.'

'Then it's rude of you to lie to the Christians about what you believe.'

'Oh, they won't mind. They'll just try harder to save me. They are very hopeful when it comes to saving souls. They never give up. That's something I've learnt about believers, they just never give up, and they always look on the bright side, and they love everything. The best ones do, at least.'

'I would find that endlessly irritating. And it would have irritated you, once.'

'Oh, it does. They can be very irritating. The thing is, it seems forced, at first. But then you begin to see it isn't. They are driven by something. They keep asking me when I'm going to bring you along.'

'Don't you dare even think about asking me. I wouldn't be seen dead . . .'

There was nothing in her past that could explain Polly's aversion to religion. Her parents were both born-again atheists, and the school she had attended, though C of E by name, paid almost no attention to religious matters outside of the once a week RE lesson, which, as far as she could remember, was taught by secular teachers as bored with their subject as their pupils. At university there had been the encounters with the Christian Union, targets of mockery and scorn from most of her friends, the feeling of dread whenever one of them caught you in conversation – and yes, there had been a friendship with a woman who left to become a nun. An English student, like her. The student had befriended someone from the Christian Union and been lost to them. She dropped out in the third year. Did she really become a nun, or was that just a rumour? Well, she can't have been a very close friend, or she would have known. Now she couldn't even remember her name. But what she did remember was the apparent disappearance of this friend. The way she dropped out of view completely. Given that she had been a quiet, unassuming woman in the first place, meant the vanishing had not been so noticeable, and maybe the friend had been more susceptible than most, but still – the complete disappearance, as though she had never existed in the first place was, looking back on it, rather shocking. But Polly's aversion to religion had little to do with that particular incident. It was already there, ready formed by the time she got to university. The Christians were like another species, pure and clean of heart, when she and her friends were into punk and its aftermath, the Christians maintained a timeless decorum, and looked at the world around them with continual disapproval. In many ways Vera was the perfect adult incarnation of those happy clappy students, but somehow, because they were both mothers, a deeper bond existed between them, that superseded spiritual beliefs.

Perhaps she had to go back further into her family to understand the origins of her aversion. She knew little about her grandparents, but perhaps it stemmed from them, giving her own parents an innate aversion bordering on disgust, which had been passed on to her.

———

She began looking for signs that Arnold had become a Christian. It seemed ludicrous at first, to be thinking of this question at all, because surely if he had become a true Christian, he would not be ashamed of the fact and would announce it with pride. He would not lie about it. Lying was a sin. She knew that such reasoning was rather simplistic, and that being a Christian didn't mean you were unable to do anything but blurt the truth, but at the same time she thought Arnold might be in some sort of transitional phase. And knowing her distaste for religion he might well be reluctant to proclaim his conversion. Yet he couldn't conceal those tell-tale signs – the peaceableness, the calmness, the optimism. These were qualities she had noticed in him, that had grown in recent weeks. Or so she felt. Hadn't he always been an optimist? What about his lack of complaint when doing household chores, his performance of good works around the house? What had happened to his domestic laziness?

She made the decision to delve into his study to see what she could find there. Normally she would not have had any qualms about doing this. She quite often ventured in there if she happened to be passing, usually after running out of coffee mugs downstairs. She would find a trove of half-finished mugs, each with a stone-cold puddle of coffee at the bottom – occasionally full cups frosted over with particulated milk. And during these forays she might glance at whatever was left open on his desk. Unfortunately his handwriting was so difficult to read she could only tell from the shape of the words on the page whether she was looking at a poem or not. She had not noticed the pages of solid prose that would indicate a novel was in the making, but then maybe he was writing it straight onto his laptop.

The safest time for her to investigate his study now was, of course, Sunday mornings, when he was regularly and reliably away for four hours, giving her all the time she needed. Yet she still felt a sense of guilt when venturing in there, not as a casually interested observer of her husband's workspace, but as someone entering what could now be thought of as hostile territory, looking for clues to something she couldn't understand. His laptop was on the desk, closed up like an oyster. To her annoyance, when she woke it up, she found it was password protected. There were the usual stacks of books and manuscripts – the fat envelope that contained Martin Guerre's poems was on the floor by the chair, still, it seemed, awaiting Arnold's response. To her surprise, the sight of it made her smile. She was tempted to read through those poems again to see if they were as she remembered them, and picked the envelope up for a moment, but then put it back down again, not wanting to be distracted. She looked through various notebooks – the handwriting was barely legible, she couldn't read it. To her surprise there were several folders of what looked like new poems, stapled together with their early drafts. Conveniently he was in the habit of dating them, and so she could see that he had been busy with poetry, at a gradually increasing rate over the last few years. She wasn't inclined to spend too long looking through them for clues, though she could gather from their titles (which were legible) that he was exploring the already well-charted territory of his first book, and gave no evidence of sudden Christian conversion. She looked through his bookshelves instead. Poetry, poetry criticism, some novels. Dante's *Inferno*. And a little book that froze her. The Bible, a pocket edition. She picked it up and examined it. It was old and well thumbed, but was not something that had always been in the house. She remembered Arnold saying something about a favourite poet of his who used to read the King James Bible every day for an hour just to get his poetry voice working. He was a secular poet, not a religious poet. Was this what Arnold was doing? And if he was writing a novel about a religious person, then of course he would want to look at the Bible. What was really surprising was the fact there weren't more books on religion evident. All this research he was doing, and there wasn't a single work of theology on his desk nor on his shelves, apart from this one little pocket Bible. And where were the notebooks for this new novel? Although she couldn't read much of the handwriting, she could read enough to tell that his notebooks were full of the sort of random observations that he kept all the time.

She remembered the occasion when she was working in the publicity department of Carpenter and Wylde, when many of the desks in the office looked like this, until a new management broom came in and swept them clean, making everyone keep tidy work spaces.

She had never had to read so much, not even for her finals at university. She would be handed a manuscript in the afternoon and then asked for her opinion the following morning, and if she couldn't give a detailed, insightful reply her standing in the office would soon begin to fall. She had begun to master the art of reading a novel in a few hours. She could get through a manuscript in a day and absorb probably about forty per cent of it, and given that in most novels it seemed that only about forty per cent of the writing was worth reading, she felt she could talk about such a novel with confidence.

Then one slow afternoon she took a call from the organizers of the W. H. Auden Awards.

'Hello, I'm so thrilled to be able to tell you that one of your authors has been shortlisted for our award.'

'Fantastic, who is it?'

'Isn't it fantastic? The author is a poet, Arnold Proctor.'

'Wonderful.'

'And we were hoping that you would be able to send us some publicity information, perhaps a photograph of the author, that we can use on our promotional material.'

'Arnold Broccoli?'

'Arnold Proctor. I'm so sorry. This is quite a bad line isn't it? Just for the record, could you tell me something about his background? This is his first publication, isn't it?'

'Do you mind if I get back to you on that? I'll just need to go through our publicity files.'

'Of course not, I'll look forward to hearing from you.'

This was in the days when computers were still in their infancy, all the information was kept in folders held in filing cabinets. She could find no trace of anyone called Arnold Proctor.

She found the head of publicity, having had to wait for her to come out of a meeting.

'I've had a phone call from someone wanting publicity information about a writer called Arnold Broccoli. I mean Proctor. Arnold Proctor.'

'Are you sure he's one of ours?'

There were other publishers under the same umbrella company, occupying different floors of the one building. She phoned upstairs and downstairs, but no one had heard of Arnold Proctor. She wondered if she should phone the W. H. Auden Awards to make sure they had the right poet, or publisher. But then she found one of the senior editors.

'You should ask Vita, she does the poetry list.'

'Vita?'

'Vita Cartwright. She doesn't come in much, once a month to have a long lunch with her old Bloomsbury friends, less so now that we've moved out of Bloomsbury. If she remembers she pops in here to look at the submissions, usually leaves without opening anything. She used to be a poet herself, but nothing published since about 1938.'

She went to Vita's desk, which had somehow escaped the new management broom. There was simply a heap of stuff on it, roughly conical in form, consisting of manuscripts, envelopes, magazines, pictures, dried flowers and box files. She couldn't touch anything for fear of causing an avalanche. Vita's filing cabinet contained no files but instead ornate and empty wine bottles, articles of clothing and an empty bird cage. She asked another editor, at the neighbouring desk,

'Do you have Vita Cartwright's phone number?'

'Oh no, she doesn't use the phone. She only responds to letters.'

'Does she live in London?'

'Somewhere in Surrey, I think.'

She had no choice in the end but go into the managing director's office, Miranda Mulholland, the only person in the company to have her own door, which was nearly always closed.

'I'm trying to contact Vita Cartwright, one of her authors is up for a prize.'

'Oh, Vita's dead dear. Who is the author you are talking about?'

'Arnold Proctor.'

Mulholland looked blank. 'It does ring a bell. What is the prize he has won?'

'He's been shortlisted for the W. H. Auden Award.'

'Oh, that's quite good. We should let him know as soon as possible. He'd be very happy.'

'That's what I was wanting to contact Vita for – I'm so sorry she's dead.' Without warning, and without feeling at all sad, Polly felt the seep of tears.

'I'm sorry, dear. I forget there may be people in the

office who have known Vita. She was such a secretive old sweetheart. I thought to make a proper announcement but she was here so rarely I truly forgot all about it. Did you know her well?'

'Not at all, actually. I hadn't heard her name until today.'

The thought that Arnold might be having an affair occurred to her now and then. In the past there had been one or two occasions when she had had cause to wonder – when she caught the way he was looking at a woman or, more rarely, the other way round. He claimed invisibility as far as the opposite sex was concerned, but she knew there was a certain type of woman who found him attractive. Women like her, for example. She couldn't be unique. This time she doubted it because she detected little sign of unhappiness or guilt in him. He seemed blasé and calm in everything he did. Their lovemaking continued in the precautionary and routine way they had adapted since the birth of their daughter – nothing too elaborate or extravagant that couldn't be instantly covered up if their child intruded, which she often did. She read that one of the first signs that a man was having an affair was the sudden appearance of new sexual techniques or interests in the bedroom. Well, there certainly hadn't been any of those. But then she read somewhere else that a certain man is duplicitous and conscientious enough to make sure he doesn't bring any new habits into a well-established lovemaking routine. She strongly doubted whether Arnold was duplicitous and conscientious enough.

She thought about the time she finally met him, at the awards ceremony. It was a tight-lipped do, the award presented by a celebrated poet she was embarrassed to find she'd never heard of. She saw her own poet standing awkwardly, a little drunkenly, with the other shortlisted authors. Something about the awkwardness attracted her. She went over to him.

'You must be Arnold, I'm Polly.'

She had grown used to meeting distinguished authors, so meeting an unknown poet was easy enough to handle.

'Hello, Polly.'

'I'm one of the publicity assistants at Carpenter's. We've spoken on the phone.'

'Oh, right.'

'Many congratulations.' She felt suddenly tongue-tied.

'Thanks. Is anyone else here? From Carpenter's, I mean.'

'No, but they all send their warmest congratulations, I'm afraid they are tied up with other things tonight.'

'All of them?'

'Yes, except me.'

'Even the poetry editor?'

'Oh, didn't you know?'

'Know what?'

'Your editor is dead.'

Arnold gave a shrugging laugh, as if to say, That's all I needed.

'I'm so sorry – someone should have informed you, I can't believe they haven't. Did you know her well?'

'I never met her actually, so no, I didn't know her at all.'

'That's good. No one in the office seems to have known her either. But she must have had a great affection for your work, she would have been so pleased that your book is on this shortlist, I'm sure.'

'Actually, I'm beginning to wonder if she published me by mistake. She may have thought I was someone else.'

'Oh I'm sure that's not the case.'

'There is another poet, called Andrew Porter. He has been very successful in the magazines and with the competitions, but he has never had a book published. I wondered if she got our names mixed up. She was very old, and she once called me Andrew, in one of her letters.'

'Well, you can rest assured, all of us at Carpenter's know you are Arnold Broccoli, not Andrew Porter, and that you are a much better poet.' She put forward a jokingly clenched, comradely fist.

'Did you say Broccoli?'

'No, I said Proctor. Andrew Proctor. Arnold Proctor.'

'Now that the poetry editor is dead, will they carry on publishing poetry?'

'I'm not sure, Arnold. I expect so.'

'The rumour is that they were running down the poetry list anyway. Now that Vita's gone, they have the perfect opportunity to dump the list.'

He was quite drunk, and his teeth were stained with red wine. They slept together that night, literally, as Arnold went out like a light as soon as he was under the covers. Polly had never slept with a man so soon after meeting them even though, as a frequent attender of literary events like this one, she had been given countless opportunities. Perhaps it was that he, unlike the other men, had made so little effort in trying to impress her. In fact, she found it so hard to keep his attention or interest, she wondered at first if he was gay. No, he wasn't gay, instead he seemed to live in a state of permanent distraction. Even so, she soon found that he would, without showing any obvious signs of affection, do absolutely anything for her. He would heel, or roll over like a dog. One phone call and he would drop everything to be by her side. The devotion baffled her. And he seemed almost painfully honest and trustworthy. The idea of him deceiving her, it was too troubling to even contemplate.

She sometimes wondered, on the mornings when it was quiet in the shop and she was alone in the back with her tanks of pulp, lifting pages out of the stewed fibres, if what she was doing bore any relationship at all to what happens in a church. She had read the lazy articles about artists in their studios, and writers at their desks, talking about sacred spaces. The cave of making. Arnold's desk was such a space, but one that was unadorned and un-ritualized. He was not the kind of writer who filled his space with mementoes and talismans. His desk was little more than a pile of rubbish, somewhere in the midst of which art was being slowly put together. Yet even in that seemingly random configuration of codexes, mugs of pens, newspapers and half-eaten food, there seemed a kind of precious order of things. Then she realized what it was – in giving no thought to how things were arranged, Arnold's placement of objects was perfectly aligned with his thought processes – when he finished reading something, he placed it somewhere, in relation to all the other things he had placed. In this way, the desk was an extension of his mind. It was his consciousness solidified. And that was what made it seem precious, or sacred.

Her own space was more ordered – the long benches for working and cutting, the drying racks, the shelves of inks, dyes and glues, the pulp tanks, the sink area, the storage bins with their bales of materials, the tubs of dried rose petals, leaves, bark. It was a space dedicated to a process of production that reminded her, in the very few times in her life she'd been to church, of the careful and considered orderliness of the Christian sacrament. When she lowered a frame into the pulp, it sank into an impenetrable morass of broken-down matter, and when she lifted it out, a perfect rectangle of paper held within the frame, dripping. It had to be treated as carefully and as respectfully as new-born life. If she thought about its origins, from the unstitching of the carbon dioxide molecule to the felling of an elderly tree, it seemed a miracle more wonderful than anything dreamt up by religion.

———

She hardly saw Vera now. The sewing evenings had petered out over the summer with few people able to make the commitment, and Vera had stopped attending before then anyway. Evelyn and Irina's always turbulent relationship seemed to have passed a point of redemption and the regular invitations to stay at Irina's house were no longer offered, and Evelyn had no inclination to invite Irina to hers. The mothers in Evelyn's year no longer waited in the school playground but saw their children off at the gates. They were old enough now to find their own way into the school. So the little community that came into existence for ten or fifteen minutes every morning had ended, except for those with children in a lower year. She missed it. It was a chore that had become a special part of her life, and its passing marked another small moment of transition, another step taken in Evelyn's progress towards independent adulthood, which had once seemed impossibly remote. And the thread that connected her to the community of other mothers had become ever so slightly weaker.

She did try to find out if something had happened between Evelyn and Vera's daughter, but no amount of questions brought any satisfactory answers.

'Aren't you friends with Irina any more?'

'No.'

'Why not?'

'I don't know.'

'Did something happen between you? Did she upset you?'

'No.'

'Did you upset her?'

'No.'

'Why then? What's wrong?'

'Mother – don't you know anything about relationships? For God's sake!'

She managed to catch Vera at the school gates one morning. They had walked past each other, Vera showing no sign of recognition. On an impulse Polly turned and ran to catch up.

'I'm so sorry about Evelyn and Irina, they seem to have fallen out.'

'Yes,' Vera said thoughtfully, as though she hadn't noticed before, and had just been made aware of the fact, 'it's a shame.'

'I wonder what happened. Evelyn doesn't seem to know . . .'

'Well, Irina has stopped talking to me about anything to do with her personal life.'

'Isn't it strange? They seem to have decided to become teenagers before their time – over the summer holiday, just like that. The things Evelyn comes out with, I can't help laughing at her.'

'Irina's the same. They are growing up fast.'

'It's a pity when that happens – it means we have less chance to meet for a chat.'

Vera agreed in a non-committal sort of way. 'Yes, we should still meet up, but without the children.'

She started moving away. Polly understood that the promise to meet up was an empty one. As their conversation had progressed, she saw that their friendship was over. There was a new and uneasy formality to how they spoke. They spoke in generalizations and clichés, not the intimate language of friendship. They no longer spoke with the expectation of mutual comprehension. They spoke, she later realized, like former lovers who meet unexpectedly.

She also realized that she had to grab this moment, so before Vera was fully on her way, she held on to her physically, laying a hand on her forearm.

'You are aware of Arnold's situation, aren't you?'

'Situation?'

'I mean the fact that he is doing research for a novel. That is why he is going to your church, he is writing about it.'

Vera looked confused, in a genuine way. She gave a short, uncomfortable laugh and set her head quizzically aslant. 'I'm sorry, Polly. Where has this come from? What are you saying about Arnold?'

'Your church, whatever it is . . . Arnold is researching a novel with a religious theme, that's why he's attending. He's not a believer, not a convert.'

'Oka-ay . . .' Vera said, drawing the word out with a querying cautiousness, as though she was unsure if she was talking to someone who was mad. 'I'm not sure what this . . .'

'If he is pretending he is there for religious reasons,

I don't think it's fair of him to deceive you. If he joins in, if he prays and sings and kneels and gives thanks to the creator of all things or whatever it is you do, then I think he is being too devious for anyone's good. I just don't think it's on, that's all. There are limits. There are boundaries. I think you should know.'

There was a pause, during which it was clearly Vera's turn to say something, but she seemed to be waiting for more from Polly. So she said, 'I'm probably speaking out of turn. It's nothing really.'

'No, it's OK. I'm glad you've said something. Arnold has taken a lot of interest in us. Perhaps things will be clarified at the retreat.'

It took a moment for Polly to realize she didn't understand that last remark.

'I'm sorry? What retreat?'

Vera looked uncomfortable again, as if she had said something she shouldn't.

'Oh – just this thing we are having at the end of the month. We go to Wales, some of us. For a weekend of prayer and reflection.'

'And Arnold's going on this, is he?'

'I'm sorry, Polly. I thought he would have told you.'

That evening, with Evelyn in bed, she confronted him in his study. He spent all his time in there now, giving them rare opportunities to talk freely.

'How long are you going to go on pretending,' she said to him.

'Pretending what?' He had turned round in the black Mastermind armchair they had bought in Ikea.

'That you haven't become a Christian.'

He closed his eyes and shook his head sadly, as if to say, not that old chestnut.

'How many times do I have to tell you, I'm not a Christian, I'm not thinking of becoming a Christian, I'm not even thinking of thinking of it.'

'I spoke to Vera this morning. She said you'd booked yourself in for some sort of religious retreat?'

'Oh that. What about it?'

'Weren't you going to tell me?'

'Of course, when I had a moment. It's not something that's at the top of my mind.'

'You're going on a religious retreat, you'll be praying and singing and praising the Lord.'

'Like everything else, it's just for research.'

'Vera didn't seem to think you were doing research. She seems to think you're a believer.'

'Did she say that?'

'No, but I could see it in her face, the look of discomfort when I said why you were really there.'

'She already knows why I'm there. You don't think I'd really lie to them about it, do you? I've told them I just want to observe, for research purposes. You were making a fool of yourself.'

He added that last comment under his breath. She chose to ignore it.

'I've come up here to tell you that you aren't going.'

'Aren't I?'

'No. I've had enough, Arnold. You're definitely not going to that retreat, it's just a step too far. And you can stop going to that church now as well. You've been going for months. How much research do you need to do for God's sake? You must know more about that church than the regular believers by now.'

Arnold didn't say anything but sat in his chair sulkily, swinging gently on the pivot.

'You don't understand,' he said quietly, 'I've got to go.'

'Got to? Got to? What does that mean?'

As though snapping himself out of something he said, 'It's too good an opportunity. They only do it once a year. I need to see what happens there.'

Polly felt weakened slightly in her resolve. But she couldn't just let him go to the retreat, she had to have something in return.

'This novel of yours,' she said, 'tell me about it.'

He looked at her in shock. 'You know I can't do that.'

'Then show it to me. I don't need to read it, just show me the pages you've written, show me the computer files. Show me the notes.'

Arnold looked at his laptop, tapped tentatively at the touchpad, stirred the cursor around the screen.

'I can't really even do that, I'm sorry. What is it? Don't you believe I'm writing a novel?'

What she wanted to say was – no one is entitled to that amount of privacy, in a marriage. You can have your separate space, your study, your notebooks, but you can't have places from which I'm totally banned. I don't care if you are a writer, I have a right to know what you are doing in here. I have a right to see the evidence. What other type of man would claim such privilege? Not even the obsessive railway modellers or woodworkers would shut their wives out completely. But this claim to artistic privacy put Arnold – it came to Polly in a sudden flash of unwanted inspiration – in the same category as the husbands who mined new cellarage beneath their houses and lived secret lives there. She had recently read about one such who had kept a place like that for years. Or worse, it put him in league with the dungeon-keepers who raise whole families enslaved in a secret basement. But it was an unsayable thought – to liken the profession of writing to the worst of human behaviour – it would have been a terrible insult. Yet she could not help thinking it, and after she left the study in exasperation, she continually had the thought that Arnold was constructing such a space in their lives. Invisibly, he was working at some sort of structure that she could only sense as an architectural presence. And one day, it would be revealed, a gleaming towering church in her back garden.

There was another reason Arnold couldn't go to the retreat, and that was because it was on a weekend when they were meant to visit her parents. On the Friday, they talked about it. He repeated that he would not get the opportunity again, that he had to go. Her parents wouldn't mind if he wasn't there, he said. What did it matter, it wouldn't be the first time he'd missed a Sunday at the ugly house. Polly felt suddenly weak in her argument. It was true that occasionally Arnold was unable to go because he was away at a conference, or attending a literary festival or was just too busy with teaching-related work, and Polly had gone to her parents without him, taking Evelyn with her. She didn't like going alone to visit her parents because it made her feel like a child again, and she hadn't enjoyed her childhood. They had had a number of rows about it, over the years. Arnold thought that they visited her parents far too frequently. Because he was an orphan, he felt frustrated that he wasn't able to counter their influence on Evelyn with his own parents. How Evelyn would have loved them, he sometimes lamented, and the house they lived in, with all its art and music and books. Had they still been around, Evelyn might have been more interested in such things.

'Just promise me,' she said to him on the Friday evening, 'once you come back from this retreat, you will be finished with your research. No more going to Vera's church on Sunday. Ever. Do you understand?'

'Not ever?'

'No. If you go back, I'll have to assume you've become a Christian.'

'And then what?'

Was he teasing her? Did he still think it was a joke?

At the ugly house she felt vulnerable and afraid. She had thought about cancelling her visit, but something made her decide to keep to the normal routine. Evelyn was happy to find that some of her young cousins were there, as both brothers had come this time, and brought their whole families. But when Evelyn went off to another part of the house, Polly felt even more alone, and prey to the old values. Her birth family seemed to tower over her, in the absence of her own. Without Arnold they seemed to think themselves more entitled than ever to offer any advice and criticism they wished, and there was no end to it. How much money was the shop making? Why didn't she branch out into gifts and souvenirs – they lived near a popular tourist attraction, why didn't she sell pictures of the cathedral, or porcelain plates with the cathedral on, or Union Jacks?

'The age of paper is dead, sweetheart,' said her mother, who had never shown much interest in paper when it was an abundant thing. 'Only a fool would throw everything into making paper at a time when everything is going onto the internet. No one writes letters now, no one writes on paper. Haven't you heard of computers? There is such a thing as email. You are a funny girl.'

It should have earned their respect, as a daughter of builders, that she was earning money as a capitalist, making something with her hands. But they seemed to think paper was not something of any proper value. Not the paper she made, at least. Why make paper, they wondered, when there were mills that could turn out rolls of perfect, pure white paper thousands of miles long, day after day, against which her paper was like some awful

recycled rough-textured stuff from the bottom of a pack-
ing crate. Trying to compete with the big boys when paper
was in decline and the market was sewn up by the con-
glomerates – it was crazy. It seemed to them like someone
trying to compete with Sony by knocking up home-made
televisions. It was pointless and doomed to fail.

'No Arnold, this month?'

'No, Arnold's gone away.'

'Oh? Where's he gone?'

'Wales.'

'Wales? What on earth for?'

'He's doing research.'

She braced herself for the opinions that would be sure
to come, about the folly of writing anything other than
potboilers.

'What's he researching?'

She decided to be honest.

'He's writing a novel with a religious theme, and he's
gone to Wales on a religious retreat.' In the hush of
puzzled silence that followed this statement she felt it
necessary to add, 'To do the research.'

They were seated around the table for lunch. She
noticed odd looks askance from other members of the
family – her sisters-in-law exchanged glances across a bowl
of steaming sprouts.

'It's a funny old thing, religion,' said her father, using
the phrase, word for word, that she had heard come from
his lips whenever the subject of religion was raised in his
presence, 'you either believe it, or you . . .' And as ever, he

left the sentence unfinished, hanging. For some reason, it seemed, he could never quite bring himself to utter the negative, with regard to religion.

'He's been going to church for the same reason,' she tried saying this in as relaxed and unconcerned a way as possible, 'joining in with prayers and singing hymns.' She laughed. No one else did. They looked rather concerned.

'Have you been going as well?' said her mother.

'Me? No. I couldn't bring myself, not even for research. I'm not sure how Arnold can stand it actually. He hates it as well. The hypocrisy . . .'

'They're all just in it for themselves,' said her mother, to general nods of agreement around the table, as she set off on one of her favourite hobby-horses. 'The priests, the Catholic Church. It's all a racket. Like everything else . . .'

It had not occurred to her before, but she now saw that her parents' aversion to religion had, like everything else in their lives, an economic source. It was all to do with money. Nothing that came into their lives or came out of it did so on anything other than a river of cash. They hated this fact, but they put up with it. They did more than put up with it, they let it completely govern their lives, so that doing anything that didn't make economic sense was utterly pointless. This meant that they regarded anything they did for recreational pleasure as simply a way of using up money that had been earned. They had taken a pragmatic approach to life to a vulgar extreme. She had tried to put her view across many times over the years – that just because money is important doesn't mean it is everything. Her father would lean back in his chair and laugh meanly at such a sentiment. Of course, now she understood. Their hatred of religion stemmed from its claim that money wasn't everything. She could make that claim because she had the security of her comfortable upbringing. The Church could make it because it was wallowing in gold stolen during the Crusades. Or whenever. But her parents couldn't make that claim because they had nothing else to fall back on. They were frustrated. Deep down they knew that money wasn't everything, but they just couldn't fathom what else there was. Polly felt a flutter of nervousness at the thought that her opposition to her parents put her on the side of God.

It was a showery day. Rain would pound the plastic roof of the conservatory where they ate, for a few minutes, and then be replaced by bright sunshine. Under the strain of the sudden changes in temperature the whole conservatory seemed to creak and crack arthritically. The weather was all around them and yet they could hardly seem further from it. Around the table people constantly changed colour, went in and out of shadow. Later the sky opened up and sunshine established itself and the lawn quickly began to dry out.

'It would be quite nice to sit outside,' said Polly.

Her mother wasn't keen. 'Would it be worth getting the furniture out? You'll be going soon.'

It seemed they couldn't just go in the garden. It had to be prepared for them, the garden furniture had to be got out of the garage, the swinging bench thing that they had

bought recently, which Polly thought looked like a float-
ing settee, under a gondola-like canopy, had to be set up.
Sunshades had to be erected and correctly positioned. At
home, if they used the garden, they just went out there,
maybe taking a blanket to sit on.

'I might just go out anyway, I need some air.'

And so she stepped out onto the lawn alone. It was a
large, well-kept garden, almost all the work of a hired gar-
dener, and the view across the Weald was mesmerizing. It
was not a house she had known as a child. She had grown
up somewhere much smaller, and every time she came to
her parents' house now she had to readjust her conception
of the family home.

At first she remained alone in the garden, everyone else
seemed to be busy with something, but soon she was
joined by her sister-in-law Holly, Mikey's wife. Of her two
sisters-in-law she was more wary of Holly. She trusted
her less. She was the worldlier of the two, always dressed
fashionably, always fabulously turned out. She had been
flirty with Arnold when she first appeared at the ugly
house, and somewhere deep inside herself she had never
forgiven her for this, even though she understood that
she was just a flirty sort of woman who communicated
with most men that way. She had brought two children
with her from a previous marriage, and now her daughter
with Mikey, Tabitha, was three years old. The little girl
was with her now; she was beautiful but seemed quietly
nervous of everything. She hardly ever spoke, and then
only in soft murmurs in her mother's ear. Polly didn't

really know what to do with her whenever she encountered her, she was so different from Evelyn.

'I'm sorry I haven't read any of Arnold's novels,' said Holly, as she guided Tabitha by the hand round the edge of a flowerbed, 'I don't get a lot of time for reading.'

'Arnold hasn't written any novels. This would be his first. He usually writes poetry.'

'Well in that case I'm sorry I haven't read any of his poetry anthologies.'

'And he's only written one of those.'

'Oh . . .' She didn't seem to know where to take the conversation next, and Polly, a little meanly she acknowledged to herself, didn't want to help her. She had come out here to be alone, and to not worry about Arnold.

'I lost a husband to religion once. It was weird.'

This piece of news, delivered so tritely, seemed too big for the mouth it had come out of.

'I haven't lost him. Didn't you hear what I was saying in there? He's doing research. I haven't lost him to religion.'

'I didn't say you had. I'm just saying, I had a husband who went over to religion.'

'As though that gave us something in common. But it doesn't.' Polly had to recalibrate her tone of voice. 'I'm sorry for snapping. I'm tired.'

Holly was silent for a few moments, and Polly could almost hear her thinking how to frame the next statement, how to present her thoughts about Arnold. She approached closely, still with Tabitha in her hand, who was trying to reach out to pick the flower heads.

'On the other hand, I can tell you're worried he's gone over. You put on a good act in there, laughing about it, but I can see it in your eyes. You're worried he's become religious. Believe me I know the signs, I've been there.'

Fury rose up in Polly's chest, at the effrontery of this woman to make assumptions about her marriage, but the anger would not express itself and instead held back at the brink. She realized that, presumptuous though this woman's remarks were, she had valuable knowledge. Polly wanted to hear more.

'What happened to your husband?'

Holly shook her head at the memory of it.

'Our son Jamie nearly died from meningitis when he was six. Tom said prayers by his bedside every day. Constantly. He'd never prayed before, though he did go to a religious school, but he'd never prayed like that. And Jamie got better, thanks to the antibiotics, but Tom insisted it was a miracle. From then on he became a true believer, started going to church, reading the Bible. I didn't know what to do, where to look. He made this separate space for himself in our lives that was nothing to do with me. OK, it was only an hour or so every Sunday, and I wouldn't have minded if he was playing golf or going to the gym, but going to church was different. I wondered if I should join him, to be supportive, but I just couldn't bring myself to. I don't have strong objections to religion, but I can't sit in a church and be told what to do and how to live my life by a man wearing a dress. So I stayed out of it, and we didn't talk about it and things just carried on for a while. But it was never the same again. Tom had changed. It was almost like he was having an affair, and in a way he was, but with God. God took priority in everything that went on in our lives from then on. It was like there was a stranger in the house, someone in the room with us all the time – at meals, watching the TV. At times I was scared. He stopped drinking. He'd always liked a pint with his mates, but he stopped going to the pub. He started seeing less of his friends, and more of the people at the church. Then the criticism started. If I wore anything too revealing in public, and I'm not talking tarty, just a normal bit of cleavage – he would start getting upset. If I went out with my friends and came home a bit drunk he would give me these filthy looks. Then he started trying to turn the children against me, using me as an example of how not to behave – "You don't want to end up like your mother . . ." I actually heard him say that to our daughter. Then he wanted them baptized, and then he wanted me to start coming to church. He said I needed to be saved. He got more and more fanatical. In the end I just had to leave.'

Polly was touched by Holly's openness, and her obvious desire to share her experience in order to help.

'Thank you for telling me all this, Holly. And I'm so sorry about Jamie, it must have been terrifying.'

'In some ways it was. But I knew we'd caught it in time, and I just had complete trust in the doctors that they would cure him. My doubt in them never wavered. But for some reason, Tom didn't think science was enough to save

Jamie. It was almost like he was waiting for an excuse to become religious.'

By now Holly had let go of Tabitha's hand and the child was now roaming the edge of the flowerbed, talking to the flowers as though they were a class of children and she was their teacher, her quiet voice making very little sense, as far as Polly could hear.

'Like I said, Arnold hasn't become religious. If he had, why would he hide it?'

'I'm sure you're right, Polly. Arnold hasn't got the religious spark in him that was triggered in my Tom. There has to be something there in the first place for religion to do its work. You look at Arnold, you can see there's nothing there.'

Polly began wondering if she should get offended all over again at these remarks, but by now Buzz had come into the garden, with a can of beer in his hand. He and his father headed over to the garage and began work on filling the lawn with furniture.


Arnold didn't get back on Sunday night till very late. It was a long drive from Wales and he had texted her regularly to give her updates on his journey. But she was in bed and pretending to be asleep when he got home, at half-past one in the morning. She could follow through sound the entire progress of his journey through the house, even though he was doing his best to be quiet. She heard the front door go, then the soft hiss of the pipes as he filled the kettle in the kitchen. Then more sound from the plumbing as he used the downstairs loo. She heard the stairs creak and the study door click as he poked around in there for a while. Then the closer sound of the bathroom, where she could monitor the brushing of his teeth, more tap noise, more rinsing. He was in the bathroom for longer than normal, making no sound at all.

And then he was in the bedroom. She could hear his feet on the carpet, hear his breathing, the rustling of his clothes, the clink of his belt, the rasp of his fly, the momentary pauses now and then when he was watching to see if she was awake. Then the covers were lifted and he was inside, bringing cold air with him. She could sense him craning his neck to check on her once again. She could have murmured a goodnight to him, but she decided to maintain the pretence of being asleep. She could always tell the difference between when he was asleep and when he was lying there awake but with his eyes closed. But he couldn't. As far as he could tell she was dead to the world, and he was soon asleep himself.

In some ways, what she feared most was that she might become someone who had feelings of bitterness towards men in general. She didn't want to be like some of the women she knew, the worn-out, faded women who'd nurtured their good looks and had used them ruthlessly to ensnare and captivate, only then to wonder why they had been treated so thoughtlessly by those they had captured. She didn't want to be weary of men, to be cynical, to be dismissive, and yet she couldn't help feeling that she would become so if Arnold betrayed her. She had never been betrayed like that before, by a man. She had parted company with previous boyfriends and lovers painlessly and politely. She had lately begun to visualize her state of unbetrayal as a kind of pearl that she carried inside her, of innocence and loving trustfulness, that was perfectly beautiful and solid and hard at the same time. Over the years the cultivation of this pearl had come to matter to her more than anything, and the work of carrying it throughout her entire life seemed the most urgent and important task that she had assigned herself, after the successful raising of Evelyn. It was important because it fed all her energy, all her resourcefulness, it gave her the ability to face up to the daily challenges of life and to see them as things of potential reward. She thought that betrayal by Arnold would dash this pearl from her grasp and risk it being damaged or lost for ever. For that reason she would treat any misdemeanour by Arnold with severity, before it could damage her. That was just how she thought about things. Cultivating herself meant being in proximity to beautiful and nourishing things. Arnold had been one of these things, and his new venture into things separate from her she regarded with suspicion and fear.

She didn't ask him about the retreat, and he didn't volunteer any information. The next morning he was only just getting out of bed, groggy from his late night and long travelling, as she was taking Evelyn to school. They didn't see each other till the evening. Over dinner she couldn't hold back, it would have seemed odd not to have asked anything, so she asked how it went at the retreat.

'It was useful,' he replied.

'Oh good.'

'Very useful. Funny. And interesting.'

'Funny in what way?'

'Oh, you know. Christians are funny . . .' He couldn't explain.

'So you got a lot of material?'

'Yes. The dynamics are very interesting. You start to see the underlying structures. Who has the real power. I found out a lot more about how the church is organized. The politics behind it all. The money.'

'Do they have a lot of money?'

'There's quite a lot of money about, yes. Or there certainly seems to be. They have some wealthy donors. They have a sister church in Rwanda. Out in the bush. They are working on building a new, bigger one on the site of the old one, with a school and a sort of seminary attached.'

'That's interesting.'

'Vera and her family go out there every year for a few weeks, to help.'

'Do they?'

'They suggested, just as a joke I think, that we should go out there with them, or any time we like.'

'A joke?'

'Well, I don't think they were entirely serious, but they did say it would be a very cheap holiday, we would only have to pay the air fares, everything else would be free, and actually I could get the university to pay mine, if I make a claim for research funding.'

'So you've given it some thought, then . . .' Again the feeling of fury that rose in Polly's chest, that she had to hold back, almost as if she was having an attack of reflux acidity, this burning sensation deep inside her. Had he heard nothing that she had said about this retreat being his last thing to do with research? She tried to speak calmly. 'What would we do out there, exactly?'

'Well, strictly speaking, we would be there as volunteers helping with the building of the church, but that could be anything really – just helping with the running of things, most of the time we could be just holidaying . . .'

'Are you suggesting that for our holiday we should go and build a church in Africa?'

'Wouldn't you like to go to Africa?'

'Yes, but not to build a church. Isn't that something practising Christians do?'

'Daddy,' said Evelyn, who had been following the conversation closely, 'I'm not going to Africa with Irina.'

'We wouldn't even have to go at the same time as Vera's family, we could just go on our own.'

'Daddy,' said Evelyn again, in an accusatory tone of voice this time, 'do you actually believe in God?'

In the flow of conversation Arnold was able to pass over this question.

'It's dangerous,' said Polly, speaking against her own instinctive understanding that Rwanda was now a safe country to visit, she wanted to use whatever weapon she had to throw against this idea of going to Africa on a mission, 'it's not a place to take young children.'

'Well like I said, it was just a jokey suggestion that Vera made, she didn't really think you would want to go . . .'

'Oh really? Why not?'

'She knows you're not religious.'

'That's something you talk about, is it? My religious beliefs, or lack of them?'

'We don't need to, you make it obvious.'

She waited with increasing anxiety for Sunday, without saying anything more on the subject. The night before, she could hardly sleep, and would wake every hour, almost on the hour, all through until dawn, when she gave up any attempt to sleep again. And her heart sank when she heard Arnold begin to stir at 8 a.m., and then rise a few moments later.

'What are you doing?' she said quietly as he headed for the shower. Her voice froze him, he seemed to think she had been deeply asleep.

'I'm going to have a shower.'

'And then what?'

'What I normally do. Go to church.'

'But we agreed, after you went to that retreat, there would be no more. You would be finished with your research.'

'Did we?'

'Yes, don't you remember?'

'I remember you saying that, I don't remember agreeing.'

'Well I'm telling you now, you're not going to church.'

He seemed rooted to the floor, unable to move forwards or backwards.

'What's your reason?'

Polly sat upright. 'The reason is that I did not marry a Christian, and if you go to church today you are proving to me that you are one.'

'Are you saying people are not allowed to change their beliefs, over the entire course of their life?'

'This sounds like you are telling me that you have become a Christian.'

He made no move to deny it.

'Have you?' she said.

He stood for a moment looking at her, motionless. She guessed he was trying to judge if this was the right moment to answer honestly. And she felt sick when he gave her that answer, in the form of a small, frightened nod.

'Say it,' she said. 'So that there's no misunderstanding. Say it loud and clear, that you believe in God.'

Again he took the moment to judge if the time was right.

'I believe in our Lord Jesus Christ.'

It wasn't just the words, but the voice. The flat seriousness of it. The absence of irony. He tried to reassure her that it made no difference to them, that he wasn't going to think of her differently, or even their lives. He wasn't going to start imposing strange rules on how they behaved. She asked him if he was going to start saying grace before meals and he said that if he did he would do it silently, to himself. Her feelings of fury subsided and his reassurances had worked in part by giving her a sense of relief that at least he had decided to be honest with her and tell her the truth and she had asked him how long he had been a believer and he said vague things like it had been stirring in him for a while, he had been harbouring thoughts about a spiritual dimension to life, and that no, he didn't believe in the literal truth of the Bible or the miracles or even the resurrection though he was still finding his way through the tenets of the faith. Attending a church meant agreeing to certain basic principles of faith, but that didn't mean you had to believe them, belief could still be a personal thing. It was too long to go into it there and then, he needed to get ready to go to church, they could talk about it later. But Polly didn't want to talk about it later, not with him. The problem was, she still didn't believe him, when he said it didn't matter, that he was the same person, that he didn't believe in the literal truth of the scriptures. He might say that now, but his faith was probably growing, he had entered a path and he didn't know himself where it might lead.

And the worst thing was, he had lessened in her eyes. He had become someone weaker and slighter than she had previously known. She had always admired his cleverness before, but she had always wondered about its strength.

How susceptible was he, after all, to persuasion, to propaganda? Was it strong enough to resist succumbing to something that he might encounter first as a detached observer? Evidently not. She hated to think it, but the truth was she now regarded Arnold as a little bit weak and a little bit stupid.

And his faith was a stranger in the household. An uninvited guest. An admonishing angel present everywhere.

She kept thinking of her sister-in-law's words – that she had lost a husband to religion. She almost wished he had had an affair instead. At least then she would know what she was dealing with, she would comprehend the situation. She could do battle with a scarlet woman, throw her cheating husband out on his ear, be confident that she was in the right and he was in the wrong. But in giving himself to God, Arnold had done nothing bad. The opposite, in fact. He was behaving like a good man. Like a paragon of goodness. And he wanted to go to Africa and build a church for the poor Africans, when he was someone who she had never seen put so much as a penny in a charity tin before, who avoided beggars on the street as though they were carriers of the plague. Now he would be washing their feet. So what should she do? She couldn't throw him out of the house for being religious. There seemed no help available. The advice columns were full of salacious letters about women whose husbands had turned out to be gay, or transvestites. There was no shortage of husbands who, as soon as they were married, turned themselves into women. But there seemed nothing she could read anywhere about the husbands who run off to join a church, or who are overtaken by a sudden urge to build a seminary in the African bush.

Now, at home, she observed him carefully, trying to understand him, what he had become. He had changed remarkably. The initial smallness she had seen in him on the morning of his confession was now replaced by a sort of nimbleness, a sprightliness. He would spring up from the table after dinner and take the plates to the kitchen. He would talk with Evelyn just as he had before, but in a more relaxed and cheerful way. He was still funny, but it was a different kind of funny. A less prickly form of humour seemed to have emerged in him. He reminded her of those magazine articles she had seen around the house when she was little, that talked about humour as medicine, a tonic. He was all good clean fun now. Or was she just thinking that because of what she knew about him?

Before meals she watched for signs that he was saying grace. It was impossible to be sure, but there were quiet moments as the food was being served when he didn't say anything, and he could have been praying, or he could have been just keeping quiet.

Evelyn, she could see, saw nothing changed in her father. And so she wondered if this was how it would continue, with the slightly more cheerful, positive, energetic Arnold, from now and for ever, and if she could accept it. Her aversion to religion was deep and visceral, almost organic. She hated the touch and feel of it, the smell of incense, the dreary groaning of hymns. She hated the smell of religion. But although she tried to find it on Arnold, she had to admit, he did not carry that smell with him, not really. In fact, he smelt sweeter and fresher than he had ever done.

These were the thoughts that filled her mind every morning at the shop now, when she was in the back with the pulp tanks, lifting the poor, soaking pages out of the water. Rescuing them, perhaps. Giving life back to the broken-down sheets, lifting them out of the water as if they were drowned kittens. To be making something was good. To be making anything.

Two people came into the shop one morning, a few days after Arnold's confession. She could glimpse them from her bench in the workshop, through the doorway. She had never seen them before. They were a late-middle-aged couple who looked oddly paired. Her first impression was of a Native American princess married to a railway ticket inspector. She had long black hair that hung in crimped, paranoid curtains either side of her face. Heavy, dark brows, her eyes almost hidden in shadow. Her mouth was a lipless slit turned down at the ends. A square jaw. She seemed beautiful against the odds. The man was small and apologetic-looking, with small, baggy, slightly bad-tempered eyes. His hair was tatty and balding. He wore sexless greys and browns in contrast to his partner's moody purples and greens.

She took no more notice of them until Tamsin poked

her head around the door and said that there were some people asking to see her, by name. She came out of the workshop and found the pair, standing closely and expectantly together by the counter. The man spoke first.

'Are you Mrs Proctor?'

He spoke awkwardly, not knowing where to put his words.

'I am. Can I help you?'

'Do you publish poems?'

'Yes, we run a small press here, we publish booklets of poems, and other things, sometimes.' Polly said this while trying to wipe glue off her fingers with a rag.

'We believe you know my son,' said the woman, 'our son. You might know him as Martin Guerre. His real name is Ryan.'

'He told us he sent you some of his poems. He said you had promised to publish them. And now you haven't and are refusing to return them.'

'He thinks you might be trying to publish them under someone else's name – your husband's, he says.'

'He says your husband hasn't been able to write a new book of poems, and so he is going to publish our son's work under his own name.'

The couple delivered these statements as though they had memorized them. There was no anger in their voices, but rather a sense of genuine puzzlement and wonder. Polly was affected by the gentleness of their tones.

'That's quite an accusation to make,' she said, equally puzzled. She remembered seeing the manuscript of Martin's poems when she had delved into Arnold's study, but that was weeks ago. What had become of them since?

'We understand that, and we didn't think it likely. But we trust our son and we always take the trouble to believe him when he says unlikely things.'

'I don't really know anything about poetry,' the man said, 'my wife knows more than me, but I tend to have old-fashioned ideas about poems. So I can't really tell if Ryan's writing is very good or not.'

'Well, it is good, I assure you.'

The couple seemed comforted by this, and smiled, but didn't ask her to elaborate on this simple evaluation.

'I like Elizabeth Barrett Browning,' said the woman, 'and Emily Dickinson. But no one else. I don't know why. When Ryan hurt himself, I found myself reading them both, one after the other. It made me feel better.'

The horrible piece of information, tucked away inside the woman's voice, snagged on Polly's mind like a thorn.

'Is Martin – Ryan all right?'

The man nodded, closing his eyes in a tired way again.

'He did something silly last week. It's not the first time. It was quite bad. He's in hospital at the moment, but he's doing well.'

Polly put her hand over her mouth. By now she had walked Martin's parents through to the privacy of the workshop.

'I'm so sorry,' she said, feeling that dragging sensation she experienced whenever confronted with a stranger's misfortune, born of a fear that anything she said might be misconstrued or lack sufficient sympathy. Oddly it was Vera who sprang to her mind as a role model of sympathetic listening. It was the way her face registered exactly what she was thinking, the way the brow would furrow with concern, the eyes intensify. Polly could feel herself willing her own brow to furrow, and hoping Martin's parents would recognize her concern.

But her statement seemed to have absolutely no effect on the couple. They continued as though she hadn't spoken.

'Do you have Ryan's poems here? We could take them back to him. He wants to see them again.'

Having successfully stifled the urge to weep, Polly was able to talk coherently.

'I didn't think we had reached a decision on Martin's poems. Sorry – Ryan's poems. If he is still interested in having them published, I think we could make a decision very soon. This week, in fact – I can promise you.'

The couple looked at each other. They were a little taken aback, having neither sought nor expected such an offer. They didn't say anything, but looked at Polly suspiciously. To break the silence, Polly indicated the shelf where Papyrus's published works were displayed.

'These are some of the books we have published,' she said. Being mostly thin volumes Papyrus's output didn't take up a lot of shelf space when only one copy of each was displayed. In all they had produced just over twenty poetry pamphlets. 'We make the paper ourselves.'

Martin Guerre's parents looked impressed. Polly was

proud of the Papyrus Press, more so than she realized, until that moment.

'You make the paper by hand?' the woman asked. 'A page at a time? That must take for ever.'

'No, I make large sheets of paper that can take eight pages of print, then they're cut up and folded to make the book. You only need to do two sheets for a pamphlet of sixteen pages. We have done some larger ones of twenty-four pages.'

'But even so, it must take a long time.'

Polly wasn't sure how to take this woman's insistence that large amounts of time were involved. Later she supposed it meant that she valued time more than anything else.

'We only do limited runs, sometimes only fifty copies. So I have to make a hundred sheets. It takes a while, yes.'

'It makes it quite special I suppose,' the man said, in his sad, slightly croaky voice, 'when you've made the paper yourself.'

'That's the idea,' said Polly. 'And I usually try and do something with the paper that responds to the poems in some way. For instance this book here has several poems about the sea. And so I added seaweed to the paper pulp. You can see it's given the paper a slightly yellowy, greeny tint. But also a rather evocative smell, if you hold it to your nose . . .'

'I can smell the sea!' the woman said, after engulfing herself in the pamphlet. 'That's quite wonderful.' She held it out to her husband, who didn't look impressed. 'My sense of smell isn't what it was,' he said, sniffing deeply at the words.

Polly, delighted, continued her tour of their publications. 'This other book has rather a lot of references to blood in it . . .' She saw the looks of mild horror in the faces of the couple as they wondered what she might say next, 'and my husband seriously suggested I mix blood in with the pulp. Human blood. I drew the line at that. I used stewed rosehips instead. Unfortunately they turned out to be a bit yellowy as well. But never mind.'

'These are very beautiful books,' said the woman. 'I wonder what you would do with the paper for Ryan's book.'

'Well, that's an interesting question. His main subject, as far as I can tell, is paper. And our books are already made of that.'

'Would you publish him under his pen name?' the husband said, ignoring this dilemma.

'Yes, unless he suggests otherwise. It's the author's choice how they would like to be known, usually.'

'We would like to have a proper contract drawn up,' said Martin's mother, 'so that everything is above board.'

'Of course.'

'And we don't want you to feel that you've been black-mailed into publishing his book. He would have cut his wrists anyway, it was nothing to do with you . . .'

'. . . It doesn't seem to matter what happens in his life, when his mood gets dark, nothing can bring him round. Nothing.'

'He lost quite a bit of blood this time. He hasn't done that before. He's taken pills before . . .'

Polly felt terrible for talking earlier about the blood paper. She tried to think of how to make up for it. She would produce the most beautiful paper for Martin's book. She didn't know what, yet, but it would be something special.

'We don't want you to publish them just out of sympathy for him. We want you to publish them because you think they are good poems. Otherwise it's a waste of time.'

Polly nodded obediently.

'And of course we'll have to speak to Ryan about it. I'm sure he would be pleased to have them published, whatever he may say. His mood can change so quickly. It would help him. Give him something solid to point to and say I did that.'

They talked a little more, but the parents soon seemed to exhaust themselves of words. They continued to thank Polly for taking an interest in their son's poems, to such an extent that she felt embarrassed. She had the awkward feeling that the conversation had somehow transformed her original offer to give them a quick decision on Martin's poems into a firm promise to publish them.

As the couple made to leave she felt suddenly compelled to ask them a question that had sprung to her mind.

'Do you mind if I ask you something? You said your son cut his wrists. It may seem odd, but can you tell me what he used?'

The couple looked so untroubled by this question you might have assumed they were asked it every few hours.

'He used scissors,' said the woman. 'That's one reason he was unsuccessful. They weren't very sharp.'

She had wondered for a while whether or not to tell Arnold about Martin Guerre. Since he had declared himself a Christian, she no longer trusted him. She was interested, on the other hand, to see how he would react to the news of Martin's attempted suicide. Knowing now how closely the boy trod the margins of rational existence, would Arnold feel some retrospective guilt at his treatment of the young man? Might he be racked with remorse for the things he wrote on his first submission of poems? If so, did he deserve to be? Now that he was a Christian, would he have a different strategy for dealing with it? The old Arnold would have felt sorry for the boy, but then nothing more. He would have tried to dismiss it as something beyond his control. What would the new Arnold do? Pray, presumably. And perhaps go and visit the boy in his sickbed, and pray by his side. As far as Polly was concerned, that was the last thing Martin Guerre needed, a born-again Christian poet who had previously written nasty comments on his poems, praying for his soul.

She also feared that, as a Christian, he would object even more strongly to the publication of the poems, emerging, as they did, from what he regarded as immoral desires. He might now share the sensibilities of that student he'd told her about, who would leave the room whenever sex was mentioned. He had seen Martin's poems (mistakenly, in her view) as thinly veiled expressions of sexual obsession for her, Polly. His fear, she supposed, was that they would release into the world a plausible narrative of his wife's infidelity that people might actually believe.

On the other hand, might it not be a rather cruel thing to withhold the information about Martin? Arnold had shown signs that he cared about him. She wrestled with this problem for a while, and it was forgotten about in the little storm that was whipped up by the different news that Arnold had to tell her.

He was going to Africa.

She had been in her office at home, the corner of the living room that she had furnished with a small desk and a set of shelves. She had been working on her monthly accounts, entering the data from her receipts and invoices onto a spreadsheet, when he casually dropped the news.

'When?'

'Probably next month. Before Christmas, at the latest.'

She turned in her chair to face him.

'How long for?'

'Just a couple of weeks. Maybe a bit longer, it depends. I've made a bid for some research leave, I'm owed a lot, so I should be free from teaching for the rest of the term.'

He seemed to think she should be pleased for him.

'Only it's not research now, is it? You're going there because you want to spread the word. You're a missionary.'

'I'm helping out with a building project.'

'Ha! What have you ever built?'

She didn't like the way she said this, and felt ashamed at being so scornful. But the anger was mounting.

'Tell me the truth. Was there ever a novel?'

'Of course.' She could hear the strain in his voice, he was lying in a new way, he was lying in a way he had never lied before, as someone who believed in sin. 'There still might be.'

His trip to Africa loomed before her like a bare hill. He had been in agony for so long with his writing that she had tolerated this venture into religious territory if it was to provide him with a creative breakthrough. The thought that it might not lead to the novel he had proposed, that the novel might never have been in his mind, that this whole episode had been, from the start, a quest for some sort of spiritual fulfilment, gave her a feeling of having been betrayed. Yet there seemed no object she could fix her anger upon. She longed more than ever for the scarlet woman, someone she could scream at. But there was only God.

Polly thought – people (apart from my birth family) think I am a strong person, they think I am brave for setting up my own business, for learning how to make paper and how to sell it. They see me as someone to be admired, as someone feisty and indefatigable. But they don't know what I'm feeling, and when Arnold told me he was going to Africa it was almost as though he had told me he was going to heaven. That he was going to die. I can't live with this man, she thought. Now that he believes in eternal life he exists in another place.

Then there was the terror that was to come, according to her sister-in-law, when Arnold would eventually turn his thoughts towards saving her. She didn't want to be saved. More than anything she didn't want to be saved. I don't want to go to heaven. If she could put her opposition to religion into a single sentence, that was it.

She needed someone she could talk to about these feelings. She wondered if she should go back to Holly, yet she dreaded it, because Holly represented the failure of this kind of relationship, the living proof that a Christian and an atheist cannot live together. Yet there must be some who do, successfully.

She became aware of churches – as buildings – as if for the first time. As if they had suddenly appeared in her neighbourhood, had sprung up like mushrooms overnight. Recent events had made them visible to her in a way they hadn't been before. Everywhere she went she saw them, some ancient, some new, most of them in between. If she walked past one she found herself slowing down, lingering outside, reading the posters and notices on the boards, as if they could provide any answers. She wondered if she should venture in, see if she could find anyone to talk to, but the churches were locked and showed little sign that anyone ever came and went.

She decided to see Vera. In the months since their friendship had faded, she realized she had missed her. It was not that they had ever talked in a deeply personal way about anything, but rather they seemed kindred spirits, despite their different outlooks. In her absence a space had opened up in Polly's life that could only be filled by the one who had caused it, Vera. She was proof that she could talk to and be friends with a Christian. Perhaps, therefore, she could also be married to one. And if there was anyone she would feel comfortable talking about religion with, it was Vera. And now, with the prospect of Arnold leaving her not only spiritually but physically, going away somewhere that she couldn't follow, she thought of Vera as the only one who could offer her advice.

So she went to Vera's unannounced. Walking up the little path to her door she felt a sudden nostalgia for the familiarity of the house, so similar to her own. She began crying, and wondered about turning back, but she had already rung the bell. When Vera opened the door, Polly could hardly see her through the warp of her own tears. And what must Vera have thought, to find tearful Polly on her doorstep, saying, 'I need to talk to you about Arnold.'

Wordlessly she had invited her into the house, though Polly noticed a cautiousness in her manner. If it had been the other way round, Polly would have offered Vera comfort even before asking what the problem was, she would have given her a hug, a cup of tea, tissues. But instead, Vera simply placed Polly in the centre of the room where she had to deal with her own tears, while Vera stood before her, her arms folded.

'What has Arnold told you?'

And Polly had replied, 'Everything. He's confessed.'

A long silence, and then Polly noticed that Vera too was crying. It seemed so odd. It was she, Polly, who was the unhappy one in this scenario. What on earth had happened to Vera?

'I'm so sorry, Polly. I'm so sorry. I hope you will forgive me.'

'Forgive you?'

'I never wanted to hurt you. It wasn't even that I was unhappy with Angus. Don't blame Arnold. He's sweet. He still loves you deeply. I don't deserve your forgiveness. I hope I can make myself worthy of it. I didn't want to hurt you. I never wanted to hurt you. Something had taken me over.'

Polly had found a tissue and was holding it to her eyes while Vera was speaking, and had only been listening with half her attention, waiting for her to begin making sense. In the silence that followed she realized she had it. All of it. The whole sense.

Suddenly in command of her voice again, she spoke. 'What are you saying to me, Vera?'

That was how it came out. A misunderstanding. A simple misunderstanding. Vera had thought she was talking about something else, and in so doing, had apologized for something Polly had never imagined. The news so wrong-footed her that the tears she had been shedding since her arrival dried instantly. It was as though she drank the emotional outpouring back into her body. As though she was resetting herself. She felt her most urgent task now was to concentrate all her attention to the words that were coming from Vera's mouth.

'We lost control,' she said. 'It was like a madness. Only that doesn't excuse us, because we always had the power to stop it. Arnold was always frightened by what we were doing, because he didn't want to lose you.'

'How long?' said Polly, astounded by her own self-control.

'Since early spring. And then we ended it in July, just before the summer holidays.'

'Why?'

Vera seemed to have trouble answering this question. She made several attempts, but came to a halt each time, then she cried again. 'Shall we sit down?' she said, when she had recovered a little. They were still standing in the centre of the room, facing each other.

'I don't want to sit down,' said Polly. But Vera had already taken a seat at the table.

Polly took a moment to look at Vera's face, suddenly seeing it as Arnold must have seen it, and a thread of recent memories suddenly lit up in her mind, connecting together the moments Arnold had mentioned Vera over the past few months, the times he had casually dropped her into the conversation, the looks she had seen pass between them when they were in proximity. How had she failed to notice them, when now they were towering land-marks in her memory? For a moment long-suppressed schoolday thoughts came back to her, of older girls, beautiful and contemptuous, the frailty of her school-self, of everyone but her knowing things.

Vera, recomposed, spoke again.

'We aren't made for having affairs, Polly. Arnold even less so than me. We didn't know what to do about what we were doing.'

'But you still did it.'

'It was as though we didn't know how to stop. We didn't know the language.'

'The language is very simple.'

So she had the scarlet woman, she had her right in front of her, to scream at, to scratch at. She had always imagined that she would fight in a situation like this. That she would raise hell, be violent, vocal. She always believed she had it in her power to do those things, but now, in the curdled reality that had accreted around her, she felt frightened, more than anything. Frightened for herself, that she was in danger of losing the thing she most treasured about herself, that pearl of pure, trusting innocence that had somehow survived all these years.

'We couldn't be our proper selves with each other, because we realized that out proper selves were with our families. We realized the most important thing was to protect our marriages. That is why Angus and I encouraged Arnold to come to our church. We felt it would give him the strength to tell you what he had done.'

Other paths in her memory lit up. This woman had been behind everything that had been happening in her family for months. The lonely Sunday mornings, the distracted presence at the dinner table. And she had thought he was worrying about his writing.

'So, not content with stealing my husband's body, you are now trying to steal his soul.'

'I'm trying to save his soul . . . and yours . . .'

She had had enough.

'You must never, ever come anywhere near me again.' She said it quietly, but with thundering emphasis. Her instinct was to scream the words but she had to remain dignified. She let the words hang in the silence for a few moments, during which she saw Vera's face, wet and puffy, looking at her with a loose, bewildered expression. Then she repeated the words, this time pointing a finger at the seated woman. 'You must never, ever come anywhere near me again.'

And she left the house.


Her eyes were so full of tears that she had trouble finding her car. She wiped them away angrily, feeling betrayed by her own body, that it should express feelings she thought were under control. Anger was what she wanted to feel, not sadness. She was worried that someone on the street might see her drenched face and take pity on her. She didn't want to be pitied. She wanted to be furious. She wanted to be a giant.

In the car she took some time to compose herself. Deep breaths. Checking her eyes in the mirror. The tears had stopped, but their traces remained, like washed-out river-bank grass after a flood. Her mind was having trouble catching up with her body, which seemed to have reacted in its own way to the revelation. She had to keep reliving moments from her recent past to see if there were clues that she should have noticed, but had missed. She suddenly remembered the school run, and Arnold's sudden eagerness to undertake that particular chore. That must have been when it started. All those months ago. It was like history being rewritten. Every action, every word he'd spoken in all those months had been carefully chosen to conceal what was really happening. Now she knew, she had to relive those months again in her mind as they really were, with Arnold coming and going from wherever he'd been, hiding the traces, covering up the facts. The cleverness of his lying, the skill of his subterfuge. It made her feel physically sick. And then the anger came again, engulfing her. Then the tears. Then the anger at the tears.

It was half an hour or more before she felt stable enough to start the car. She didn't know where to go or what to do. She didn't want to go home. She had taken time away from the shop to visit Vera, and so she went there. As she drove she felt her old self recovering, taking charge. She hadn't realized before quite what a sanctuary Papyrus had become. Had she gone home she would have been in uncontrollable fits of sorrow, but at Papyrus she felt composed and sane. She carried on with her work as though everything was fine, she chatted with Tamsin and Terri, aware that she was a different woman from the woman who had been in the shop a couple of hours ago, but she was able to pass herself off as normal. She wasn't yet ready to confide anything, nor did she feel the need for support, not yet. There would be a time when she would cry on Terri's shoulder, but not now. Now she had the shop to take care of. She had felt, on her way back from Vera's house, suddenly concerned for the paper she had made. All those fragile leaves, thin and vulnerable. Blank sheets, nothing written on them. Unreadable. No one could take these and read them, as Vera had done Arnold. She wanted to be there to take care of them.

In the evening, she could see that Arnold was oblivious to what she knew. She had given no sign, no clue. It amazed her, her own capacity for calm self-control. She cooked a normal meal. A home-made pizza. It was something they had nearly every week, on a Wednesday or Thursday. Of all their meals, it was probably the one they most enjoyed. It was the most fun. Evelyn loved her mother's pizzas, the colourfulness of them, the slapdash extravagance of them, the way they could be eaten without a knife and fork in a fiesta of hand-to-mouth gobbling. Polly watched Evelyn and her father enjoying their slices, playing little games about who had chosen the best portion, whose mozzarella was the stretchiest. All through the meal she maintained her composure, she had managed to lock down her rage, and had built up reserves of strength to see her through whatever was to follow.

After dinner the evening dragged on. Still he had noticed nothing different or odd in her mood. She felt as though she was in some terrible endurance contest, like in one of those ghastly TV shows Arnold enjoyed, where famous people are buried alive with rats. She sang songs quietly to herself, went about her business of clearing up and tidying away, found things to occupy herself. And then, when finally Arnold went upstairs to read to Evelyn, she got the suitcase she'd earlier packed, down from the bedroom, and awaited Arnold's return to the living room.

'I've booked you a hotel,' she said.

She noted the way he looked at her, then at the suitcase, which sat upright on the floor like an obedient little bodybuilder, then back at her. He was working out what strategy to follow. He made a stab at incomprehension.

'What? What are you talking about?'

'I want you out of the house, tonight.'

'I don't understand.'

'You do. I've spoken to Vera. She told me everything.'

He stared at her for several seconds. The light went out of his eyes.

'She had no right.'

'She had no right not to. You, apparently, were going to keep it a secret for ever.'

'I would have told you in my own way. What else could I do?' He was raising his voice. She cast her eyes upwards to remind him that Evelyn should not have to hear them.

'You could have told the truth.'

'And would things have been any better?'

'I don't care. It's too late to care about that question. If you'd told me, there might have been a chance to talk. But not now. Not now that I've found out this way.'

'There's still time to talk. We have to talk.'

She ignored this remark, and instead handed him a piece of paper on which was written the details of the hotel she'd booked.

She didn't understand why he smiled to himself when he saw that she had booked the hotel on the bypass. She didn't realize it was the same hotel he had used on his night away in an imaginary Birmingham. He thought she had chosen it for its cheapness and its seediness, but it was the hotel Arnold would have used again, if he had had to make the choice.

'You've booked me a week at this place?'

'Yes. I booked it with your card.'

'And after the week's over?'

'Then you'll have found somewhere else to live. Or you can stay on in the hotel for as long as you like.'

'I won't be able to find somewhere else to live. I've got nowhere else to go.'

'Perhaps your church will help you.'

He was shaking his head, looking at her pleadingly. 'All that church business – you don't understand – they forced me . . .' As though realizing how pathetic it sounded, he stopped mid-sentence. Every avenue of explanation seemed blocked to him.

He begged for a few more minutes to sort out some papers in his study. He had lectures to give, student work to mark. She told him to go. He could collect his stuff at some future date, but he had to go now. His students would have to suffer. His lectures would have to be off the cuff. Or he could phone in sick. It wasn't her problem. There was a moment when she could see he was thinking about whether or not to protest. Any moment he was going to say that she was being unreasonable. To pre-empt this, she said:

'Do you really want Evelyn to hear us fighting? Are you waiting for me to smash something? I think we can do this like civilized people, but if you want blood, I'll give you blood.'

The words seemed to empty Arnold of any colour, though she too was terrified by what she had said, and by the fact that she meant it.

With one final but long drawn out stream of apologies during which Arnold did his best to produce tears (but failed), he was gone.

When he went, in that manner of meek obedience that had somehow become his hallmark, she didn't shed the flood of tears she was expecting to. Instead she felt a beautiful hardness settle within her. In removing Arnold from her presence, she had protected herself. After listening to the sad coughing of his car starting up, and then the engine fading out into the distance, she experienced for the first time the house without Arnold. It was silent. The TV was off. There was nothing but the remote, within-the-walls hum of the house doing its own work, those noises she was never quite sure about – refrigeration? Central heating? The expansion tank filling? She let it settle about her for a moment, wondering what sort of person she was, in this new, few-minutes-old life. She put aside thoughts of whether she had been fair and reasonable in her actions, and instead tested the weather of her own feelings. Did she feel better for what she had done? Yes she did. Was this a permanent or a momentary feeling? Permanent, she thought.

The House Without Arnold, she discovered, was a very different place from The House From Which Arnold Is Temporarily Absent. The silence of that house was sometimes awkward and uncomfortable, even frightening. But the silence of the House Without Arnold was comforting and luxuriant. A very different place. The House Without Arnold opened up around her, the walls seemed to recede, enlarging the space within, the lights brightened. She was shocked by the feeling, the sense of release, of relief, of something dark having lifted. Later she thought it was the departure of that unwanted and invisible guest who'd taken up residence since Arnold's conversion. The weight of Arnold's faith had lifted, there was no one watching her now.

She walked about the house as if to experience it for the first time, opening doors and peeping into rooms to see if they were the same, surprised to find that they were, but only literally. Otherwise they were transformed. Evelyn's bedroom, into which she dared herself to glance, seemed actually to be the fairytale princess's boudoir to which it aspired. Lately Evelyn had been asking for it to be redecorated, as she had outgrown its prettily clashing colour schemes. Arnold had always been in charge of redecorating his daughter's bedroom. Polly realized that she would now have to do this herself. And in reflecting on that fact she realized that she had thoroughly written Arnold out of the future history of the house. She had had no hesitation in accepting this new dispensation and adapting to it. There could be no second chance for Arnold. He would be back, probably as soon as tomorrow, with some sort of angle or strategy to excuse what he had done, to make her think less badly of him. But she was firm – firmer than she actually thought she would be – in putting her plan into action, of protecting the pearl that was so close to being dashed, by giving Arnold no quarter.

The phone call came at about eleven that night, just as she had expected. She read his name on the screen of her mobile. He was ringing, presumably, from the hotel, having settled in, and having had time to think of something new to say. Some new line of argument. It only reassured her that she had done the right thing. She switched her phone off without answering the call, and watched the screen go dark.

At the back of Papyrus, in her workshop, Polly took more time than usual in tearing the paper for pulping. Tamsin was helping her. At first Polly was doubtful about letting her help, but Tamsin was bored, the customers had gone and the shop was empty. And so Polly had agreed, and allowed Tamsin to do some paper-tearing. They sat alongside each other, letting rip through the heap of material on the bench. Polly watched her assistant to see if she was taking any interest in the paper itself. It was unusual paper to be making pulp from. Loose sheets, covered in handwriting. Anyone else might have paused to try and read some of it, to wonder where it had come from, who had written all these words. But she was soon chatting about her favourite subject, which was the failings and weaknesses of her current boyfriend. Polly half-listened, having heard much of it before. She had met the boyfriend a couple of times, when he had come to the shop to meet Tamsin, and he had struck her instinctively as someone Tamsin should avoid at all costs – a loping, bejewelled, tattooed man-child who seemed to speak a language of his own devising. Tamsin's main complaint, that evening, was that he had become addicted to computer games to the extent that he was losing interest in sex. She laughed at the right moments when Tamsin gave her account of the row they'd had. She had picked up his Xbox and had threatened to throw it out of the window.

'You should have,' said Polly, when Tamsin told her she didn't have the heart to carry out her threat.

She felt sorry for the fact that she couldn't offer her own story in return. Tamsin was clearly expecting some sort of disclosure as the next part of the conversation. But it would have been impossible to talk about what had happened in her own relationship. But then, if Tamsin had taken the briefest of moments to look at the paper she was tearing into strips, then smaller strips, then crossways into little squares, she might have been given a chance to begin talking about it. She would need to talk to someone soon.

When, on the night of his departure, she had gone into Arnold's study, she'd felt immediately that it no longer possessed any sort of power to exclude her. It was no sort of shrine or sacred space. It was a room full of objects. She had a right to do in there whatever she wanted. She had packed his laptop in his suitcase, but everything else was left as it was. The mess of his so called creative life. His writing. In the drawers she found lots of it. The folders of new poems that he had been working on with painstaking slowness for ten years. There were dozens of them. He had almost enough for a new book. He still wrote on paper, using his laptop only for university work, and for final drafts. Here were the pen-and-paper versions of each poem, A4 pages closely lined and criss-crossed with black ink, crossings out, marginal notes and arrows pointing to and from portions of circled text. It had been his characteristic habit, to write like this, on loose sheets of A4. When he finished a new draft, he fastened it on top of the old one with a paper clip. This was so that he could immediately refer back to previous drafts as he worked on the new one. He had shown her once, his system. As the successive drafts mounted up, the wad of paper held by the paper clip could become very thick. Finally the typed draft would go on top, and all the pages stapled together, as a permanent record of how the poem was made. On average he made about twenty drafts of each poem. He saved them all in the outlandish hope that they might one day be worth some money to a collector of manuscripts. There were all the manuscripts of the poems that were published in his first book, they filled a large cardboard box. The poems that he had written since filled another box. Then there were the diaries and notebooks. He was a prolific note-taker and diary keeper. The diaries were in large A4 bound notebooks that he had bought during a trip to China. Cheap, manila-coloured, thin paper, but the books were hundreds of pages thick. In other notebooks were journals that went back to when he was a teenager. All of them written in his crabbed, indecipherable hand. She went through the whole room. She found other folders. Other boxes of rough drafts. Things she'd never seen before – it looked as though he had made several attempts at writing a novel after all. Tiny handwriting filling hundreds of lined pages. The paper was, apart from the Chinese notebooks, standard white writing paper, the type of mass-produced paper Papyrus had reacted against. She spent most of the evening sorting through it, finding boxes and carrier bags to stuff the papers in. She took these out to the car and, in the dark of approaching midnight, filled the boot to its brim.

She remembered that there was probably a document among all his official papers, which she hadn't bothered to go through, that gave legal notice of the fact that she had been designated the executor of his literary estate. In the event of his death it would be she who would be waiting for the requests to quote, the requests to biographize, the requests to peruse the manuscripts. It was laughable to think that even a single person on the planet might be stirred enough to make such a request. She had thought that at the time but hadn't said it. In fact she had said the opposite, yes, you must designate a literary executor, you just never know what might happen after you've gone. There might be people – scholars, the idly curious, the intrepid waders through forgotten troughs of literary sludge – interested enough to want to see your handwritten works.

She broke the hardback covers of the notebooks and diaries and disposed of them, leaving the loose pages to add to all the other loose material. There would be enough to fill several tanks, she thought. Tamsin left her to it when some customers arrived. By now they had torn through most of the paper, reducing it almost to fluff. Her fingers were grey with ink and a little tired. She filled the tanks with water and then began adding the paper, lifting heaps of it in her cupped hands and scattering it in. The ink separated from the paper, darkening the water. She added bleach, which dissolved the ink further, clearing the water and whitening the pulp that remained. By the time it had properly soaked there wouldn't be a trace of Arnold's writing left, not even its chemical make-up.

A few weeks before, Polly had ordered papyrus sheets from a manufacturer in Egypt. The parcel had arrived earlier that day. Though they had named the shop after this product, they had never given much thought to the material itself, or the fact that it might still be manufactured, but a brief search found that specialist manufacturers still made it on the banks of the Nile. She and Terri thought they would have to stock some. But now that she had it, she wondered if it could be added to ordinary paper pulp, to make a new kind of paper. She did this to the tanks in which Arnold's collected works had dissolved and when, some days later, she began making paper from the pulp, she found these new sheets had a colour and texture quite unlike anything she had made before – they seemed almost to be golden. It was going to be beautiful paper to print *The Paper Lovers* on.

There were moments when she felt bad about what she had done to him, and in all her imaginings of such an event, the destruction of irreplaceable written matter, the record of someone's life, the expression of their imagination, had not occurred to her. She had changed the locks by the time Arnold returned to the house, but she let him in so that he could get some of his things. She followed him upstairs. He ignored the bedroom where the rest of his clothes were and went straight to the study. She waited on the landing, behind him. She heard him opening and closing the drawers. When he emerged he looked white and blank.

'What have you done?' he said, quietly.

She said nothing. In rehearsing this moment, she discovered there was a danger in making it seem as though the debt of Arnold's crime had been repaid by her destruction of his life's work, and they could now be thought of as equal. He didn't seem to be seeing it that way.

'Everything?' he said. 'You've got rid of everything? What did you do, make a bonfire? Do you realize . . .' He looked again at the bareness of the room, 'Do you realize what you've done?'

She remained silent. When she was actually doing it she had relished the thought of telling him precisely what she had done with his writing, but now she couldn't. She was not sure if she would ever be able to. He couldn't summon any anger. He just looked tired and sad. He returned to the room to sort out a few books and collect the student work that she had carefully separated from his own material.

They talked briefly about Evelyn. She told him that, so far, she was fine, but it was early days. Yes, of course he could see her. They would arrange something. He mentioned going to Africa. He would be going soon, he said. Given the situation, perhaps it was just as well. He might stay out there for longer than he originally planned. When the time came to leave he paused at the front door, and delivered a short speech that he had clearly been working hard on.

'There are things about this situation that you don't understand, Polly. I know you don't want to listen to me now, but I hope that in the future . . .' Instinctively she shut the door on him, cutting off anything further he had to say.

Apart from the student work, there was one other item of written material that Polly saved from the pulp tanks, and that was the collection of poems, still in their large padded envelope, by Martin Guerre. On the night of Arnold's departure she had taken them downstairs, feeling as though she'd saved them from a catastrophe. She read them again. Perhaps it was the memory of her recent encounter with his parents, or the awful news they'd borne of his suffering, but she fell deeply in love with Martin's poems. Their obsession with paper, through which she could better understand her own love of the material. Their humanizing of it. The extraordinary way in which paper and people seemed interchangeable. As for Arnold's worry that they serenaded her, that was pure fantasy on his part. Martin's paper lovers were universal, archetypal. For Martin paper was always a living breathing substance. She would publish these poems as soon as she could. She would organize a proper launch party, everything they did for their best poets, all would be laid on for Martin and his parents.

The publication of *The Paper Lovers* was something that gave her both a point of focus and a pleasing distraction in the fraught weeks following her separation from Arnold. At first she feared she would have to involve him because she had no way of contacting Martin or his parents, there was no address on the manuscript and there was no sign of him online. Only Arnold knew where he lived. Fortunately, the boy's parents made a second visit to the shop that week, following up on her promise to make a quick decision.

'We don't mean to press you, Mrs Proctor, but this matter does need to be resolved as soon as possible. It can't be allowed to carry on any longer.'

'It's fine,' said Polly, unable to conceal her delight that they had appeared in her shop at just the right moment, 'we've made our decision. We would like to publish *The Paper Lovers* immediately. I've already started making the paper.'

When Martin arrived at the shop this time, he was like a man who had returned from a wilderness. In the weeks leading up to this moment, she had not met him. He had given her free reign to select whichever poems she liked for the pamphlet, he only asked that no changes be made to the poems themselves. Fortunately, no changes were needed, as far as she was concerned. There weren't even any typos. She sent proofs to his parents, and they came back by return of post, with no corrections. She asked him for a list of people to invite to the launch party. After a few days, a list was sent. It read

> *Mum*
> *Dad*
> *David*

David, it turned out, was his brother, who had emigrated to Australia. What about his friends from college, she asked his parents. Was there no one else? Yes, they said, there were other people they could ask. Ryan seems to have forgotten he has any friends, his mother said, but they are still there, and they still love him. They would be proud of him. And so his parents handled the delicate task of inviting people who loved Ryan. Would Ryan be prepared to read some of his own poems at the launch? His mother thought that yes, if he felt strong enough, he would love to be able to read some his poems aloud.

The regular attenders of their book launches could be relied upon to provide additional audience. She invited some of her own friends. People from the sewing evenings came, wearing their latest creations. It didn't take many people to fill the little venue, once they had cleared away the display tables and put out the chairs. There was already a buzzing crowd by the time Martin arrived. He came with his parents. It wasn't that they were holding him up, rather they were standing either side of him, as if ready to be there if he should fall. He was still visibly the young man she had last seen dressed in a suit of paper, haranguing her customers. Yet he looked older now. Perhaps it was the beard, fuller than it had been then. He was thin, or thinner. She glimpsed fresh scars on his wrists.

Polly hugged him. He almost disappeared under the pressure of her embrace, and he gave a little sigh. She had pushed the air out of his lungs.

'I am so glad you have agreed to read some of your

poems. Are you pleased with the book? I can't believe we haven't met before.'

'It's beautiful,' he replied. He was holding a copy in his slender, slightly trembling fingers, and he admired it again. 'I never thought I would see it.'

His parents were nearby, close to the table where some olives and nuts had been put out. She acknowledged them and they smiled. They had a slightly dazed air about them, as if unable to quite believe what had happened and so quickly, from making a simple enquiry about a stray manuscript, to the launch of their son's first book of poetry.

'I'm so looking forward to hearing you read these,' Polly said.

There was a calmness about Martin now. She wondered if he was on tranquillizers, or whether having his book published had had a soothing effect on him. The only moment of agitation was when he mentioned Arnold.

'Is Mr Proctor here?'

'No, he's not.'

Martin looked disappointed.

'He didn't seem to have any hand in making this book. Mum and Dad said they only dealt with you.'

'That's right, Arnold's gone away.'

'Someone told me he is in Africa.'

'Yes, I believe he is.'

'You're not sure?'

'I am sure he would be very happy with the book we've produced. It will always be special to him. I know that.'

---

Later, Polly took her place at the front, before the audience that was now seated.

'Thank you all so much for coming this evening. As you know, we at the Papyrus Press specialize in producing poetry pamphlets of the highest quality, both in terms of their poetry – and I think there can be none higher where Martin's poems are concerned – and in terms of their paper. We produce paper specifically for the book. In that way, every one of our publications is unique, not only for the words they contain, but for the paper on which they are printed. I feel the Papyrus Press has been very lucky, privileged even, to have the opportunity to publish Martin's poetry. When I first read his poems – I have to say I fell in love. They were poems by someone who had a very special feeling for paper itself. When you read these beautiful poems, and when you hear them later, you will see that Martin – I think some of you will know him as Ryan – thinks about paper in a way that is very original and very unusual. I'm not sure that I have met someone who thinks about paper so deeply. And so I realized that the paper we made for Martin's book would have to be very special indeed. And so we made the paper from a very special pulp that incorporates real papyrus, grown on the banks of the Nile, which I have had imported specially from an Egyptian manufacturer – yes, you can still find it and indeed there are papyri still being made to this day. But despite the fact that the name of this shop is Papyrus, we have never used papyrus in our paper before. So I am glad to say that not only does Martin's book represent a wonderful new addition to the family of Papyrus Press Poets, it actually legitimates the press and the shop by using the product after which it is named. What can be more wonderful and fitting than that, for a book made of paper, about paper, by people who love paper?' There was a pause while the audience nodded agreement, and murmured interestedly. The poet was sitting a little nervously on the front row, ready to take his place before the audience. 'And so now, I would like to introduce the extraordinary poet whose debut collection, *The Paper Lovers*, is launched tonight – please welcome, Martin Guerre.'

There was vigorous applause and some whoops from the back of the room as Martin shakily lifted himself from his seat, stepped to the front and then turned to face the audience. A silence fell. Then, in a hesitant, at times barely audible but beautiful voice, he read his poems.

# picador.com

blog
videos
interviews
extracts